Dying for Love

Also by Gwen Moffat

DYING FOR LOVE

Gwen Moffat

Constable • London

Constable & Robinson Ltd
3 The Lanchesters
162 Fulham Palace Road
London W6 9ER
www.constablerobinson.com

First published in the UK by Constable,
an imprint of Constable & Robinson Ltd 2005

ISBN 1-84529-046-1

Printed and bound in the EU

For Christopher:
friend and climbing partner

Acknowledgement

I am indebted to Christopher Goodall for his advice on medical matters.

Chapter One

The country was ripe for violence. Alice Potter could feel it in her bones: the hazy escarpment looming above the village, not a breath of air down here – early heatwaves seemed wrong in the Vale of Eden. Driving rain was what suited the Northern Pennines: wind, and cloud skimming the tops; these explosions of warmth and colour loosened inhibitions. Small children were sent out to play unsupervised in the long light evenings. Their big sisters walked home in the owl light, and occasionally throughout the border country one or two of them never made it home. People went missing in winter too but everything was so much easier in summer, warmth indulging fantasy and inducing lust . . . Alice came back to reality with a start, astonished at herself and a little uncomfortable.

Stocky, pushing fifty, well-preserved but giving the impression of permanent dishevelment, Alice was a copy editor and a good one at that, but not today. The ambience killed concentration. She looked out from the shade of the apple trees to the kitchen window framed in candy-striped clematis. It was the wrong colour, like a stick of rock; against a red sandstone wall you should have something subtle, like lavender. Pink and white had been Win's choice, she had no colour sense; Alice was the artistic one. With a sigh she turned back to Hart's latest novel. Phoenix in a heatwave and *noir*, small wonder she'd drifted off into a reverie of sex and violence in Cumbria. She stared at a page of typescript, thinking a drink might help, hearing the beck talking in the ghyll below Back Lane – She was suddenly alert; the water level was too low for the sound to carry . . . then she distinguished children's voices – angry children?

One of them approached, unseen, talking now, recognizable, the gist not surprising given the speaker: 'It's not fair! I'll tell. I hate him. I swear, on my heart I swear, if he touches me –'

Alice stood up, stretched, and walked to the gate that gave access to the path between her house and the holiday place next door. Kim Butler came round the corner of Back Lane, trudging through the dust, clutching the flaxen-haired doll that was the image of herself, stopping dead at sight of Miss Potter, the furious little face momentarily alarmed, then truculent.

'Why are you on your own, Kim?' Alice asked brightly.

The child blinked. 'I got V'ronica.' Presenting the doll, playing dumb, playing for time. She was as wily as all the rest of her dysfunctional family.

Alice looked towards Back Lane and the ghyll. 'Someone down there, in the trees?'

'The black beast.' Getting no reaction to this Kim pushed on: 'Him's got huge shiny green eyes, like on a car, and pointy ears and he's got – there's blood running all over – his mouth is all bloody – where he's been eating someone?' Wrong, and she knew it immediately. 'Lambs,' she corrected. 'Him's been in the sheep, but he could kill little kids. Him's scary.'

'Mr Carrick's Lab's loose again, crashing through the bushes, that's what you heard. The black beast is just a big tomcat, and it's hundreds of miles away –'

'He's not a cat, he's like – a dragon!'

Alice nodded dismissively. 'Where's Jason?'

Kim stared at her, licking her lips delicately. 'I run away.'

'You ran away from Jason? He's going to be –'

'No, I ran away from home.'

But she was going towards home – more or less, she'd have been quicker turning right on Back Lane instead of left and coming out here. Alice pushed the gate open. 'Come inside,' she ordered, 'you look as if you could use a drink.' And after that she'd send the child home, not take her, it would be enough to watch her go down the green to Dubb's Close, no way would she turn up at the Butlers' door with their youngest in tow: too broad a hint that Maureen Butler should take better care of a five-year-old.

Without warning Kim pushed past her and ran through the garden towards the back door. Larry Payne had turned the corner.

Alice's eyes widened. He approached, smiling his thin smile, his gaze intent. 'Like it?' he asked, preening himself.

The new hairstyle was cropped short but a cockscomb had been left and the whole dyed palest blonde. His tan had to have come from a sunbed so early in the year but it looked natural and was a delightful foil for the black singlet. He was wearing his gold ear-ring this afternoon and there was a large abstract tattoo decorating one upper arm. A hunk was the only way to describe him, thought Alice, wondering as usual about Larry's private life.

'It suits you,' she said honestly, admiring the hair. 'Is this the estate agent's current leisure wear? If your boss could see you now!'

'I'm a good salesman,' he protested, and she knew it was true. 'But I don't wear the ear-ring to the office.'

Actually she'd seen him dressed, was more used to that; today he looked a trifle – indecent – and even though no more flesh was exposed than his arms he still looked like a Chippendale and ready to strip at the blink of an eyelid. 'Larry!' She was reminded of small children on the loose. 'Kim's talking about a black beast. Is Graham's dog loose again?'

'I didn't see anything in the ghyll.'

'Only Kim' – a fractional pause – 'and Jason.'

'Right. She ran off.'

'Scared of you no doubt. You're no stranger of course but – the haircut? The tattoo? You startled her.'

'No.' He was serious. 'It was Jason who sent her packing.'

9

Alice frowned. 'Why? He's supposed to take care of his kid sister. He'll be in for a beating if his father's home. You shouldn't have separated them.'

'That sounds improper.' He was amused. 'As if I had designs . . . Actually Jason wanted to chat.' He frowned then, echoing her perplexity. 'They won't talk much to him at home, I suppose, and kids need to communicate . . . But why did he have to get rid of Kim?' he asked himself. 'He didn't say anything *private*; I mean, that he wouldn't want her to repeat.' He spread his hands. 'What am I saying? Odd, isn't it?' He was appealing to Alice, eyeing her doubtfully.

She raised an eyebrow. 'Scouting the ground? Casing the joints?' She'd lost him. 'Which holiday cottages are currently occupied?'

'Surely the Butlers would be more interested in them when they were empty.'

'No. Owners lock up securely and remove all the valuable and portable items. You won't find a toaster or a food mixer and such in any empty cottage over winter. But in summer, when tourists are away for the day, leaving back windows open, think of all the goodies they leave lying around – My God!'

'What?'

'Kim's in there' – a glance at her cottage – 'and Win's still at the pub.'

'Kim can't conceal anything in jeans and a T-shirt. You reckon she's tarred with the same brush then?'

'At five years old? All Butlers are born thieves.'

'Isn't that just a trifle incorrect politically, dear?'

'If Jason was trying to get something from you, aged ten, his little sister won't be immune. In fact, with her looks she's likely to surpass him.'

'Jason's not short on looks either. And he knows it.'

She looked at him sharply. 'Be careful, Larry. Petty theft is one thing but that boy's as clever as a monkey; you need to watch your back.'

'Knowledgeable but not experienced.' She gaped at him. He went on quickly, 'I mean, he's half-baked. He may –

probably has picked up a lot of information at home one way and another, and I realize now that he could have been trying to pick my brains about holiday people, but that's it: opportunist thieving.' He stopped, then asked silkily, 'What did you have in mind?'

She held his eye. 'Blackmail? Everyone has secrets.'

He shook his head, refusing to be fazed. 'He could try but he'll get nowhere with me. I'm pure as the driven snow. But there you are: he's inexperienced, and if young Jason did ferret out a dangerous secret who would you put your money on? With your criminal background you know as much about the way people's minds work as anyone in this village. Who would you back: the holder of the guilty secret or a ten-year-old?'

'What exactly did he want to talk about?'

'I said: holiday cottages. You don't think –?' He checked and eyed her warily. 'There were one or two probing questions,' he admitted slowly, 'but I put it down to prurience, like he'd heard something at home and wanted it explained.'

'Something – of a sexual nature? He was asking – hinting –'

'No, no. Look, you'd better go indoors, make sure all your little ornaments are safe. As for Jason' – he looked back at the ghyll distractedly and she knew he was worried – 'he'll be home by now, and Kim should be too or there'll be trouble, them turning up separately.' They were going to turn up separately anyway, Alice thought, but didn't say so. 'As for me,' he went on, suddenly brisk, 'I promised Mum I'd do Mughlai chicken tonight. I'm away.' And he was off with his jaunty swagger. Alice thought that however complicated Mughlai chicken might be it surely didn't demand three hours' preparation. The Paynes ate at seven.

Kim wasn't in the cottage. Alice was coming downstairs when the front door burst open and Win stumbled in, flushed and sweaty and still wearing her striped apron. 'My God!' she gasped. 'It's bloody roasting in that kitchen. We'll have to buy fans. I told Freda I'll be suffering from

11

heat exhaustion come June, laid it on thick; where are they going to find another gourmet chef, I said, when I collapse? Who else is going to work in this oven of a place? She promised to speak to him this evening . . .' She went along the passage grumbling to herself and Alice followed. Their own kitchen was warm but fresh, redolent of flowery smells, the blinds closed but the back door open to the garden.

'You been working down there,' Win observed, glimpsing the chair under the apple trees, the typescript on the seat. 'All right for some.' She went to the fridge for bottles of Budweiser.

'You should have been over here too,' Alice told her. The afternoon was Chef's free time. She fetched a glass as Win subsided on a chair that creaked under the strain of twelve stones of solid flesh. 'Look at me,' she protested, 'crossing the green in me pinny, would you believe. Rachel Payne would have something to say.' She drank from the bottle and wiped her mouth with the back of a pudgy hand. 'Been baking,' she explained. 'Birthday shindig this evening. Some county councillor's mum: party of sixteen. I was doing zucchini bread. I'll bring a loaf over tonight. What are you looking for?' Alice was moving about the kitchen peering at cluttered counters.

'Just making sure nothing's missing. Kim Butler was in here.'

'You should know better than to take your eyes off that young devil for one moment.'

'I was out in the lane talking to Larry. He came up from the ghyll after her.'

Win gasped. 'You mean he was chasing her? What on earth are you saying?'

'No! Jason was with her but he wanted to speak to Larry and he sent Kim on ahead.' Win scowled. She was a big, powerful woman and, shining and unkempt as she was at this moment, sleeves pushed up, muscular forearms on the table, she was the picture of aggression. Alice thought again that the situation, as depicted first by Kim, then

Larry, had indeed been odd. She sketched the background for her friend's benefit.

Win listened, studying her face. She said thoughtfully, 'You're worried – but there's never been any talk about him.'

'We'd have heard.' Alice was relieved, a haunting doubt was out in the open; no longer sinister, it could be discussed. 'Between your kitchen and the bar we hear everything,' she said firmly, 'and there's never been a breath of suspicion. They were quick enough to talk about us.'

They grinned. When they'd come to the village talk was inevitable but the locals soon tired of speculation about a possible lesbian relationship, and that was years ago.

'With Redneck Butler in Dubb's Close,' Win was saying, 'no paedophile would have lasted a day in this place. No, our Larry's a walking advert for machismo, despite being Mummy's golden boy. And not a bad cook at that.'

'Did you see him?' Alice breathed, eyes shining. 'No, he'd be home by the time you came over. He's had a new haircut with a quiff like a Mohican, and bleached the palest lemon. A black singlet, my dear, and a beautiful tattoo, kind of Arabic' – she stroked her arm, demonstrating – 'and the ear-ring –'

'You're a bit long in the tooth for Larry.'

'Don't be daft. But he *exuded* sex. A woman of eighty would have seen it, let alone one of fifty. He was quite disturbing. Why, even Kim –' She stopped. Win's eyebrows climbed. 'That had to be why she left them,' Alice breathed. 'She was scared, knew there was something – dangerous? Couldn't cope. Like Larry said of Jason.'

'Here, what's this? What about Jason?'

'We were talking villainy, not sex.' Alice turned prim. 'Larry was saying that Jason might be knowledgeable but he didn't have the experience to use the knowledge. I took him to mean blackmail. Yes, that was it: he said if Jason were to try it, he'd put his money on the blackmailee. He also said, Larry said, he was pure as the driven snow.'

They giggled conspiratorially.

* * *

Larry was transferring the chicken to the oven when his mother came in from the garden with a bunch of coriander. 'Bart's just back,' she announced. 'Where's he been, this time of a Friday evening?'

'Avoiding June,' Larry murmured, taking the coriander and inspecting it critically.

'You mean deliberately not coming home until she'd left? And where's she this evening?'

'Parish council? "Keep Eden Clean"? Dialect Society? You name it.'

'Poor man.' Rachel glanced at the window that looked towards the Hall next door, its walls mostly obscured by birches and sycamores in full leaf. 'She'll have left something for his supper no doubt.' The tone was only a mite short of contempt. Larry's lips tightened but he said nothing, concentrating on easing the foil off a carton of yoghurt. 'Ask him over,' Rachel said sharply.

'It's an idea.' He decanted the yoghurt into a basin. 'You give him a bell. He'd appreciate it.'

'I shall. We can't have him eating alone in that great place.'

'It's only a house, Mum.'

'It's huge and it's a tip, a pretentious tip. How Bart can be expected to turn it into a graceful home . . .' She strode purposefully to the telephone.

He regarded her back speculatively, alert to her end of the conversation. She was a small trim woman, tonight in gun-metal trousers and an emerald camisole. Only the mature mousy face framed by curls that were a trifle too black gave the lie to the impression of a girl below the age of consent.

She replaced the phone. 'He says give him five minutes. We do have enough chicken?'

'Heaps. Mum, next time I do your hair, right?'

'Sweetie!' She was devastated. 'It's too dark?'

He appeared to consider. 'Maybe you left it on a shade too long. Perhaps we should try another brand.'

'You're the expert.' She studied his own style. 'It's ultra sexy, dear; you'll be a sensation in the pub.'

He shrugged. 'Whisk the yoghurt for me, will you?'

Their guest arrived on time, crossing their adjoining gardens, dressed casually in polo shirt and scrubbed jeans: Bart Milburn, owner – or rather, part-owner – of Culchet Hall, but definitely not the squire. He was by way of being a builder at the moment, as he turned a hand to renovating this seventeenth-century mansion bought for a song two years ago. He didn't look like a builder, at least not the overblown, overripe prototype; he was tall and well muscled, an indulgent alcohol intake mostly cancelled out by hard physical labour. Close to forty he showed little sign of ageing, his hair thick and well-cut (he and Larry used the same barber), his teeth all his own and his eyelashes so long Alice Potter opined they had enchanted his wife. 'It wasn't his eyes,' was Win's retort. They were cool blue eyes. Win had been jilted by a blue-eyed man and as a consequence distrusted all of them. True to the myth Bart was a charmer. Rachel Payne adored him.

'You've been in the pub,' Larry stated as they manoeuvred round each other in the kitchen.

'Is it so obvious?'

'Scotch!' Larry wrinkled his nose. 'You stink of it.'

'Manners!' Rachel placed a slim hand on the small of Bart's back, thrilling to the feel of warm muscle under thin cotton. 'Come along, Bart, we'll have our drinks in peace and let the boy finish here.'

She propelled him towards the dining room where they turned their chairs to face windows that were wide to the still evening. The room was shaded by one of the huge horse chestnuts that gave the village green the air of parkland; all it needed was a herd of fallow deer to complete the illusion. Inside the room chance specks of sunlight caught polished wood and glass and struck amber glints from their whisky.

Bart regarded his hostess benignly. 'Rather more comfortable than the pub,' he assured her.

She nodded. It was her due. 'Who was over there?'

'No one. Well, a couple of visitors.' He smiled ruefully. 'Joely behind the bar.'

She was suddenly coy. 'You'll have to watch yourself in that department.'

'*I* don't do anything.'

'You don't have to. You're the nearest thing to a movie star in little Joely's firmament and, at sixteen, passions run high. Remember what it was like?'

He was thoughtful. 'I had other interests,' he pointed out. 'Boys do, you know.' His tone lightened. 'She's a very pretty child however. And sixteen – not under-age any longer, is she?"

'Bart Milburn, you'd never dare!'

'Never dare to what?' said Larry from the doorway, approaching, reaching for the Glenfiddich and the third glass. 'What are you up to now?' Turning to Bart.

'We were discussing the gorgeous Joely.'

'Oh yes. And?'

'He pointed out that she's not under-age any longer.' Rachel feigned disapproval. 'A moot point: who would you have to fear most, Bart – Graham Carrick or Freda – or June?'

'June wouldn't give a damn.'

For a moment no one spoke. It was Larry who broke the tension. 'This,' he said coldly, 'is a sleazy subject, don't you think? Right, I'm going to dish up.'

'In a moment, sweetie,' Rachel protested as he turned, carrying his drink. 'Let's take our time over the whisky. We have Chardonnay to come,' she told Bart.

'It was in bad taste,' he murmured as Larry returned to the kitchen. 'Joely's a joke, she means nothing to me –'

'Of course not, dear! I was only teasing. Larry takes everything so seriously.'

He wasn't listening. 'She can be a nuisance though,' he mused. 'I'm wary of going in the Stag these days. Thank God she doesn't follow me across to the Hall. I have to admit, that little girl scares me stiff at times. She's so blatant, even in front of Graham and Freda. Or do you think they can't see it? Surely they do. So why –'

'Oh, they'll see, but Graham will be guided by Freda and she'll have assured him it's just a crush, which it is: puppy love. And Freda knows that the child would never dare come across to the Hall, she'd be far too scared of June.'

'Who isn't?' She wasn't meant to hear that and she gave no indication that she had. She wasn't surprised, the Milburns were such an ill-matched couple: him with his looks and his restlessness, a multitude of jobs behind him and no career, something vague about dropping out of university but giving a general impression of dissatisfaction, a man who'd not yet found his niche. And then there was June: heavy, plain, even dowdy, a pillar of the community, with a hand in everything: the parish council, the environment, youth, farming regeneration after foot-and-mouth, gardens, the local agricultural show – there was nothing that June wasn't involved in, nothing that didn't interest her – except her husband.

Widowed for five years, Rachel remembered her overbearing but predictable husband with a fondness she'd never felt for him when he was alive, not realizing that it was quite common for the bereft to invest the departed with virtues they didn't possess. Leo Payne had been a cold man but conventionally correct. He was a textile manufacturer, finishing garments imported from the Third World (sweated labour, Larry called it), so he had left them well provided for. In fact, although she would never admit it, Rachel felt that her lifestyle had improved when her son assumed the role of head of the family. Leo had never been affectionate but Larry was kind, he brought her flowers and chocolates, took her to good restaurants, came with her when she bought clothes; in short she was cosseted, treated as an attentive young fellow of her generation would have treated his fiancée. People told her how lucky she was to have such a good son, what on earth would she do when he married, they asked. Rachel assured them that he wouldn't move far away. Discerning folk knew that Larry would never move *out*. Moreover they were quite sure that no partner of Larry's would ever move into Todbank Cottage, not while his mother was alive.

*　　*　　*

17

It was dusk when June Milburn came home from a parish council meeting in the next village. The main item on the agenda had been consideration of a proposal for a trail biking course at the foot of the escarpment. Discussion had been heated and drawn out. June returned home tired, feeling threatened. She didn't want bikers but the mood of the council was against her and she'd been accused of self-interest, which wasn't far from the truth. She might maintain that her opposition was on general grounds but there was no denying that it was also specific. Her aim in renovating Culchet Hall was to establish a superior Bed and Breakfast place, the kind that would attract discriminating tourists: wilderness walkers, naturalists, university courses – people for whom bikers and four-tracks were anathema. If the East Fellside were thrown open to such traffic visitors would go elsewhere; the Southern Uplands were only a few miles away over the Scottish border. The Hall would become a white elephant and, in view of its size, unsaleable, even if Bart ever managed to finish the renovation. He was a slow worker; June was starting to consider calling in professionals to do the job.

The street lights glowed softly through foliage as she drove up the green. A white cat sat on the steps of the old pump washing its face. Winter here could be hell but in a good summer Culchet epitomized the charm of bucolic village life, and this particular village was rendered even more attractive by the contrast with that stark and lonely sweep of moorland two thousand feet above, and now humped black against the stars. With advertising and the internet she might attract Americans . . .

She drove into the stable yard to park neatly at the back door. The Land Rover and Bart's pick-up were not so much parked as left, as clothes – his clothes – were dropped on the bedroom floor. No lights showed in the house and the back door wasn't locked. She inhaled sharply. Before the Butler family came to Culchet people left their doors unlocked and their windows open. Now, if it was screwed down, the screws were taken as well. And if it was Bart's tools that were stolen there were no guesses as to who had to replace them. They weren't his anyway; she bought them, he merely had the use of them. She was disgruntled, she needed a drink. For a moment she considered going across to the Stag but she dismissed the thought; it smacked too much of an old cartoon wife hauling her man out of the pub by his scruff.

She went through the house switching on lights, feeling the chill strike up from stone flags. She collected brandy and a glass from the dining room and returned to the kitchen, sitting down at the big scrubbed table to taste the first strong drink of the day. Savouring it with relish she started to make a note of the tasks for tomorrow.

'June's home,' Larry observed, watching the tail lights of her Escort turn in at the Hall. 'Did you leave a note?'

They were sitting at a shadowed table outside the Stag. Around them other customers talked quietly in contrast to the hubbub inside the pub where holiday people were swelling numbers at the start of the weekend.

'Why should I leave a note?' Bart was surly, feeling a trifle nauseous after malt whisky and wine, not to speak of spicy chicken, now beer. Bart didn't hold his liquor well. 'I've had it up to here,' he muttered. 'I'm sick of it.'

He could have been referring to the drink but Larry knew he wasn't. The situation was deteriorating but the man was short on decision-making, and Larry was never averse to playing Iago. 'You have to do something,' he said tartly, not for the first time. 'You're heading for a break-down otherwise. Get out while the going's good.'

'Move out?' Bart's head turned and his eyes gleamed. He'd been looking towards the Hall, hidden from here by the chestnuts. 'It's my home, man!'

'That's not the only way out.' There was a long silence. '*She* could leave,' Larry said softly.

'It's her house. She's got plans. You know that.'

'Buy her out.'

'You're joking. It cost peanuts but I don't have a hundred to my name. She supports me. I'm a gigolo and that's it.'

'Oh, for God's sake!' Larry moved violently, jogging the table, spilling beer. He said wildly, 'That place is too big; she has to admit it, force her to admit it. Show her somewhere manageable, smaller, in good nick – *I'll* show her; we've got plenty on our books: in the Lakes –'

'Yeah, costing a fortune –'

'Over the border then –'

'Your firm don't go across the border.'

'Bart, you're being obstructive. What's with you?' Larry's voice dropped. 'You want rid of her; ever since I knew you you've been depressed. You can't go on like this, you've got all your life before you, are you going to stay –'

'You want me to leave.'

'No, you goon! I want you to stay. What you have to do –'

'I want to stay too. I love this place. I could be very happy here' – his face was pale in the gloom, his tone warm – 'you know that. I put yew berries in the stew.'

'Then that's settled. You're not leaving and – *What?* What was that? Yew berries in the *stew*?'

'Keep your voice down! It was a joke.'

'Well . . .' Larry subsided, then stiffened. 'You mean you just made a joke, or putting' – he glanced round and leaned close – 'what you did was meant as a joke?'

'An experiment,' Bart conceded. 'I tried it to see what would happen, what effect it would have.'

'Yew's lethal, man! She could have been –'

'She didn't touch it, only a taste, not enough. She said something had gone off. Threw it out. I pretended my helping tasted queer too although of course I hadn't put any of the stuff in mine.'

'Are you telling me you meant to . . .' Larry stopped and waited.

'It was to make her ill just.' Bart continued in an innocent, artificial tone: 'To drive her away. I tried ground glass once. In the sugar. She puts sugar on porridge. She said there was grit in the oatmeal. She threw that out too.'

After a while Larry asked tightly, 'How long has this been going on?'

'It started at Easter. We came over to you on the Saturday night, remember? I was a bit under the weather and I threw up when we got home. She was there, I mean, with me. She must have cleaned up after me. Never said anything about it on the Sunday when I came downstairs. I'd have preferred her to shout and throw things like any hysterical woman but not her. She never does. Just occasionally she'll say something.'

'Like what? You didn't tell me this until now.'

'She tells me what – what she maintains is wrong with our relationship.'

'With you. She lays into you.' The silence was strained. No way would Bart admit that what he'd resented most was a charge of inadequacy. Larry said lightly, as if changing the subject, 'When's Carol coming up again?' Carol was June's daughter by her first husband whom she'd divorced when she discovered him having an affair with his secretary. Carol was married to George Hammond, a publisher in a small way.

'They're in Australia,' Bart said. 'Something to do with his job, such as it is.' He lifted his glass but did no more than taste its contents. He'd had enough. 'He's a wimp,' he muttered and relapsed into silence.

Larry said, quiet but firm, 'You're not going to leave the Hall so you have to force her out.'

'That's the idea.' He was slurring his words. 'I'll come up with something, you can bet on that.'

'No, you won't, not *that* way. Now you listen to me. You're going to forget all about' – Larry lowered his voice – 'what you were saying: your naughty little jokes. I'm going to take over. I'll get rid of her for you.'

Bart was still. 'How would you do that?' he breathed.

'Don't ask questions. This is my department now.'

'I have to keep the Hall, Larry.' Bart was panicking. 'That's the whole point of the exercise far as I'm concerned. I'm not having her selling the place out from under my feet, or leaving it to Carol – ' He stopped abruptly.

'Who's talking about "leaving" anything? As in wills, d'you mean? All the same, has she left the place to Carol?'

'She hasn't made a will.'

'Oh, you discovered that. Clever boy. That's all right then. And I can deal with Carol too, any time. Mr Fixit, that's me. Let's have one more round; we're going to drink to our future.'

'Not for me. I need to get home.'

Larry gaped but he made no comment. He saw that, like a battered wife, Bart was trapped. He couldn't leave because he was committed, even more committed than the wife who can leave and take her children with her. Bart's home was here, he had to stay in Culchet, but if there were no intervention the poor guy was going to take the simplest course – and end in court charged with manslaughter at best. He'd plead provocation, of course, and juries tended to favour men with sadistic wives, but no way was Larry going to see his mate pilloried in the media as a wife killer.

Chapter Two

Maud Brunskill, short and wide but solid for all her eighty years, marched firmly across the green to the pump where Jason and Kim sat on a step. They watched her approach with the hair-trigger air of young animals considering flight, the difference being that Jason was weighing the advantages of staying put. In his view Mrs Brunskill had a nasty mind, and she talked crafty, trying to catch you out, but it could be amusing trying to beat her at her own game.

'Jason!' She had a funny voice, soft but loud somehow, and he could always understand her unlike some of the folk in the old cottages – which was how the Butlers referred, with contempt, to the houses round the green. Jason's family lived in Dubb's Close: a circle of newish, low-cost dwellings sited on the fringe of the village. 'The visitors at Rowan Tree Cottage,' Mrs Brunskill said, proclaimed rather, and waited expectantly, her eyes shaded by dark glasses and the brim of her baseball cap.

Jason said nothing. He hadn't been asked a question. Beside him Kim shifted nervously. 'They gotta yappy dog,' she said, the words overlapped quickly by her brother's, 'We don't know them, miss.' He was a polite boy when it suited.

'There was no jumble sale this weekend, nor is one planned,' Mrs Brunskill said sternly.

'What you do,' Jason was suddenly earnest, 'is you collect enough things so it makes a good load, and when a sale do come along, you got something worth taking there, see?'

'You went inside Rowan Tree.' He swallowed. 'With Kim. The people didn't invite you, you pushed your way in.' The dark glasses were turned on the little sister.

'No!' she protested. 'I never. I never go in folk's houses. I'm not supposed to, not strangers –'

'I see she don't come to no harm,' Jason interrupted loudly. 'She knows not to take sweets from men nor thumb a ride –'

'You took her into Rowan Tree' – the old lady was speaking like a bobby now – 'and you demanded clothes for a jumble sale that isn't going to happen. You got a beating at Christmas from your father for the same thing –'

'He didn't then –' Kim broke in, and winced as an elbow drove into her ribs. Most little girls would have dissolved in tears at that but – 'Fucking bastard,' she hissed, and jumped up to stalk away.

'You wait for me or I'll tell our dad,' Jason shouted. 'Little madam,' he told Mrs Brunskill in a tone way beyond his years. 'Don't you worry, miss, I've done nowt wrong. All them old clothes is in our shed ready for t'next jumble.'

Maud considered. 'Perhaps I should have a word with your mother.'

'Not a good idea.' He looked mournful. 'Her's on tablets for her nerves. Doctor says as how she gotta rest up; no stress, he says.'

'If Maureen Butler's on tablets they'll be appetite-suppressors,' Maud said, drinking mid-morning coffee with her husband after recounting this exchange with the youngest Butlers. 'Even the woman's nerves must be insulated with fat.'

'There's no point in speaking to her about Jason,' Ted said, glancing up from his *Independent*. 'It would be herself who sent the children out in the first place. You've always maintained she couldn't afford to dress them in designer clothes. Obviously she picks over what they collect and keeps the best for the family. They're all into some form of villainy, it's a criminal family.' He snorted, rustling the paper. Ted was a naturalist and he classed the Butlers in the same category as toxic waste. At the moment he resembled an angry hawk with his beaky nose and large round eyes. Maud regarded him indulgently, knowing he would have erupted in fury had she acquainted him with the obscenity Kim had hurled at her brother. You couldn't blame the child, she picked up foul language at home. 'A problem family,' she corrected, 'not villains.'

'Huh! Maureen receives – if not stolen goods, then items obtained by deception. Jon's already served his first term as an adult prisoner, and how long was he in young offenders' jails? As for Hugh, all you can say for him is that he's not been convicted: caught, but got away with it. What was it: roofing slates? Stripping remote barns?'

'There was never any proof.'

'Like there was no proof of the graffiti in the school lavatories, but everyone knew it was young Jason.'

He would make no allowances for any of the Butlers; he held that Jason was responsible for vandalizing the saplings he'd planted in the ghyll, for fences broken down in order to reach fruit in back gardens, indeed for any act of vandalism that couldn't be attributed to the elder brother, but then Jon operated further afield, old enough to be wary of fouling his own doorstep.

'The close was a respectable place until they moved in.' Ted glared at his paper, unable to concentrate on it, reminded of past sins and current anxieties. He dared not watch a peregrine's nest on Wragg Scar for fear of attracting attention to it. Jon Butler was the last person you wanted to know there were young peregrines within reach of a rope, and worth a fortune in the right market. Butlers would always know the whereabouts of the right market, and the going price. He said so but Maud pointed out that Jon wasn't that clever; at twenty-two he'd already spent three years in jail.

'Fear of consequences wouldn't stop him robbing my nest,' Ted growled. 'Or shooting the nestlings like that scum in Yorkshire –'

'Ah, Rob!' Maud exclaimed, in some relief as their egg-man's bulk blocked out the light.

'I brought your order.' Rob Housby placed two boxes on the table. 'Hope you had enough left for breakfast. I was held up. An old cow had a bit of trouble.'

Maud was concerned. 'Is she all right?'

'She's fine now. Breech birth – but Jill's home so we managed, the two of us. What was that about Yorkshire scum?'

'The bugger who shot the peregrines in that quarry,' Ted told him. 'We'd got on to the Butlers: same mentality.'

'They've discovered the nest on Wragg Scar?'

'No, no, we were talking generally. One set of villains puts you in mind of another.' Ted glowered at his wife. 'What started this? It's a beautiful morning, why bring up such a nasty subject?'

'I met Kim,' Maud said shortly, pouring coffee for Rob as he pulled out a chair. 'It'll be nice to have Jill home. Is this a holiday or . . .' She trailed off; her generation could never come to accept the speed with which youngsters changed jobs these days, and a girl being home on a Monday could mean redundancy, even teachers were being forced out of their posts. Jill Housby took physical education in a Manchester school.

'Half-term,' Rob told her. 'And is she glad to be home, this weather and all. She can't wait till the heat goes out of the day to have her horse out and work some of the fat off him. She says I've got to keep him up to scratch when she goes back.'

'You're too heavy for him,' Tom said.

He was heavy, not fat but tall and solid like many of the country people in Cumbria, women too, descended from Viking settlers. Ted himself had the big frame but where he never put on weight (out on the hill most days and Maud serving good healthy food), Rob, widowed and living alone, was slack about his diet and did much of his shep-herding on a farm bike. Even his face was filled out and, where Ted's features were predatory, Rob had the look of a genial bear. He was a contented man, although happier when Jill was home. Without her there were only the collies and a monstrous cross between some Italian hound and an Alsatian. There was Australian blood in that animal too which had produced strange pale eyes. He had the roar of a tiger and a trick of stretching his jaws in a soundless snarl that produced the fear of death in strangers. Jill had christened him Baz, for Baskerville.

Maud mentioned that Jason was up to his familiar ploy of conning people into parting with clothes that were not necessarily old but relinquished in order to get rid of the children.

'Extortion,' Ted muttered.

'We've all suffered once,' Maud admitted, 'or until we've cottoned on to it. Jason will be talking to you, oh, so persuasively – and politely, it has to be said – and then you notice that Kim is moving behind your back, quietly picking up little objects – I actually saw her in a mirror. I turned before she could pocket anything but I wonder how many people are missing small trinkets . . . It could happen the other way of course: Jason inspecting bric-a-brac while a person talks to Kim. Depends which you find most winning: small boys or little girls. Did they ever try it on with you?' Maud never considered that her words might be misinterpreted.

Rob laughed hugely. 'Not on your life! They did come, yes, but I wasn't in the house and I wouldn't have known until I was accosted by Hugh Butler in the pub and he accused me of keeping a savage guard dog, loose, that would kill a child one day. It had attacked Kim – he said.'

'Ah.' Maud smiled knowingly. Everyone knew – that is, Rob's friends knew – that Baz was all bluff; if you stood your ground he would close those massive jaws, soft as a gundog's mouth, and slobber all over you. One wore old clothes when visiting Rob.

'I asked Butler,' he told them, 'what Kim was doing at my house. Visiting, he said, couldn't a little girl visit neighbours without being savaged? I looked him straight in the eye, and the pub was quiet at that moment, and I said it depended what she'd come for, visiting a man who lives on his own. "You allow that?" I asked, innocent-like. It took him a while to get the import, then he walked out.'

Even Ted had to grin at that. Rob stood and picked up his cap. 'I'm away to the Stag. Any message for them?'

Maud had taken Win a bundle of herbs already this morning. 'That poor girl,' she said, 'working in that kitchen over the weekend, and no fans! Graham's away to Carlisle to see what he can find. Win's threatening to leave if he doesn't come back with something efficient.'

'He will. The Carricks aren't about to lose the best chef outside the Lake District.'

He drove the short distance past the holiday cottage next door and into the pub's car park, sited discreetly at the rear and occupying space that would once have been stables and a cobbled yard. He collected trays of eggs from the back of his van and entered the kitchen. Win was taking a sheet of rolls out of the oven while Joely, in white tank top and skintight jeans, was stirring soup. Rob, who was comfortable around young girls, having raised one, regarded her indulgently. At sixteen she'd lost the puppy fat but her cheeks still held the plumpness of adolescence and with the long pale hair tied back with a black ribbon she was arresting: a childish face above a ravishing body. He thought that she'd wreak havoc when she grew up, forgetting that Jill had done as much at sixteen.

'Soup?' he queried. 'I'd have thought it would be all salads this weather.' The kitchen faced east and was stifling.

'The salad's done,' Win told him. 'But if this was the tropics there'd still be folk wanting soup. Men,' she added pointedly.

'Well, I could eat your soup any time.' He was heavily gallant.

'What kept you?'

'Cow calving.'

'Is she all right?'

'Fine. Jill helped. It's half-term.'

Joely turned eagerly. 'Is she taking Sherry out? I could borrow Thornthwaites' pony.'

'You do that, she'll be glad of the company. She's out every evening. Sherry's as fat as butter.'

'You should take him out, Rob; you could lose a few pounds yourself,' Win said carelessly: the pot calling the kettle black.

'I'm too heavy.'

'I can!' Joely cried. 'When Jill goes back I'll take him out summer evenings.'

'Yes, well, you'll have to speak to her about that.' No way would his daughter allow Joely to exercise her precious horse. Exercise! She'd gallop him home and turn him out sweating like a pig. But Rob avoided confrontations with women; attacking him was like shouting at his Hereford bull: man and bull would walk away. He turned to leave and at that moment Freda Carrick came in from the front of the house, flustered, hair awry, looking drawn. 'A party of geologists wanting lunch – 'Morning, Rob, another lovely day – they've settled for bar meals, Win: soup and salad. OK?'

'Can do.' Win wiped moisture out of her eyes, undid the bandanna at her throat and tied it round her forehead. Joely giggled.

Freda acknowledged the hint, crude as it was. 'If he doesn't come back with fans, I'll go in and find some myself.'

'Funny thing,' Rob observed. 'The Hall strikes chill. Their flags are sweating.'

'No damp course,' Win said.

'They've got cellars. Bart's working down there at the moment, him and Hugh Butler: pouring concrete.'

Joely licked her lips and her eyes shone. 'Pouring concrete?'

'For a wine cellar.' Rob grinned. 'B and B *and* evening meal, he says. But – a wine cellar?'

'We've got competition,' Win said, and smiled thinly, knowing her own worth.

'June's away looking at more properties,' he told them.

'More?' Freda was astonished. 'Are they moving – no, they're renovating. Or are –'

'They're never moving!' Joely was stricken.

The women ignored her and focused on Rob. 'June's got the bit between her teeth,' he said. 'She's proposing to buy more property for letting: short-term and holidays. That's where the money is, according to Bart – in property. Presumably he's quoting June.'

'He's right.' Freda nodded sagely. 'It's certainly a lot safer, things as they are, and June thinks things through, she's a very practical lady. Where's she looking?'

'Bart didn't say.'

Hugh Butler, gross but powerful, balding, and shifty as a buffalo, started up the cellar steps in the face of Bart's protests. 'I told you I could only spare the morning,' he whinged, 'I got them beasts to shift. I could come back this evening.' He waited for an offer of extra money: overtime pay.

Bart said tightly, 'You could at least call in for the cement.'

'I'm no taking a girt cattle wagon into town! Where'd I find a spot to park? I'd be hours, man; you'd need to pay us for a full afternoon.' Again he waited hopefully.

'The wife'd have something to say about that.' Bart let the sledgehammer fall on the cracked slabs. 'I'll need to go myself then. So I'll see you tomorrow.'

'Do me best.' It was no more than a response, definitely not assurance. Bart expected nothing else; he'd known it was going to be himself collecting the cement.

Hugh climbed into his Land Rover and started down the green. His younger son was standing near Thrushgill, Alice Potter's place that she shared with Win Langley. Jason was talking to the Thornthwaite kids. 'Where's Kim?' Hugh demanded.

'She's here.' Jason glanced down the side of Thrushgill. 'Kim!' he shouted. 'Where you gone?'

She appeared to emerge straight out of Thrushgill's garden wall. 'Shut gate!' Hugh bawled. 'Come 'ere.'

She took her time latching the gate and advanced slowly.

'What you doing in Potter's garden then?'

'Her told us to come in for a drink.' Her eyes were guileless.

Hugh scowled, looking for a grievance. 'You stay with your brother,' he ordered, glaring at Jason who sketched a nod to show the Thornthwaites he wasn't intimidated.

Hugh was in a bad mood because Bart had been unable to pay him for the morning's work, maintaining he had no cash in the house until June returned from town. Hugh was deep in debt, he had no credit cards and was dependent on illegal work and sickness benefit. He had fallen in a hole when drunk one night in Brimstock. The hole had been in a car park, adequately railed and lit but his mates had smashed the lights and kicked away the rails and Hugh insisted that vandals had done that before he fell – which was why he fell. He was trying to sue the council and getting nowhere because of the quality of the original safety measures and the difficulty of determining the exact nature of his persistent injury. Meanwhile he was so skint he hadn't enough for a tankful of petrol. He was to be paid cash to take some old cows to the abattoir but he hadn't enough fuel to reach the farm. Maybe Maureen had something in her bag. He'd need to be crafty there, wait for an opportunity – or Jason might have a few quid squirrelled away in the room he shared with Jon. Or Jon himself for that matter, the kids were better off than their dad. The thought crossed his mind that they might be more successful at acquiring money in the first place, he couldn't see Jon breaking flags with a sledgehammer all morning and not getting paid for it. Even Kim: only her word for it that Alice Potter was home. Maybe Kim was learning from her brothers, he thought, coming quietly up the step to his kitchen in the close, noting a new bike leaning against the wall, smelling bacon and black pudding. Past noon and his wife was frying the lad's breakfast!

'Thought you was at the Hall today,' Maureen said, turning from the stove, still in her dressing gown, a skimpy thing, mostly lace and parting at the seams. She hadn't washed and her hair was like an old crow's nest.

'I finished there.'

'Did he pay you?'

'He paid.' If he told the truth she'd know he was looking for cash. He glanced round the kitchen. No bag; with himself out of the house she'd have thought it safe to leave it upstairs, although there was Jon . . .

The front room was hazy with cigarette smoke, curtains permanently drawn because the television was in the window. The news was on but the sound turned off. Jon sprawled on the sofa under an ornate standard lamp, reading *The Sun*, wearing jeans and nothing else. Even prone you could see that he was a tall fellow and you'd have thought, with his parentage, he'd put some flesh on his bones once he reached maturity, but he was all angles and his ribs showed like a starved beast's. Even his face was long under a high forehead, the features squeezed together: small eyes, a child's nose, prim lips. The stubble that he tended so carefully made him look unfinished rather than sophisticated.

'The bike,' Hugh said, peering round out of habit. Her bag wouldn't be here.

'What bike?'

'New mountain job outside back door. Who's it belong to?'

'Me.'

'How d'you manage that?'

Jon shrugged. 'Sold summat.'

'You'd best keep it in shed. Leave it there, in plain view, that's asking for trouble.' No question but that both items – 'summat' and the bike – had not been legally acquired.

'I'm going out on it.' Jon sat up languidly as his mother

came in with a plate piled with food. 'Where's me tea?' he protested.

'I'm fetching it, aren't I?' Maureen blundered back to the kitchen. Behind her Hugh slipped upstairs, hurrying to find what might be left of the family benefit before she realized what he was about.

Kim came in the back door grizzling, found no one in the kitchen, checked to see if any food was immediately available, heard her mother returning and broke into low sobs.

'Now what?' Maureen cried. Communication among the older Butlers was habitually conducted at full volume.

'Jason hit me.'

'Why? Show me!' Maureen pulled tiny hands from the blotched face. 'He hit you in the face? What d'you do?'

'I didn't do nothing. He knocked me flat. He called me an 'ore.'

Jason appeared. 'Her fell,' he told his mother. 'She were running across green and a car were coming like the clappers. I caught her before her reached road.'

'It weren't –'

'Why d'you have to hit her then?'

'He called me an 'ore.'

'You shut up,' Maureen snapped. 'I got a headache fit to split me skull. You deal with these,' she shot at Hugh as he appeared in the inner doorway. 'I'm going up and take me pills and have a lie-down. I've had it up to here with the lot of you. Them's your kids, I have 'em all day, if it isn't one thing, it's another.'

'Who belongs to t'bike?' Jason asked.

No one answered. Maureen had realized that her husband had been out of her sight for several minutes and here he was sidling towards the back door – 'Where you going?' she shouted.

'Gotta take beasts to slaughter.'

He was gone. Maureen clambered up the stairs to find out how much money was left in her bag.

Jason and Kim knew better than to look for crisps or biscuits (fast as they came into the house, they went); they drifted into the front room to sit on the floor in front of the TV. The sound was on now and Jon was staring blankly at *Brain Teaser* while he ate. Jason reached for the remote.

'Leave it,' Jon growled automatically.

Jason started to whine, knowing it would have his brother climbing the wall. Kim walked out.

In the small town of Harras some ten miles from Culchet three boys, aged around fourteen, came quickly down a ginnel looking for a place to hole up for an hour or two. They wore shell suit tops the better to conceal cans of cider and cigarettes, not nicked but acquired through the offices of an older sister.

The ginnel debouched on a weedy plot below high walls set with small barred windows: the rear aspect of stores fronting on the street. Ragwort and willow herb flourished in the cracks of steps leading up to doors that looked as if they hadn't been opened for decades. Apart from the path down the ginnel the yard could be approached by an arched tunnel through the buildings but it was seldom used simply because people who worked in the stores preferred to keep their cars in the market place at the front where they were overlooked and therefore more secure. So the boys were surprised to see a relatively new Escort in the yard. Surprise mounted to interest as they sauntered casually past it, to excitement when they saw that the keys were in the ignition. One of them could drive.

Chapter Three

Rachel Payne tried to replace the phone but she was too shaken. It fell and dangled on its cord. She knew she should sit down but she couldn't just sit, doing nothing. She staggered through the kitchen gripping objects as she went: the refrigerator, the table, feeling her way to the door and the coal bunker. She looked towards the Hall and tried to shout but her mouth was dry and she couldn't make a sound. She drew deep breaths although the first were sobs.

Bart was in the stable yard, seated on the mounting block in the shade, drinking Carlsberg Special, three full cans beside him. His eyes narrowed as she approached, still unsteady, and against the raven hair her face was so pale it looked as if she'd been bled. 'My boy,' she whispered, and held her hands out to him.

Anyone would have thought she was drunk and coming on to him but, 'Larry?' he asked on a rising note. 'What's happened? Here, sit down.'

He held her, guiding her to the block. She pushed at him feebly. 'Take me to the hospital. I can't drive, I'm too shaky. Please, Bart, you're his friend. Take me.'

'What's happened to him, Rachel?'

'A crash. He's unconscious. They say he's all right, he's alive. I'll get a taxi – phone for me, Bart.'

'I'll drive you of course –'

'Or June could.'

'She's not here. Hang on a moment while I fetch the keys to the Land Rover.'

*   *   *

Larry seemed to have shrunk. He lay like a thin robot, connected to machines, bruises on one cheekbone and his forehead, dried blood in his pale hair. Bart wondered why they hadn't washed it out but he supposed that wasn't a priority. The ventilator was doing the essential work. He left Rachel sitting there holding a limp hand, her other hand hovering over the hair that had been so arresting, still was, but no longer amusing. He found a nurse and asked how it had happened, *what* had happened.

Evidently Larry had hit a tractor in a lane close to the motorway. The tractor driver was uninjured but he'd been treated for shock and allowed to go home.

Bart stayed for an hour, talking at rather than to Rachel across the pathetically slight form. Her eyes were fixed on her son's face and she murmured to him between acknowledging Bart with automatic and sometimes senseless responses. She wouldn't leave. She had come straight from home just as she'd returned from shopping in Kendal. The hospital had been trying to reach her for hours; Larry had been identified from his car's registration. Bart said he would drive home and ask June to go into Todbank and pack an overnight bag. 'That would be kind,' Rachel said vaguely, and asked the nurse if she could wash Larry's hair, at least wipe it with a damp cloth. The nurse said it was better to leave it for the time being.

It was eight o'clock when Bart reached the Hall. It had been a long day and he was tired and hungry. June wasn't home and he had no idea what kind of things an elderly woman would need in an overnight bag. He went across to the pub, still in his working clothes – which he'd never wear in the Stag in the normal way. People had looked askance at him in the hospital: covered with cement dust and smelling, making eye contact with everyone, desperately concerned about Larry.

Joely, collecting glasses from outside the pub, stared as he passed without speaking. At the bar her mother stiffened at his approach, alarm bells ringing. 'Larry's had a smash,' he told her roughly. 'He's in a coma. I just got back from taking Rachel to the hospital.'

There was momentary silence as visitors caught the tension from the locals, then broken questions: 'How bad –?' 'Will he –?'' 'Where did it happen?' 'What happened?'

'It was on the local news,' someone exclaimed. 'Chap hit a tractor up Keld way. That was *Larry*? They never said.'

'They don't release names till next of kin's been informed.'

'That's when someone's – when it's serious like.'

'How bad is it?' Freda asked Bart quietly.

His shoulders slumped. 'Rachel needs some things,' he said. 'June isn't home yet. Do you think someone could come over to Todbank and pack a bag for her?'

'I'll come!' This from Joely, pushing a tray of glasses on to the bar.

'You'll stay here,' Freda said sharply.

'I'll do it.' Alice Potter approached, pale but as collected as any of them. 'Do you have the key, Bart?'

He looked bewildered. 'I didn't ask her for it. She came straight across to me after taking the call from the hospital and she didn't go home again. I think she must have just walked out of the house, dropped everything. Probably didn't even lock up.'

She hadn't; the telephone was still dangling on its cord, her handbag and car keys on the table, upmarket carriers on a chair, tissue protruding. Alice thought how shocking it must have been for her: returning from a spending spree to such a ghastly telephone call. And here was Bart, Larry's friend, looking like death himself.

'While I put some things together,' she said, 'you go home and get June to rustle up something for you to eat. And have a brandy while you're at it.'

'June's not back.'

'Oh yes, you said. Where is she?'

'She went to look at a house.'

It wasn't an answer. He sat down suddenly. 'I'm bushed.'

Shock, Alice thought, and seized Rachel's kettle. There was no rush to get back to the hospital and she wasn't about to allow him to drive in this state. In fact she'd go with him.

In the event she took her own car because he insisted that he would stay in Carlisle. Someone had to support Rachel, he said. It was late by the time Alice returned to Culchet and Win appeared as she was putting the car away. 'We know some more about the accident,' she said quietly, drawing the other woman indoors, mothering her because the strain of coping with Bart was starting to show. Bart, said Alice, was distraught.

They sat at the kitchen table, the door open to the flickering bats and the last of the afterglow. Alice sipped brandy.

'Ebenezer Maughan,' Win announced, 'that chap with the Jacob's sheep: his cousin works with the tractor driver that Larry slammed into. He says – the tractor guy – that Larry came round a corner like a rocket, didn't stand a chance. He'd come out of a gateway and turned so that the tractor was facing Larry who crashed into its front. Even the grille's pretty sturdy on one of those big John Deeres but then there was all the engine block. That's what saved the tractor driver of course.'

'Larry must have been wearing his seat belt.'

'Alice! His Peugeot's a write-off! Concertinaed. He has to be terribly injured.'

'Bart seems obsessed with the blood in his hair.'

'I'd have thought he'd be swathed in bandages. Maybe it's all internal injuries like – what's that term when the brain bounces off the inside of the skull?'

'Contrecoup.'

Win had a sudden thought. 'What was he doing there?'

'Where?'

'Where it happened: in a lane between the motorway and Keld.'

'He'd be going to see a house. That's his job.'

'Oh, of course. Someone will have to tell his boss. Rachel and Bart won't think of it. Maybe we should give the office a ring in the morning.'

'Or June – my God, June! No one will have told her where Bart is. She'll be over there, wondering –'

'You mean she wasn't home when he had the news? But he'll have left her a note, surely.'

'I doubt it, the state he was in. I'm going up there.'

They went together, but there was no light in the Hall and no one came to the doors, front or back. June's car wasn't in the yard nor in the coach house where she kept it in winter. They looked to make sure. They went home and telephoned, letting it ring. There was no answer. It was eleven o'clock. They were puzzled.

Win asked, frowning, 'Larry *was* alone?'

'Of course he was!' Alice stared in astonishment. 'Some-one would have said: the tractor driver, the paramedics, police . . .'

There was a lengthy silence, broken again by Win. 'Her Escort's not there. Where could she have gone?'

'Bart said she went to look at a house.'

'What on earth for? They're still working on the Hall – ah! Rob said something this morning: about June looking for a place to buy and rent out; I didn't pay much atten-tion, it sounded more like some hare-brained scheme of Bart's. Plenty of ambition, that one, not much sense of application.'

Alice was following her own tack. 'If she *was* looking at property,' she said, 'she'd be most likely to go to Wharton's.' Wharton was Larry's boss.

They thought about it. 'When you call him tomorrow,' Win began, 'ask him – no, that's wild; June will be home tonight, you'll see. I know what's happened: either she's broken down, or she's gone visiting, had a few drinks and decided to stay put with her hosts rather than risk driving. She'll have tried to phone home and got no reply.'

'They both have mobiles.'

'Doesn't mean they both took them. The trouble with you is you're so involved with crime – with crime fiction – that you project it into real life. How much d'you bet we'll get a call from June asking us to go up there and tell

Bart that his phone isn't working – or something – and she won't be home till tomorrow?'

Alice regarded her brandy morosely, thinking that it had turned eleven; whatever had befallen her, June should have been in touch with someone by now.

At nine the next morning Jerry Wharton had not yet reached his office but the woman who answered the phone, although deeply affected by the news, said that she'd tell him as soon as he came in. At the time Alice felt that it was inappropriate to ask if June had called at the office yesterday, for that matter she hadn't looked to see if June was home.

Win was in bed. Taking her a cup of tea Alice said she was going to pop up to the Hall and if there were still no one home she would call in at Wharton's. Tuesday was the day for their weekly shop in Brimstock.

'Take your mobile,' Win told her. 'I'll ring the Hall off and on; if she comes home I'll call you.'

The Hall was as deserted as it had been last night. The Milburns kept no animals so Alice didn't have that to contend with. Two cartons of milk stood on the back doorstep and she took them home to keep in Thrushgill's fridge.

In Brimstock she went about her business distractedly: the supermarket, the library, the bank – listening for the chirp of her mobile, avid to know what awaited her at Wharton's, yet holding back, giving June the benefit of – what? The doubt? What doubt? Win didn't phone.

As an estate agent Jerry Wharton was accustomed to tricky situations, but today he was obviously worried. Middle-aged and balding, he was confused as to Alice's status, treating her as a relation of Larry's rather than a neighbour: commiserating, ushering her into his private office. An older woman, evidently his assistant, asked if there were any news. Alice said not as far as she knew, and wondered how she was to put the question about June without their jumping to the conclusion that there was a connection. She tried to spell it out for Wharton.

'Something else has come up,' she said diffidently. 'Nothing to do with Larry. Another neighbour, Mrs Milburn, went to look at a house yesterday and hasn't come back. We thought it might be one of your properties.'

He blinked at her as he tried to adjust to a new problem – hers, not his – and why should it interest him? Oh, as an estate agent. 'Mrs Milburn? The name doesn't mean – I'll ask the girls.'

No one had heard of a Mrs Milburn. 'Sorry, we can't help,' he said, returning. He did a double-take. 'Did you say she's missing?'

'She hasn't come home,' Alice corrected. 'You don't suppose – could she have contacted Larry outside the office and he was showing her a place without your being aware of it? Is that possible?'

He regarded her blankly. She could sense cogs meshing. He was considering a connection, and not liking it. 'He was alone when he had the accident,' she pointed out. 'But Mrs Milburn's car isn't at her house so I wondered if they met somewhere – to look at a house . . .' She trailed off, eyebrows raised.

'I see what you mean.' He didn't, and he was concerned that no shadow of scandal should fall on his business. 'Actually Larry was going to look at a property in Keld when he had the accident . . .' He paused and frowned, shaking his head as if to deny something, but Alice hadn't spoken. 'He was on his way to Keld,' he said firmly, 'definitely not meeting anyone, but inspecting a house which came on our books last week. Oh dear! I've just realized he must still have – the keys will be – er, with him. We'll have to retrieve those. Not that keys have any importance in the face of the poor chap's condition of course.'

Alice drove home thinking about roads, wondering why Larry hadn't taken the direct route to Keld from Brimstock rather than going out to use the motorway and then having to cut back cross-country: a longer way round, and speed on the motorway cancelled out by the awkward lanes at the end. Maybe he'd reckoned on there being nothing in the lanes at that hour of the morning. A thought started to rise to the surface of her mind and at that moment a string of riders appeared: Indian file but beginners. She knew the school, recognizing the leader even as she stamped on the brake.

She crawled past, grinning an apology at Hettie Lewthwaite, thinking she should take a horse out herself, her life was too sedentary. And she'd been going too fast, next thing she knew a tractor would turn out of a gateway, farmers were hay-making . . .

She passed Dubb's Close with care, alert for rolling balls, small children, bikes. She turned right and came through the narrows between the two sentinel houses. The green rose ahead, a family of geese strolling up the tarmac, people in bright tops at tables outside the Stag, more sprawled in the shade of the horse chestnuts. Also outside the pub there was a police car. Alice frowned, faltered, taking her foot off the accelerator, then creeping on to Thrushgill. None of her business.

But it was. It was everyone's business in a small village where people looked out for each other. June's car had been found, burned out, on wasteland at an abandoned pig farm.

Chapter Four

Kim and Jason were fascinated by the activity in the village. They'd been eating what passed for their lunch when Jon had alerted the family. He was a few miles from home when a patrol car passed him. It didn't stop although he was known to the police; probably they didn't recognize him since he was wearing the helmet that he'd nicked at the same time as the bike. But they were heading in the direction of the village, and paranoia told him which house they had in their sights. Jon knew of only one set of thieves in Culchet.

The patrol car had passed as he started along the Brimstock road. He pulled into the next field and called home on his – or rather *the* mobile. He never bought anything that could be acquired without cash.

Maureen took the call. Hugh was in the front room watching television with Jason and Kim; there was no point in working at the Hall when Bart wasn't there to pay him, and owing him at that. Three pairs of eyes lifted to Maureen when she appeared, exasperated, relaying the alarm.

Hugh tried to recall which recent actions on his part might merit attention from the cops – or were they after the bike? But they hadn't stopped Jon . . . Jason was expressionless, giving nothing away except by his apparent lack of excitement, but no one was noticing. Kim was enthralled; she knew that although Jason could be taken away, little kids had nothing to fear from the police.

Maureen parted the curtains a crack to look down the

close. Behind her the children slid out of the room like young stoats.

They sat on the steps of the village pump and observed events. They saw the candy-chequered cop car creep up the green and turn in at the gate of the Hall. They said nothing, Kim taking her cue from her brother, Jason considering some link with his dad because he'd been working there, down the cellars. He was also wondering whether they were conspicuous, him and Kim, but cops didn't notice little kids any more than ordinary folk did – and then their car emerged from the Hall's gate and turned left. 'Going to Todbank,' Jason muttered, and guessed that Larry had died and they'd come to tell his mum, and they'd made a mistake and gone to the house next door. Kim was tugging at his arm. 'What's happening? Who're they after?'

He ignored her. The car passed Todbank, went round the top of the green, past the track to Lonning Head and that girt killer dog, and came down towards the pump, menacing in its leisurely progress. Jason felt the sweat break out on his back.

The car stopped at the pub. It stopped there, on the grass, not going round to the car park at the back. Parking in front was a sign, it was obvious: a threat in plain view. Two uniformed men got out and walked into the Stag. They stayed a while and Jason decided that, after all, they'd gone in for a drink, which was against the rules. He wetted his lips, thinking of an anonymous telephone call to Brimstock nick.

Potter's car came through the narrows, the geese walking ahead of it. Jason saw Alice glance across the green but there was nothing remarkable in that, anyone would – a cop car in Culchet. She stopped at Thrushgill, came back to open the boot and started carrying the shopping indoors.

Next thing that happened was Win Langley coming fast over the grass, never giving the open boot a glance although there was more stuff to go indoors, they could see the Safeway's bags, and Kim hissed, 'Them's coming out!'

The police were in a hurry too. The car lurched as they jumped in, then they came down past the pump and up the other side of the green to stop behind Alice's car. They went through the garden to the porch, white shirts brilliant in the sun. Kim said, awed, 'Them's after Alice and Win?'

'Don't be daft.' Jason was thinking that with so much happening, folk rushing around like wild sheep, houses could be left unoccupied, people forgetting to lock doors. Kim would want to tag along but he could cope with Kim.

'But I don't know anything!' Alice protested. 'I'm as much in the dark as anyone. This is just shock after shock. Our neighbour crashed his car, you see, and he's on life support, and there's his mother: old, she dotes on him –' She was babbling and the stout sergeant held up a meaty hand. Win placed a mug of tea in front of her. 'Drink this.' She was gruff. 'It's June they want to know about, not Larry.'

A number plate had survived the fire so the owner, and then her address, had been discovered almost immediately. Finding no one at the Hall the police had gone to that fount of information, the pub. Told that the woman's husband was in Carlisle they'd been about to leave when Freda saw Alice drive up the green and suggested that she might have more information because she'd been to Brimstock and had intended visiting the estate agent. Apparently June Milburn had been viewing property yesterday.

Win slipped across to Thrushgill ahead of the police. She was acting on impulse; had she been asked she couldn't have specified why Alice needed support, only that even if people had nothing to hide, the arrival of cops at one's door, unannounced, was disturbing. But her hurried exit didn't escape their notice and they followed closely.

45

Win's action was counter-productive; her appearance at lunch-time and her urgent hiss, 'The police found June's car and they're coming over,' served only to confuse Alice.

They were large men and they seemed to fill the kitchen. Belatedly Win thought of moving to the sitting room but it was a dim place, shaded by the chestnuts: a room associated with winter and parties, inappropriate. The kitchen was light, much used, safe.

'The car was *burned*?' Alice was appalled. 'You mean it was taken by joyriders?'

The sergeant – his name, freakishly, was Plumpton – hesitated. 'Cars may be burned in order to destroy fingerprints,' he said heavily.

'It didn't have to be kids then.' Alice was recovering fast, her brain getting into gear. 'So where's June?' She looked from Win to Plumpton. 'Was there anyone in the car?'

Win inhaled sharply. Plumpton said, 'There was a *fire*, miss.'

'A body wouldn't be totally destroyed.'

The constable, young and callow, stared at her. Win turned to the sink.

'Are you a doctor, ma'am?' Plumpton was circumspect, not sure what he had here.

'I'm a copy editor.' Alice was dismissive, preoccupied.

Silence. Win turned round. 'Crime,' she said. 'Her job's editing crime books. She can tell you how long it takes to burn a body, what part goes first, what's likely to be left, where the seat of the fire was, how it –'

'Give over, Win.' Alice was cool. 'You haven't answered the question,' she told Plumpton, putting him in mind of a teacher he'd had in primary school. 'Was there a body?'

'No, ma'am.' A sensible fellow, she had his respect now.

'Do you have any idea where June – Mrs Milburn is?'

'That's the question we need answered. Mrs Carrick at the pub said as how you might be able to point us in the right direction.'

'We're back to square one then. All we know is that she hasn't come home. We'd been thinking in terms of her car breaking down or her staying the night with friends but now' – Alice turned to Win – 'this is puzzling.' No one spoke for a moment, then, 'It's sinister,' she amended. 'If kids – if anyone had stolen her car, she'd have phoned someone. Her husband first of course, but then she couldn't get through, he was at the hospital. You do know about his neighbour crashing his car?' Plumpton nodded. 'So if she couldn't contact Bart – her husband,' Alice persisted, 'why didn't she phone us – or the Stag – and surely she'd call you to report the car being stolen?'

'Where did her husband think she'd gone?'

'He didn't know she was missing!' Alice was amazed at the question. 'He still doesn't – that is, unless he's been told about the car.'

'I think he's been told.' Plumpton was vague on that score.

Bart had left the hospital at lunch-time and when he returned to the ward he was approached by a man with an unmistakable air of authority who asked if they could have a word. A second fellow, thickset, young, built like a rugby player, had materialized at Bart's elbow, standing rather too close. The man who'd addressed him indicated an open door and the rugby player nudged his arm. Bart shrugged him off but he yielded and entered a room furnished with tacky easy chairs and low tables where used styrofoam containers spoke of staff shortages. The slighter chap introduced himself as Detective Sergeant Blake. The other was DC Ware. The sergeant told him that his wife's car had been found.

Bart blinked, trying to orientate himself. 'My friend's in there' – gesturing – 'he's in a coma.'

'It had been set on fire,' Blake said clearly, holding the other's eye.

Bart shook his head. 'Look, a chap's dying. A car was stolen. So what?' The police said nothing. Awareness dawned on him, the whites of his eyes showing all round the iris. 'June?' he breathed. 'June – oh no!'

'She wasn't in it,' Blake said.

'Jesus!' Bart went limp. 'You bastard!' He groped for a chair, fell into it like a sack of beans and leaned back, gaping, breathing heavily. Ware walked out of the room.

'Where did she go?' Blake asked.

'Stolen,' Bart stated, as if it were a revelation. 'That's what happened: the car was stolen while she was – where?' He glared at the detective. 'Where did she go?' he repeated. 'She went to see a house.'

'Where was the house?'

'She never said.'

Ware returned with tea in a styrofoam cup. He placed it on a table in front of Bart who thanked him automatically.

'Wouldn't it be unusual,' Blake asked, 'for a wife to go to view a house and not tell her husband where it was? You might not approve the location.'

Bart looked surprised. 'She would have done, when she left, but I wasn't there – not upstairs, I mean. We were working in the cellars. The cement mixer was running in the yard; if she did call out to me, I wouldn't have heard.'

The time to discuss it would have been prior to her leaving but Blake didn't push it. 'What time did you expect her back?' he asked.

'Expect her? That would depend on what she was doing.'

'She was viewing a house.'

'That would be just one item in her day. June's a busy lady. Me' – he grinned – 'I'm only a builder, at least until we've renovated our present place. She going to do B and B.'

'I see. So you were working all day and she never phoned to say she'd be late – or anything?'

'She could have done but I wouldn't hear with the row we were making, even if I'd had a mobile down there. I don't think I did have it. Hugh was mixing and pouring

48

concrete; I was breaking up the old flags, levelling the floor.'

'Hugh?'

'Butler. He works for me part-time, just the morning yesterday.'

'Then what?'

'He had to take some cattle to the abattoir. I went to Brimstock for a load of cement.'

'Could your wife have come home while you were away?'

'If she did there was no sign. And how could she if her car had been stolen?'

'Taxi?' Blake didn't point out that no one knew when the car had been stolen.

Bart nodded. 'But if she'd come home in a taxi and gone off again she'd have left a note. She's a very responsible person. Besides, someone would have seen a taxi. We watch out for each other in the village. Specially in summer time. You don't know who's about.'

There was a pause. Bart held his cup in both hands, staring into it, missing Blake's signal. 'You must be concerned about your wife,' Ware told him.

The man looked up, startled by the different voice – and Ware had a Geordie accent. 'I wasn't bothered – then. I thought she must be with friends, and then I forgot her.' His eyes went to the door. 'The hospital called. It's not only Larry, but his mother. She's old and she needs support. I have to get back to her, try to persuade her to take a break.'

'*We're* concerned about your wife.' Ware was emphatic.

Bart nodded. 'So am I – now.' Then the other's tone reached him. About to rise from his chair he sank back and stared at the detective. 'Are you thinking that – because of the car . . .' He clenched his fists. 'Did you look in the boot?' It was a shout.

'She's not in the car,' Blake said flatly. 'We don't know where she is. That's what we need to find out. She hasn't contacted anyone – to our knowledge; we have no idea where she was going when she left home, where the car was stolen or by whom. These questions are bothering us.' The inference was that they should be bothering Bart too.

'I'm sorry.' He knuckled his skull. 'Here I've been focused on my friends; it's difficult to reorientate myself. What should I do?'

Blake became businesslike. 'The first thing we need is the names and numbers of your wife's friends; DC Ware will take them down, then her other contacts, the shops she uses in town and so on. Who was the agent that dealt with the sale of Culchet Hall?'

'Oliver Airey. Why?'

'Because the house Mrs Milburn went to view could have been on his list; she could well have gone back to a firm she knew.' Obviously Blake had discovered that the Milburns were not long-established residents. He'd been checking.

Bart returned to the ward and sat down on the other side of the bed. Larry's position hadn't changed, only the bruises were darker. Rachel looked across at him without expression. 'I have to go home,' he told her. 'They've found June's car, burned out.'

'Crashed.' There was no feeling in the tone, no emotion.

'No. It had been stolen and set on fire. June's missing, apparently.' Bart's eyes were on Larry, fiercely intent. 'I have to tell the police what she's taken – with her. Clothes and so on. Maybe her passport.' He paused, turning things over in his mind. 'There could be a man.' Rachel didn't react. 'Did she ever say anything to you?' he pressed. 'That she was seeing someone – someone special?'

'Who?' Rachel took Larry's hand in both of hers, stroking it as if it were a newborn kitten. She started to croon softly.

Back at the Hall Bart seemed confused and helpless, disinclined to take the initiative. Asked which clothes were missing from June's wardrobe he regarded the contents blankly and said nothing was gone so far as he could see. When pressed he couldn't say what she'd been wearing yesterday since he hadn't seen her leave. The police noted, poker-faced, that from the evidence of male occupation, the Milburns shared a bedroom.

He left them going through her papers. They found her passport and they glanced through her correspondence: filed neatly in a two-drawer cabinet. They discovered nothing personal. It appeared that she destroyed letters once she had replied to them. There was nothing from her daughter who, they understood from Bart, was in Australia with her husband. They glanced at her financial statements. The Milburns didn't have a joint account, which might not be significant; lots of married couples didn't have joint accounts. Blake didn't ask to see Bart's statements. June had £35,460 in a Base Rate Tracker, £2,500 in her current account, and £2,300-worth of Premium Bonds. There was no mortgage on the Hall. Bart told them as much but he didn't tell them the purchase price and they didn't ask.

They sat in the kitchen, the police refusing whisky, Bart taking a discreet measure in his tea. He had pulled himself together to some extent but he was still in need of direction. 'Where do I start to look for her?' he asked Blake. 'At some point I have to find Carol – her daughter – but I'm sure that's premature, aren't you? She'd only be worried. I'm sure June's just – well, almost sure – look, couldn't it be that she was doing too much: something snapped, I mean, she's fifty, it could be the – her time of life. She's gone away to find some space.'

'And doesn't know her car's been stolen, like left at a railway station?' Blake went along with it, knowing all the arguments against. He reminded the man that the police had nothing to go on but if Bart could remember anything that might point them in the right direction, a name they'd missed, an indication concerning the locality of the house she'd been intending to view . . .

Bart shook his head weakly. 'I'll drive around,' he said, evidently dismissing the theory of June's needing to find space, 'but what do I look for? Not the car. You found the car.'

Blake suggested he go back to work. 'In the cellar,' he said, watching the man's eyes. Bart said he'd no heart for it, how could he work in the circumstances? He said he ought to return to the hospital to tell Rachel how things were, that he had to look for his wife. They let him go.

He left first in an old Land Rover. The detectives stood by their car in the stable yard in no hurry to follow. 'I don't like that cement mixer,' Ware said, staring at it.

'It's too obvious,' Blake demurred. 'Everyone knows that when a wife goes missing the first suspect is the husband, and the first action on our part, if he's been laying concrete, is to dig it up. No, she's not in that cellar.'

'We'll be digging it up all the same.' Ware was gloomy.

'Could be, but for my money she's somewhere else.'

But where, that was the question. Bart told them his wife had a wide circle of acquaintances but he could remember only a few names. However, they'd garnered a list of organizations she was involved with and they spent an hour or two tracing people whose names had come up, and others mentioned by such primary contacts. Apparently none of them had seen June nor spoken to her on the phone, nor had anyone spotted her yesterday. The agent who'd handled the sale of the Hall had been approached without result. She hadn't been in contact with his firm recently.

The old pig farm was searched using specialist dogs that could find bodies even under the ground but no traces were found and they hadn't been expected. If the car was burned to destroy fingerprints the perpetrators must have had the sense to dispose of the body at a discreet distance; perpetrators in the plural because there had to be more than one: another driver to take them (and June Milburn?) away from the farm. But there were no tracks. The ground was iron-hard.

The sun beat down on the abandoned buildings and Blake didn't linger there. He drove away with Ware to find drinks and welcome shade in the yard of a pub in the old part of Harras, another border town with tall sandstone walls and small, almost secret alcoves. In the case of the White Hart its court had been transformed by a jungle of colour; not a space that wasn't occupied by a tub, a sink or a hanging basket dripping with fuchsias and petunias and explosions of gold and scarlet nasturtiums against the old red stone.

Blake savoured his beer and stared at a calico cat washing her face on steps that appeared to lead to a loft. Even the cats in this place were coloured. He considered a tiny window, barred and opaque, that must supply the only light in the loft.

Ware broke in on his musing. 'The reason why the car was torched in that place was because it's remote and in a bit of a hollow. If anyone did see the glow he'd take it for youngsters having a wild party, and no one's going to tackle kids these days: drunk, probably carrying knives.' There was evidence of old fires at the pig farm, along with empty flasks and bottles that had held cider and Breezers.

'What makes you think it happened at night?' Blake asked.

'Well' – momentarily checked, the DC recovered – 'if it'd been daytime the smoke would have been visible.'

'Day or night, it's immaterial. No one's reported a fire.'

'Doesn't mean to say no one saw it.'

'You got a point. Tomorrow you can check out the nearest farms. Houses too; plenty of retired people: they could be out in their gardens this time of year.' He finished his pint and looked at Ware's glass. 'Drink up, we've half an hour before business shuts down for the day. We're going to talk to estate agents.'

'We've done that.'

'Only one and that not in Harras. The pig farm is less than two miles away. June Milburn left home to view a house; it could have been one near here.'

'I don't follow – Hang on while I finish my beer!' – as Blake made to get up. 'There can't be that many estate agents in Harras, we got plenty of time. You reckon something happened here? I don't see it. She could have been looking at a property anywhere.'

'The car is close by, man! And she'd have to start with an estate agent – surely?' There was a hint of doubt now, but then another thought struck Blake. He said slowly, 'There's that estate we passed on our way in from the farm, council estate. Half-term: no school.'

'It's not a run-down area,' Ware protested, 'not like big tenement blocks. Folk on that estate would be ultra respectable.'

'Just a thought.' But Blake was thinking that respectable parents could have ultra rebellious kids.

Ware was thinking too. 'Someone knew about that farm,' he conceded. 'That suggests a local, but it's not kids, is it? I mean, two cars?'

'That's what I'm saying: the pig farm's within walking – or running distance. And why not two cars? If they can steal one, they can steal a second.'

'Then it's two different crimes,' Ware persisted. 'We're thinking foul play, right?' Blake stared at him moodily. 'So if joyriders – kids – took a car – or two . . . Are you suggesting they're responsible for what's happened to the woman?'

'We don't know what's happened to her. But kids do kill.' Blake paused and they thought about it. 'Or it could be someone wants us to *assume* it was kids,' he pointed out.

'Muggers? A mugging gone wrong?'

'If they're going to rob, they're going to take the car too and sell it, not torch it. It was nearly new. But if she was mugged in the street' – Blake looked round the yard – 'or in some quiet corner, muggers wouldn't necessarily know where her car was. Joyriders could have come across it . . .'

'Like I said: two separate crimes: most unlikely. And muggers' – Ware grinned – 'in *Harras* don't usually kill their victims. And where's her body? OK, you're going to say we don't know she's dead, but why hasn't she –'

'Maybe she's unconscious.'

There were only two estate agents in Harras and the name of June Milburn meant nothing to either of them. In the early evening they trawled the council estate eliciting expected reactions from the youths they spoke to: wary responses, ostensible boredom, nonchalance only a hair's breadth from contempt. And, predictably, no one admitted knowledge of joyriding or vandals, least of all, of muggers.

There was no manned police station in the town and Brimstock's record of recent juvenile crime here amounted to two youths cautioned for under-age drinking. All the same they tried the addresses they were given. There was no reply at the first house and at the second they found a tired single mother who told them her son was out and she had no idea where. 'It's half-term,' she said. 'He's got a life.'

'I bet he's got a mobile too,' Blake said as they returned to the car. 'She had one there on the table. She looked towards it when you were asking where he was. We'll go back later.' He had a feeling about this one, at the same time admitting to himself that it could hardly be called a lead: a boy cautioned for drinking Breezers in a yard.

Chapter Five

Jill Housby came quietly through the ghyll: a slim tanned girl on a glossy little horse who'd look better when he lost some weight. Although the temperature had dropped with evening he was sweating buckets and Jill, hatless, never one for the conventions, was exercising responsibility here, walking home, cooling him off after the ride. The hound Baskerville had been with them but he'd run ahead as they came down from the escarpment, scenting a bitch no doubt. Jill wasn't bothered; Baz wasn't a sheep chaser, on the contrary, when he walked through a flock they took less notice of him than they'd pay to a hare.

A thrush was shouting from the top of an ash and wood warblers were singing below the thrush. Jill missed all this in Manchester, she should come home more often . . . Then a child shrieked in the green wood and the gelding's ears flicked forward. Not a frightened child but an angry one. Bullying? The teacher in Jill was alerted. She pushed along the path, hoofs muffled by thick dust, and heard: 'I'll tell –'

'You do and I'll put you in –' The rest was lost.

'Our dad's gonna beat you raw!'

'I'm gonna kill you –'

'What's going on here?' The horse towered over them, Jill Housby still higher, a woman never soft-spoken or silly, always someone to be watching out for, and now carrying a *whip*. Jason shrank into himself.

'Why are you going to kill your kid sister?' she asked pleasantly, and the tone made it worse.

Jason thought about the answer. 'Joke,' he ventured.

'Are you going to tell on him?' Jill asked of Kim.

'No, miss.' Kim's eyes were huge as she edged away.

'We was playing,' Jason said, thinking that she'd never dare use that whip, anyway he'd done nowt wrong – that she could possibly know about. Moreover, that horse couldn't follow him through the trees – if it tried she'd be knocked off. 'We gotta get back for ours supper,' he said, reaching for his sister's hand, but she turned and started to run.

There was a crashing in the undergrowth, a roaring bark, and Baz blundered past the gelding, past Jason, knocking him into brambles, bounding after Kim, leaping . . .

'Oh, Christ!' Jill was laughing as she slid down and walked past Jason who, flat on his back, stared at her in mute horror, not daring to move. Kim was on the ground, Baz licking her neck, her ears, trying to get at her face.

'Leave her!' Jill commanded, gripping his scruff. 'Get off her, you great gowk.'

He stood back reluctantly and watched with interest as she lifted Kim who clung to her knees, too terrified to scream, even to cry. 'You're all right,' Jill chided. 'You didn't even cut your legs, the dust is too soft. It's Jason who bought it, look: he fell in the blackberries.'

Kim looked, ready to crow, but she saw Baz waiting to resume his ministrations and then she did howl.

Jill sighed, made a move towards Jason but found herself anchored by strong little arms. At that moment Carrick's Labrador bitch came bounding along the path to throw herself joyfully on Baz. Behind her came Graham Carrick, pushing past the horse which was grazing, unconcerned at the commotion. 'What's all the row?' he demanded.

As the dogs cavorted, intent on each other, Jason saw his chance, tore himself out of the brambles, grabbed at Kim, and the two of them went stumbling, then running hell for leather down the path.

'Always up to some mischief, that pair,' Graham commented. 'Don't tell me you whipped 'em!' He was a large

portly fellow – the image of mine host – coping unsuccess-
fully with his weight problem, a smart black polo shirt
failing to disguise his paunch.

'They were quarrelling,' Jill told him, picking up the
reins. 'Odd, isn't it, the way they're always together in the
holidays?'

'He'd be belted by his dad otherwise.' Graham's amusement was replaced by concern. 'A bad thing about Larry –
and now there's June missing. D'you think there could be
a man in it somewhere?'

'Which one are you talking about?' He was dumbfoun-
ded. 'That's a joke,' she said quickly. He frowned; every
reaction was reflected in his fleshy features. 'OK,' she
sighed: 'no joke, but they *are* alive.'

'Only just in Larry's case.'

'You're suggesting June's dead?'

'Of course not; you're too quick, young lady, you jump
the gun. I asked: do you think June's with a man?'

'She's too busy to have a lover. I mean, she'd have to go
to him in the daytime, wouldn't she – that is, before this
last time? At a guess the only man in June's life apart from
her husband, parish councillors, church wardens, et al,
is Rob.'

'Rob!'

'And you. She's friendly with you.'

'What I meant was – a boyfriend.'

'Graham!' The man was obsessed with sex. 'She's fifty if
she's a day!'

He was resentful. 'Sex doesn't stop when you reach
middle age.'

'It doesn't?' She moved to the far side of her horse,
hiding her grin.

He said, 'She hasn't contacted anyone. Don't you think
that's disturbing?'

She mounted and settled herself, hesitating, seeing that
he was less prurient than worried. 'Maybe she's done a
runner – temporarily; wants to get away for a while.
Maybe –' She checked, picturing Bart Milburn, ten years
younger than his wife, quite a looker for his age, and Joely

58

– this old guy's daughter – crazy for him. Graham's worry could originate close to home.

'Maybe what?' he demanded.

'Maybe she'll call within the next few days.' It wasn't what she'd been about to say, wondering if it wasn't a man in the case but a woman, or rather a young girl.

'Who burned her car?'

'Graham! How would I know? That's a job for the cops. Where was it found?'

'At an old pig farm out Harras way. It was stolen so why hasn't June reported it to the police?'

'You're asking me?'

'Not really. These are the questions people are asking. Hadn't you thought of them yourself? What's Rob's opinion?'

She blinked. 'I don't know. Rob's not one for gossip.' A lie, and he knew it. Rob drank tea in most of the places where he delivered eggs, and tea was oil on the wheels of gossip.

'You said he was a friend of June's.' It sounded like an accusation.

'I meant "friendly" as opposed to "unfriendly". Like she'd hardly be friendly with Hugh Butler.'

'No,' Graham agreed, 'she wouldn't.'

For the second time that evening Jill heard angry voices, or rather one, but this time it was a man's. She was coming up the track to Lonning Head and there was a Land Rover parked in front of the house and Hugh Butler out on the gravel shouting at her father. Predictably Baz galloped ahead, his bark alerting Hugh who dived for his truck and slammed the door. 'You see!' he shouted as, his legs trapped in the well, he tried to shrink away from the open window where Baz pawed the sill like an excited bear. 'He'd kill *me*! If he's not shot tonight, then I'll be up and do the job meself. You!' He was addressing Jill now who, still mounted, had edged up to stand beside her father. 'You set this brute on my little baby!'

59

'Down, lad,' Rob ordered. 'Heel.'

Baz dropped down and came to sit on his feet, grinning. 'He's harmless,' Rob said. 'And if you come on my land with a gun, in fact, if you have a gun, you'd better be showing the licence.' It was a shrewd guess; with the suspicions if not convictions associated with Hugh, it was unlikely that he'd been granted a licence.

Jill wasn't thinking straight and, aghast at the threat to harm Baz, she waded in, frightened but controlled. 'Why does Jason say he'll kill Kim?' she asked, in a voice like a court prosecutor.

Hugh gaped. 'He don't!' He caught his breath. 'You're lying. And that beast of yourn savaged my boy too!'

'Jason fell in some brambles,' Jill told her father. 'Kim tumbled in the dust and Baz licked her.'

'She'm traumatized! Her come 'ome torn to bits, her little shirt all covered with blood and dirt, her mam's having a panic attack – that brute there loose, could come after anyone. My kids – my littluns got away only because Carrick's bitch come up and distracted un.'

Jill said harshly, 'Baz had plenty of time to kill both of them before Mr Carrick arrived. There's not a mark on Kim, only dust where she fell. As for Jason, any blood will be from the brambles. All the violence was between the kids: Kim saying she'd tell you, and that you'd beat Jason raw – her words – and him saying he'd kill her. What's their story? What's the awful crime that's worth killing for?'

Hugh's mouth opened and closed. He was behind the steering wheel now, the round head sunk between massive shoulders.

Rob said thoughtfully, 'You're working at the Hall.'

'So?' But the belligerence failed to mask trepidation.

'Mrs Milburn is missing.' Rob drew it out. Jill stared at him in amazement.

'And?' It was shaky.

Rob seemed to be following a defined track. 'Have the police been to you?'

'What *is* it with Jason and Kim?' Jill put in tentatively.

60

Hugh fumbled for the ignition and the engine roared.

'What on earth did you mean by that?' Rob asked as the Land Rover lurched down the track.

'I was following your lead. You were suggesting he knew something about June's disappearance so I hinted that the secret the kids were quarrelling about could have a connection. We were trying to scare him, right? Because he threatened to shoot Baz. Dad, you weren't serious?'

They started to walk round to the stable. 'There's the cellars at the Hall,' he reminded her. 'They've had a cement mixer going for days: concrete, cellars, a missing woman: put you in mind of anything?'

'Rob Housby, you're a wicked old man! And there's Graham Carrick speculating on whether she's got a lover. What do you really think – honestly? That she's gone off with some man – or she's in her own cellar? Oh no, that's over the top.'

Joely dressed carefully, settling for her baggy trousers with the grey vest. Her nails matched the shocking pink strap on her new watch and, trying out different effects with her hair, she chose a style worn by some old film star, a blonde curtain on one side of her face. Maud Brunskill would have recognized an echo of Veronica Lake but there was no one to observe her as she left the pub by the back stairs and slipped through the car park to Back Lane.

Bart was in his kitchen, sitting at the table on a hard chair, a tumbler and bottle of Glenfiddich in front of him. Joely hesitated, posed in the doorway, feeling irresistible. He caught sight of her and for a moment he looked severe: narrowed eyes, thinned lips, then he softened, indicating the whisky. 'You've come to keep me company? This place is like a tomb.' He winced at his own words.

She wondered how long he'd been drinking. She hadn't seen him come home. She came round the table and started to knead his shoulders. 'You've got to relax. You're all knotted.' She was exulting, she'd never touched him so intimately before. It was her fantasy coming to life; this was how it happened in the movies: the massage, sweet talk . . . He sighed, her eyes shone, she willed her desire to reach him through her hands.

'Where did she go?' he asked miserably. 'Can *you* think where she might have gone? Why?'

'Relax, Bart, forget it –'

'*What!*'

'For a while, just for a while; build up your strength again. You're no good to anyone right now. Tell me, what did you do today?'

'Oh, backwards and forwards.' He was slurring his consonants. 'There's no change at the hospital. Rachel needs me but what can I do? What am I doing here? I'm no good to her either.'

'They'll find her,' Joely said, praying that they wouldn't. Her hands were still, resting on powerful muscle. He shivered. 'What?' she murmured.

'I keep thinking the worst.'

'Oh, Bart!' She pulled a chair out and slid on to it, turning to face him, very close. She was wearing her mother's Chanel. He looked at her with a face of despair. She held out slim arms; now he should collapse with a sob, and once they were embracing his body would take over, he couldn't resist. Technically Joely was a virgin but she had watched too many late night movies not to know how it was done.

He didn't come to her arms, instead he held her hands in his. 'You're a sweet kid, Jo. I can't tell you how much it means to me: you coming over to keep me company.'

She tried to smile, grabbed at her flagging confidence and assumed the candid expression of a child. 'It's the least I can do. I thought you'd be lonely and look at you: solitary drinking. How long would this have gone on?' He blinked at her. 'I mean, you have to go to bed sometime.'

'Not necessarily.'

She gasped in frustration. 'Why don't we –' she began, and stopped as Win Langley stepped into the kitchen, a casserole in her gloved hands. Joely glowered.

'Brought you some supper,' Win stated, ignoring the girl. 'Not the weather for hot-pot, true, but Alice was sure you wouldn't touch a salad.' She turned, looking for Alice, but there was no sign of her. She moved to the cupboards. 'Where d'you keep the plates?'

Alice came in from the yard, showing no surprise at finding Joely there, smiling at her, a smile not returned by the girl who, standing now, was obviously uncertain about her next move.

'Are you eating too, Joely?' Win asked politely.

'No. I've eaten.'

Alice leant against the sink. 'No news, Bart?' she asked.

'No one's been in touch,' he responded dully. 'About either of them. But it's me who calls the hospital.'

'A double blow,' Win murmured, spooning small portions of mutton and vegetables on to a plate.

'I can't eat,' he protested, eyeing the food, then standing and barging out of the room.

'He's full of Scotch!' Joely was indignant on his behalf: the old cow pushing hot meat at him, a night like this, turning his stomach – and who were they to say he didn't eat salads?

Alice and Win exchanged glances. 'You could be right,' Win said, dumping the food back in the casserole, replacing the lid. 'Put this in the fridge when it cools. We'll leave him to you – not that I think you'll get very far.'

'Bitch,' Alice said mildly as they strolled back to Thrushgill. 'She'd got herself up so carefully too.'

'She has to learn sometime. Where were you? You didn't come in with me.'

'Nosing around. He'd left the cellar door open and I closed it. They're working in the cellars. Can't have cats walking in wet cement, you'd never get it off their paws.'

In Dubb's Close Kim snuggled up to Maureen on the sofa,

sucking her thumb, on the edge of sleep as her parents watched *Alien* with the sound turned down. It was the score as much as the images that had terrified Kim, waking from a dream to maintain that 'that dog' was in the house. Maureen assured her that Housby's dog was chained and secure, her dad had made sure of that. Brute were going to be shot, Hugh growled, taking no thought to what he'd say when his daughter discovered that the dog was still alive, needing some peace at this moment, needing to think while he pretended to watch the film. His day had been fraught. Maureen was in no doubt that it was he who'd taken the tenner from her bag, and he'd been forced to repay her out of the cash he'd earned running the cattle to the abattoir.

Then Jon had come home without the bike and the helmet, saying he'd sold them, which in one way was good because the stuff was gone, but the fact remained that they had been in the lad's possession, and the cops who'd passed him on the road must have recognized him. They had other business at the time but they'd remember. They always remembered. And June Milburn's disappearance wasn't the godsend it appeared to be at first sight, removing attention from the Butlers in the short term; her being missing brought the cops swarming through the village, and the family could do without that. Housby had reminded him of the danger, that there *was* danger, mentioning the cellars at the Hall. Hugh was troubled, thinking of those cellars.

As if he hadn't enough trouble already, Jason, driven into a corner, had confessed he'd been up to his old trick of conning folk into parting with good clothes. True, before Christmas Maureen had been involved but he'd put a stop to that soon as he knew, pointing out that the clothing scam could be brought in as fraud. Maureen stopped but Jason had started up again, now selling stuff to his friends – not much, he told his dad: just a pair of Nikes, some T-shirts, a fake leather jacket, like that. Hugh belted him for getting caught. He shouldn't have taken Kim along neither: five years old, how could she be expected to keep her mouth shut? Jase had been sent to bed without his supper, which would have hurt as much as the thrashing – and riled as hell because Kim was downstairs being fussed over after the dog attack. Actually Maureen said there wasn't a mark on her, she thought the dog was just playful – rough maybe, but it certainly hadn't bitten Kim. All the same the child was strangely quiet, and she wouldn't leave Maureen's side, refused to go to bed, said she'd sleep with her mam tonight.

In Harras surveillance was kept on the house occupied by Sharon Barclay, the single mother, and at ten o'clock Blake was alerted. The son had come home.

The boy tried the old trick of escape by way of the back door but hadn't reckoned with another pair of cops, hadn't thought beyond the two at the front. Blake was pleased, the lad had something to hide.

Blake and Ware with the Barclays settled in the parlour, a bright spartan place but clean: a shelf of paperbacks, homework on a table, three-piece suite, the television. No sign of opulence, this didn't look like a criminal household. No one referred to the foiled escape, only Sharon was pale with tension, Lester, her son, appearing defiant, which was par for the course.

The police knew straight away that there was no call for the good cop, bad cop routine. Both were genial; Ware the sportsman, closer to the lad in age and possible interests, he opened the interview with a kind of slow motion explosion.

'We've been examining the car at the pig farm,' he told the Barclays, mother and son, who were perched on the sofa. He could have been informing them that it was a pleasant evening outside.

Lester had been stiff, now he was rigid. He licked dry lips and said nothing. Sharon threw him a glance. She was terrified. Everyone knew the car belonged to the woman who had disappeared and she was certain that any utterance of hers would serve only to incriminate her boy.

'Who else was involved?' Blake asked.

Lester gulped. 'In –' It emerged as a croak. He tried again: 'Involved in what?'

'Taking the car, son.'

The lad's mouth hung open. Sharon couldn't control herself: 'You been joyriding!'

He stared at the carpet.

'What did you do with her handbag?' Blake asked.

'I never! There weren't no handbag!' Shock was replaced by resentment. 'I ain't no thief!'

'You stole the car –'

'I didna – I just –'

'You just drove it.'

'He can't drive!' Sharon shouted. 'Someone else drove – he were just a passenger. And he never set it on fire, did you, son? *Did you?*'

'No.' He was close to tears. 'I didna torch it.'

'You drove,' Blake insisted.

'Yeah –'

'You can't –'

'I can, Mum. I learned.' His head came up. 'I can drive fine,' he boasted. 'So I drove it around – there was one of them big cowboy hats on the back seat, I put that on so's folk wouldn't know I weren't old enough. So we had a tour like and ended up at pig farm. But I didna torch it.'

'Where in hell did you learn –' Sharon shrilled, to be silenced by Ware's large palm, gently raised.

'What did Mrs Milburn say?' Blake asked conversationally.

'Who's she? We never – oh!' The import reached him. 'We never saw her,' he protested. 'We found the car: door open, keys in the ignition but no owner anywhere – and no handbag, I swear.'

'Where did you find the car?' Blake asked.

'In Buncle's Yard.'

'What time was that?'

Lester frowned. He's clean, Blake thought, except for taking and driving away; at fourteen he'd have crumbled if he'd been involved in foul play where June Milburn was concerned, but he'd pulled himself together after his initial fright, even regained some colour. He was in for something more than a caution for the car business but you could see that now he'd been caught he was relieved; he had the wit to realize he could be mixed up in something nasty and now he was putty.

'It were before dinner,' he said. Dinner being at midday here. 'Probably around noon.'

Blake didn't push it, nor did he ask for the identity of the other boys. He wanted the basics now, while this one was amenable. He glanced at the window. The street lights had come on but the sky was still pale. 'You can show us where you found the car. Perhaps you'd like to come too, Mrs Barclay.'

Buncle's Yard was approached by a dark ginnel but Ware had brought a torch. Glass crackled underfoot. There was no other noise, no echo, the texture of the stone so soft that it seemed to absorb sound rather than reflect it.

They emerged in a high open space, the sky luminous above towering walls. Flights of steps led to closed doors. Metal glinted, a can clattered in the gloom.

'Police!' Ware shouted, the torch beam swinging. 'Stop where you are!'

There was no response, no patter of running feet. 'Cat,' Blake said.

'That's where the car was.' Lester pointed.

There was nothing to show for it, only flattened weeds; as at the pig farm, the ground was too hard for tyre tracks. If the lad were telling the truth June Milburn – or someone else – had parked her Escort here, left the door open, keys in the ignition – virtually asking for it to be taken . . . There was a faint glow in one corner and the torch beam illuminated an arched cavern. 'It goes through to the street,' Lester told them superfluously. It was the only way the car could have reached here.

Sharon shivered. 'I never come through this yard. I mean, it's not a short-cut to anywhere I'd want to go, and then it's a tip: sort of place people'd shoot up – if we had a drug problem. Which we don't,' she added quickly.

'So these steps lead to the backs of shops,' Ware mused. 'And the doors aren't used?'

'I suppose. They'd be locked and bolted for security.' Sharon started to list the premises concerned.

'And what about that one?' Blake asked, taking the torch from Ware and directing the powerful beam at a studded door at the head of a stone stair. A date, 1680, had been carved in the lintel. There were more windows in this wall, the lower ones barred. Broken panes glinted jaggedly.

'I thought it was a house,' Blake said, turning away.

'I doubt it was at one time,' Ware said. 'If that door's genuine it ought to be preserved. 1680. That's old!'

They walked under the arch to the street, its brightest light coming from a pub, the Bear and Ragged Staff, diagonally across the road. Blake sent the Barclays home with Ware who was to take a statement from Lester. When they'd gone he studied the front of what he saw now was indeed an old house. It was larger than had appeared from the back: double-fronted, and it had been empty for some time; the street door and the ground-floor windows had been boarded up to deter vandals. He crossed the road to the pub.

They were closing and he learned nothing. The barman who'd been on duty yesterday at noon worked the day shift; he'd be in tomorrow, he was told. He asked about the empty house and was met with blank stares. It had been unoccupied as long as anyone could remember, for what that was worth; the publican was new and the barmaid was a student from New Zealand.

Ware had taken the torch and Blake had to find a route back to the estate through well-lit streets; no way was he going to return through Buncle's Yard, risking a sprained ankle in the dark.

Chapter Six

Bart called the hospital at nine o'clock next morning. There had been no change in Larry's condition and his mother had been persuaded to go to bed. She was mildly sedated. Bart said he needed to stay in Culchet in case he should be needed in the ongoing search for his wife; the hospital had the number of his mobile and he was assured he would be called if – if there were any alteration in his friend's condition, the spokesman ended clumsily.

Ted Brunskill was emptying his slug traps when he saw the Land Rover emerge from Back Lane and turn down through the Narrows. 'Bart's away,' he told Maud, coming in from the garden. 'He's not going to find her.'

'What makes you say that?' At the sink she paused in the act of drying a plate. 'What d'you think's happened to her?'

'If the police can't find her, what chance does Bart have?'

'They've hardly started looking yet.'

'They've had long enough. It's the first forty-eight hours that count. Alice said that.'

'What are you talking about?'

'Kidnapping.'

'Kidnapping's for ransom.' Maud emptied the washing-up bowl. 'Bart doesn't have a penny of his own. Kidnapping in Culchet! You've gone potty.'

'June's disappeared.' He nodded smugly; women didn't follow through: no lateral thinking.

'Give over!' Maureen was losing patience with Kim.

'You'm like a laal puppy dog, won't leave its mam alone. Let go me leg, will you?'

'Come 'ere.' Hugh entered the kitchen, buttoning his shirt. 'I got a minute afore I go. Come and sit on step and tell us all about it.' The geniality was sincere; Kim was still unhappy, in shock, he maintained; playing up, was Maureen's verdict but she was puzzled. The child had slept in their bed and slept well, but this morning she wouldn't let her mother out of her sight, refused to leave the house, even with Jason, said the dog was waiting for her . . .

'You *are* going out,' Maureen told her. 'I promised Mrs Carrick I'd go in and clean for 'er –'

'I'm coming with you –'

'You'll do no such thing.' Maureen relented a little: 'All right then, you can stay here and watch telly. Shut all doors, dog can't get you then.'

'*No!* I'm going with my dad!'

'You're not.' Hugh was firm. 'I got business in town.'

At eleven Blake and Ware entered the Bear and Ragged Staff and found the man who had been behind the bar Monday lunch-time. Blake had a photograph of June Milburn but it meant nothing to the fellow, and it would have done if she had been a customer: an imposing lady of fifty alone in a back street bar. He told them to try the Woolpack, people went there for morning coffee.

It was a compact little town, everything within walking distance. The Woolpack was only a few yards from where they'd parked the car in the market square. This was a hotel, not a pub: its white façade freshly painted, embellished with hanging baskets and window boxes, a cobbled roadway to one side and a discreet notice with a hand directing motorists to a car park at the rear.

The front door was wide with a ramp for wheelchairs. It opened on a panelled hall and passageway leading straight back to what would have been the stable yard. Through another wide doorway the detectives saw a rosy wall topped by yellow stonecrop above a cream Jaguar. In the hall brass gleamed on old oak and there was a smell of lemons.

A cleaner, flummoxed by their air of stolid command, summoned the manager: a neat woman in navy with her hair in a pleat. She didn't recognize June Milburn from the photograph and suggested that she wasn't the right person to ask. They tried the waitresses who served morning coffee, finding the one who was here on Monday, but without result, then they tried the barman as a long shot. At length they were accosted by the proprietor, an officious person insisting on knowing their business with his staff. By now it was public knowledge that June Milburn's car had been found at the pig farm and that the police were trying to trace her movements so Blake had no reason to conceal the latest development, although he didn't mention Lester's part in it. He said the car had been seen in Buncle's Yard on Monday morning.

'Good God!' The man's eyes went to the car park. 'That's right next door to us.'

'How's that?' Blake's eyes glazed as he tried to picture the layout of the streets.

'Well, bit of an exaggeration, but everything's close in Harras, and then you've got all the ginnels connecting the streets, and the yards themselves are passages . . . There's our way through to the ginnel' – he gestured – 'that goes down to Buncle's.'

'We'd like to see that.'

They were taken through the hall and across the car park. 'Nice car,' Ware remarked, admiring scarlet leather in the Jaguar.

'We have a good name for food,' the proprietor murmured, meaning to imply that the Woolpack was a superior hostelry all round. 'This is our annexe.' He halted at a break in the wall where a wrought iron gate gave access to a stone cottage. He opened the gate and they found themselves at the front of the house which was unpretentious but substantial. 'The resident staff have rooms here,' he told them. 'And that's the ginnel that takes you down to Buncle's Yard. Now if you'll excuse me . . .'

Blake lifted a finger detaining him. 'Why would she park in Buncle's Yard when you have a safer – and more salubrious place? Buncle's is all broken glass and rubbish.'

The man shrugged. 'There was no room here? Our guests tend to breakfast at their leisure and leave late, and then people are coming in for coffee?' he smiled deprecatingly, the tiresome question marks implying that this was police business, and why did he pay taxes?

'Why didn't she park in the market square?' Ware muttered as they walked past the front of the cottage and down the ginnel the chap had indicated, hearing the gate close behind them as if they'd been seen off the premises.

'Perhaps it was a clandestine meeting.'

'Are you serious?'

'There had to be a reason. What's over this wall? Give me a leg up.'

A clematis with small pink blooms was draped down the wall. Ware clasped his hands and hoisted the other until he could hold himself steady by the coping stones. 'Oh my,' he breathed.

Blake stayed there a few moments before asking to be lowered. 'It's a garden,' he said, dusting his trousers. 'Must belong to the house at the end, I can see garden furniture. It's beautifully kept: lawn, flower beds, azaleas. You'd never guess it was there, would you?'

'These places must be worth a fortune.' Ware looked back at the cottage belonging to the hotel. 'Town houses with secluded gardens: why, you could keep a big dog in the middle of town.' He was a dog man.

'And,' Blake said grimly, 'if youngsters – or adults for that matter – did think of climbing over your wall, they'd have a rottweiler or an Alsatian to reckon with. Nice thought.' His face changed, became thoughtful. They'd emerged in the ginnel that ran into Buncle's Yard. 'They don't all have gardens though. There's the buildings backing on to Buncle's: no gardens, no place to park.'

'There's only one house there and the owners would park in the yard.'

They stood in the open space surrounded by stone except for the two entrances: the ginnel and the tunnel affording vehicular access. 'The staff from the commercial premises don't park here,' Blake said slowly, looking around. 'And that's because of all the broken glass and nails and stuff.'

'And it's not overlooked.' Ware stated the obvious.

'True.' Blake squinted as he pictured a scene. 'She could park here the once, not realizing what a hazard it was for her tyres until she got out of the car.' They regarded the flattened willow herb. 'And left her keys in the ignition,' he mumbled.

'And the door open.'

'Someone was waiting for her?'

'Someone was *with* her . . . And they couldn't wait to be at it?' Ware was incredulous. 'A woman of fifty? Never.'

'Not impossible; we've been considering it.' Blake, in his forties, was reproving. 'But they'd have gone somewhere more discreet, like a wood out in the country. Even then –' he grimaced, glancing round in distaste. 'There's nothing inviting here.'

'They stayed in the car?'

Blake didn't respond, he was staring at the empty house. 'She came here deliberately. She took her handbag – if young Lester is telling the truth – but left the keys in the ignition, the door open, or just unlocked – that last could be immaterial. But if we're thinking that it was June drove into this yard, doesn't the fact that the car was left – accessible – say something to us?'

'Ah. Someone else put the car here: wanting it to be stolen.'

'Women of her age don't leave their cars unlocked.'

'They do in their own drives. Men too. Cars go missing from outside people's houses even when they' re unloading the shopping: the phone rings indoors and they rush to answer and forget to lock the car.'

'Outside their houses,' Blake repeated, regarding the impressive door under the date, 1680.

'This wasn't her house.'

'But she'd told people she meant to look at a house.'

'Not this place surely. It's ancient.' They thought about it. 'Could that be the attraction?' Ware mused. 'Its age?'

'It looks as if it's a tip inside, and since it's boarded up the vandals may have been in, although it could have been secured in time to keep them out. That door might be valuable. The site isn't or the place would have sold by now. But the structure looks sound enough, she could have been thinking of development: flats maybe. Remove any bits that could be restored, like panelling, that door – use them at the Hall. Who owns this place? Let's try the estate agents again.'

'We did them –'

'We were asking them if June Milburn had been in contact, now we need to know who owns this house.'

'But if she was looking at it, she had to call at the agents!'

'Right, but it could be an agent elsewhere, Carlisle, for instance.'

There was a mouth-watering smell of baking at the back of the Hall. Bart wasn't surprised, all the women seemed to be looking out for him. He came in the kitchen to find Joely turning from the Aga as she took off a pair of oven gloves. This morning she was wearing white shorts and a striped tank top. The shorts were hard pushed to cover her buttocks.

'I knew you'd be back for lunch,' she told him gaily. 'You left the door open. You shouldn't do that; Kim will have been all over the place.'

He was askance. 'Kim and Jason were here?'

'Just Kim. Not here, as far as I know, but she was in the cellars.'

There was a pause. 'Have *you* been all over my house, Joely?' he asked gently, his eyes lingering on her body. She basked in the attention; she'd been told she had fabulous legs.

'Why not?' she pouted. 'You don't mind. And who's to know? Other than you.'

'Why the cellars?' He was smiling but his eyes were still intent. She didn't think he was bothered about the cellars although he must be aware of the gossip concerning concrete and missing wives.

'That door was open too,' she said carelessly. 'Kim was there. She slipped out when I was looking for you in the stables. I saw her from a window and thought Jason was still down there so I went to root him out. He wasn't, but Kim's left footprints in the cement.'

'Shit! But it's dry now. She must have been down there Monday. It'll have to be gone over again . . .' He trailed off, his eyes looking beyond her. She was frightened, trying to follow his thoughts: could people be right? Could he have – He gave a small gasp and grinned at her, his eyes wrinkled. 'So you've been baking. What's in the oven?'

She beamed. 'Cheese muffins. You eat them hot with butter. They're full of calories but let's be devils, shall we?' They were back in the present where she was fit to be seduced and he was building up to it again, barring interruptions. June had no part in this scene.

'It's fun to be cherished,' he assured her. 'We should have something to drink but d'you know, there's nothing in the house. I accounted for the Scotch last night. I have to go to town to stock up.'

'We've got wine.' She was smug. She opened the fridge and displayed two bottles of Chardonnay. 'Fetch the glasses,' she ordered.

He felt the bottle she brought to the table. 'This is ice-cold! How long have you been here?'

'Long enough. You left early. Where did you go?'

'Looking for June, of course. Barns and that. I don't want

to talk about it, if you don't mind. To tell you the truth I need to forget. Personally I think she's with a lover.'

'That's what my dad says. He said you're too young for – I mean, June's a lot older than you, isn't she?'

'Give over, Joely.' He left the room and she scowled. Had she gone too far? But he came back with two glasses, smiling wryly, apologetic. She was struggling with a corkscrew. 'Here, I'll do that.'

He approached, crowding her. If he'd been anyone else he'd have been invading her space but touching him, arm against bare arm, was immensely exciting. She pushed against him artfully and it was as if a current passed between them; she'd felt it before, with boys, and resisted with indignation or ridicule. Now she was more than co-operative, she felt as if she might melt into him.

A timer shrilled and he started back. 'I have to take the muffins out,' she breathed.

'You do that.' He twisted the corkscrew savagely. 'And then we'll have a drink and forget all about time.'

At one o'clock Maureen came home to an empty house. She assumed that the children had come in, helped themselves to crisps and pop (although she didn't remember any being around) and left again, but before the kettle boiled for a cup of tea Jason arrived, alone and intent. She looked past him. 'Where's Kim?'

'She'm with you! She went with you –'

'I know what she did! Where is she now? I sent her out to you.'

'You didna'! Her went with you to t'pub.'

Maureen stared at him, trying to remember the sequence. 'I let her stay a whiles but she kept after me like a shadow. I saw you on green – when was it? Half an hour, an hour after I started on top landing and I told her she were to go out with you, I'd had enough of her. She saw you through winder and she went.'

'She didna come out, not to me she didna. Honest, Mam,

on my heart, I ain't seen her since she went with you after breakfast.'

'Then she's still in pub! She's locked herself in somewhere, that's what she's done. She's in a toilet. You come with me, Jase, help me find her.'

Chapter Seven

The police had no difficulty in discovering the agent responsible for the house in Buncle's Yard; the identity of the owner took a little longer but in the end that was immaterial. The agent was Wharton in Brimstock.

'Why hasn't he come forward?' Ware asked angrily as they started south. 'But then maybe June never went to him, just took one look at the outside of the place and decided against it.'

'Walked round to the front and the boys took the Escort at that moment? She'd have seen her car emerge from the tunnel and called us immediately. That is, if it was June who put it in that yard. Whatever, something's happened to stop her contacting us. Why does the name "Wharton" ring a bell? We know she was going to look at a house, and we thought of the firm who handled the sale of Culchet Hall but it wasn't them. Who is Wharton?'

'Plumpton!' Ware exclaimed, braking hard. A cattle wagon had rounded a bend ahead at the moment he was about to overtake an ancient Land Rover.

'Why Plumpton? It's too small to have an estate agent.' It was a village north of Penrith.

'Uniform: Sergeant Plumpton. He talked to one of the Culchet women about June Milburn. She'd been to Wharton's and no one there had heard of June. So someone's lying.' He accelerated to pass the Land Rover.

'Not necessarily,' Blake said. 'Not if she didn't go to the office for the keys.' Neither spoke for a while. The flowery banks flew past: drifts of cow parsley and campion and ox-eye daisies. The air was heavy with the scent of may. 'Then the keys should still be with Wharton,' Blake continued doubtfully. 'Maybe the inside of the house could tell us something.'

'You mean – How would she have got in?'

'Someone else was there. They let her in?'

Yes, said Wharton, bustling out of his office, chewing (it was lunch-time): Buncle House was on their books, was something wrong? Vandals? He paled at sight of their IDs, realizing belatedly that detectives implied something more serious than spray paint and graffiti.

'Does the name June Milburn mean anything?' Blake raised his voice and the reactions were obvious. Two younger girls stiffened but their eyes shone with excitement. An older woman was concerned. Wharton gasped.

'If you'll just step into my office . . .' His glare swept the members of his staff and the youngsters turned quickly to their computers. The older woman watched the men warily, not one to be intimidated.

'The name means a lot *now*,' Wharton emphasized, going behind a desk, waving them to chairs. 'A Miss Potter came yesterday asking about Mrs Milburn but we couldn't help her. Then the car was found – burned out – and it was traced to her: the woman Miss Potter was asking about. But still it had nothing to do with us, with this firm. Buncle House! How on earth does that come into it?'

'You still say you've never met June Milburn?' Blake pressed.

'Never. Wouldn't know her from –' Ware was passing the photograph across the desk. 'No!' Wharton protested. 'I may have met her, passed her in the street – small place – a local woman, but to my knowledge she's never come in here.'

Blake nodded to Ware who took back the photo and went out to the front office. 'Who owns Buncle House?' Blake asked.

Wharton inhaled sharply, trying to get a grip on himself. 'A Charles Nevill; old gentleman, in a nursing home.

Alzheimer's. A son has power of attorney; he's in London. We have his particulars.'

'When was the last time anyone was inside the house – legally?'

'No one illegally I hope.' He essayed a tortured grin. 'The place should be secure.' He waited for reassurance and, getting none, pushed on: 'Legally, I can't remember exactly, well over a year, I'd think. Elspeth will know.' He nodded to the front office.

Ware returned, shaking his head at Blake.

'There's a question of redevelopment,' Wharton said vaguely, his eyes on Ware as he pocketed the photo. 'Some of the properties backing on that yard are empty. They're thinking of low-cost housing. Demolish and start again. Buncle House will never sell in its present condition.'

'We'd like to take a look at it.'

Wharton gulped. 'Er, of course.' He stood up. They rose with him. 'I'll fetch the keys,' he said, implying they should wait there. Blake nodded but he was on the man's heels as he went out. Ware followed.

In an alcove in the front office there was a large board with bunches of keys hanging from hooks. These must relate to properties on offer because Wharton ignored them and, watched furtively by the girls, overtly by the older Elspeth, he opened a drawer in the desk nearest the board and took out a red metal box. Rooting in the drawer he came up with a key which he used to unlock the box. Inside were several tacky envelopes labelled in faded ink. He inspected them carefully – they were difficult to decipher – then looked up: at the detectives, at his staff, back at the box. His hand was shaking.

Elspeth moved, pushing past Ware, and studied the labels. 'Buncle House isn't here,' she said coolly, and turned on the girls who, gaping like pretty fish, shook their heads vehemently. She turned back to her employer, quite sure of herself. 'Larry took them,' she stated.

'You knew?' Blake asked.

'I had no idea, but since it wasn't any of us, it had to be him.'

Wharton blundered back to his office, hitting the door jamb with his shoulder. He collapsed behind his desk, then sat up as if jerked by strings. 'Elspeth!' he shouted.

She appeared, taking her time. 'You went to the hospital and they let you go through his possessions, right?'

'Yes, Mr Wharton.'

'To recover the keys of the property at Keld that he was on his way to look at?' She nodded. *'They* were there,' he told Blake, and turned back to the woman: 'But there were no keys to Buncle House?'

'No.'

'Thank you, Elspeth.' He looked to the detectives for comment.

'Could they be in the car?' Ware asked generally.

'Do we know which garage it was taken to?' Blake wondered. 'No. We'll get uniform on to it.' He turned to Wharton. 'No one else has access to these offices? What about cleaners?'

'The girls do the place themselves. There's someone here all the time in opening hours. At night the windows are locked: in the kitchen and the toilets. There have been no break-ins.'

For a moment they regarded each other in silence then: 'What's your explanation?' Blake asked. 'At a guess.' Wharton stared gloomily at the surface of his desk. 'Mr Wharton?' Blake pressed.

He lifted his head and they saw a new thought strike him. 'Why, it's simple! Larry came in early, took the keys, forgot to leave a note, would have told me when he came back from Keld – that's right! I wondered why he should have the accident *there*, going to Keld the long way round, why hadn't he gone direct from here? Of course! He went to Harras first.'

'He doesn't seem to have had the keys when he crashed,' Blake reminded him gently.

'That's right. Unless they're in the car. The garage would know.'

'And if they're not in the car –' Ware began.

'Right!' Blake turned on his partner, effectively silencing

him. 'We'll have a look inside the house.' He was suddenly jovial. 'People post keys back through the letter box, don't they?'

They left. 'There's no letter box in that back door,' Ware observed, settling behind the wheel. 'And the front's boarded up. And why d'you shut me up in there?'

'Because there's something fishy about those keys, and someone in that office is involved.' Blake was dialling and now he gave instructions to locate the garage and have the crashed car searched for keys.

Out on the open road Ware spoke up again. 'Larry Payne,' he mused. 'Is there a sex angle after all? He's in his twenties, she's fifty. Toy boy, you reckon?'

Kim hadn't been found in the Stag. Maureen had looked behind every door, Win Langley had searched her larders. Graham went through the outbuildings while Freda coped with the customers, regretting that she'd allowed Joely to leave after breakfast, saying she was going to visit Jill Housby.

After the pub was searched – people opening doors and calling Kim's name – Maureen started to repeat the process randomly, entering guests' bedrooms, pushing clothes aside in wardrobes, shifting beds. Alerted by Win, Freda rushed to restrain her. Meanwhile Graham, hearing Jason repeat that Kim hadn't emerged from the front of the pub, made the obvious deduction: that she'd left by the back entrance. And that gave on to Back Lane where, by turning right, she'd have only the Brunskills' place to pass and one field, and she'd be home. But she wasn't home.

Ted Brunskill was out, Maud told Graham: somewhere on the fell, but she had been in the garden for part of the morning. The wall was high however, too high for her to have seen Kim pass. Bart might have seen her, he came home for lunch – but he'd have said. Alternatively the child could have gone the opposite way from the Brunskills': up Back Lane, which would take her round the head of the village, past the gardens behind holiday cottages, over the Housbys' track, past Todbank, the Hall, Thrushgill . . . and the ghyll. Sending Jason to inquire at all the occupied houses, taking his dog, Graham went across the green to the path beside Thrushgill, crossed Back Lane and dropped down to the beck.

Back in the Stag, eased into a chair by Freda, persuaded to sit still and drink a little brandy, Maureen quietened down to state harshly that Kim had hidden deliberately in some secret place or she'd run away. The child was terrified of Housby's dog. 'I thought it were harmless,' she told Freda, stricken by guilt as each new horror engulfed her. 'Now I don't know; maybe he's took her.'

She was referring to a dog but Freda dreaded the moment when she'd be referring to a person. Freda wasn't bothered about Baz; Graham had said that although the animal had been standing over Kim when he'd come on them yesterday evening, Jill had been laughing helplessly while all the hound did was slobber over the child. On the other hand the child did seem to be frightened of something; Maureen maintained that Kim was actually clinging to her this morning.

When Hugh came back from town at three thirty he was drunk but that didn't stop him calling at the pub. Freda was behind the bar, in control now that they were no longer serving food but her heart sank when he appeared, flushed and unsteady, reeking of beer, moreover totally unaware . . . She shook her head at his demand – not a request – for a pint. He was incredulous, laughing, fumbling for cash. 'Maureen's out looking for Kim,' she told him. In the face of his condition she didn't want to say the child was missing – a sinister word.

'So?' He swayed, blinking, uncomprehending. 'What d'you mean?'

'They've been looking' – she glanced at the wall clock but still temporized – 'for some time now.'

He couldn't follow this but he sensed trouble. The bonhomie leaked away. He gripped the counter, his face blank. 'She's with Jase.'

'She was with Maureen.' Freda wanted him out of here.

She sized up two of the fellows in the bar: young, big enough to deal with a drunk. She put it to him baldly: 'Kim was here with her mother – who told her to go out to Jason at the front. Evidently Kim wasn't having any and she dodged everyone and went out the back. They're looking for her now. You weren't here.'

'I were working! Where's –'

'You've been drinking and –'

'Never you mind what I been doing!' Shock had sobered him but he was in a rage. 'When did she go?'

'Around ten o'clock I –'

'She's been missing *hours*! What's the p'lice doing?'

Freda said angrily, 'We haven't told them. That's down to –'

'You haven't – My baby's been missing five, six hours, and no one's called p'lice!' He clapped his hand to his back pocket, turned and rushed out to his pick-up. In a moment he was shouting into a mobile.

A man approached the bar. Freda mimed an apology. 'Not your responsibility,' he told her comfortably.

'It's a small village.' It was by way of being a contradiction.

Buncle House smelled. It smelled of dust and dried mould and nameless things and, once the echoes of the ram had died away, it was very quiet. After the door was broken down they hadn't gone bursting in as they would when calling on villains in the early morning because here Blake had no idea what to expect, not with the keys missing. By the time they reached Harras the garage had been located and he was assured that there had been no keys inside Larry's wrecked car. What had been there was awaiting collection. So the keys of Buncle House could be in the possession of someone inside it at this moment, which was why Ware had shouted 'Police!' when they entered, and why no one moved afterwards. There were four of them now, the party reinforced by uniformed officers.

They had torches, unnecessary at the back where the

windows were barred but not boarded; they would be needed at the front and in the hall. When there was no response to Ware's shout they proceeded carefully, one uniform with Blake staying below, Ware and the other constable climbing stairs which were just inside the back door. On Blake's left, and facing into the yard, was a room fitted with shelving and nothing else, not even a fireplace. He wondered about it. 'Pantry,' the constable told him, retreating past the foot of the stairs to the doorway of another and larger room. 'Kitchen.' He was phlegmatic. 'Nothing here, the floor's gone.'

Blake peered past him. In the light from the shattered window he saw the gaping hole, a gash rather, where several floorboards had given way leaving pale jagged edges. 'Worm-eaten.' The PC was dismissive, thinking Blake was unfamiliar with old buildings.

'That break's fresh,' the detective observed. At that moment Ware came down the stairs. 'Nothing up there,' he said. 'Only a couple of old mattresses covered with rat shit. The son must have sold the furniture. He has power of attorney. You found something?'

Blake was inching into the kitchen, testing floorboards. 'Hold hands,' he ordered. 'Make a chain.' They joined up, a constable gripping his wrist. 'Hand me a torch.'

He leaned out – 'Careful,' someone muttered – and shone the beam into the depths. They saw him stiffen. For a moment the beam moved erratically then settled, Blake cocking his head like a bird. 'Bring me back,' he said quietly.

They applied careful pressure and he retreated. Ware knew by his expression. 'We found her,' Blake said.

The entrance to the cellar was in a corner of the kitchen. The door opened into the room and planks had been nailed between the jambs. These were prised off with tyre levers and their torches revealed a flight of stone steps, worn but solid, unlike the cellar ceiling through which some daylight penetrated to show them a sprawled body. The skirt had rucked up and a pointed shaft of bone protruded through one shin. A few feet away, on top of a pile of broken wood, was a handbag.

When the doctor arrived he said she had been dead for quite a while. He lifted a limp hand, turned it and glanced back at the steps. 'I'm no pathologist,' he said, 'but I'd say she's been scraping at that door. Look.'

Blake looked and winced. Ware, peering over his shoulder, said, 'That's splinters embedded! She tried to get out and the bloody door was barred on the outside. Christ, how long did she live?'

The doctor stood up. 'Off the record, the fall killed her. *This* one.' He gestured to the steps. 'Both legs are broken so she must have dragged herself up there and lost her balance as she was clawing at the door.'

'So she lived for a while after the first fall – when the floor gave way,' Blake mused.

Ware was incredulous. 'Why didn't she shout?'

'Who'd hear her?' Blake asked.

'Maybe she couldn't shout loud enough to make anyone hear,' the doctor pointed out. 'She was a heavy woman, there may well be internal injuries, and concussion. She wouldn't be thinking straight.'

'That's why she went through the floor,' Ware said. 'Being so heavy. *You* had to be careful' – to Blake who was standing by the fallen rubble, slapping at his trousers, frowning. He picked up the handbag. It was made of rich brown leather, with compartments. 'No mobile,' he murmured, and opened a wallet, glancing at credit cards. 'June Milburn,' he pronounced. 'There's no mistake.'

'Keys?' Ware asked.

Blake shook his head and stepped back to the body, feeling delicately in the pockets of her jacket, once lemon, now much begrimed. Metal clinked and he held up a bunch of keys.

The doctor had started up the steps but he stopped and looked back. 'What on earth was she doing in this place? Viewing it? On her own? Someone's for the chop.'

*   *   *

At Culchet Hall Bart took them to his kitchen, apologizing: 'We're casual around here, you don't mind? Have you – has there been a development?'

'Yes, sir.' Blake was cautious. 'I'm afraid there has.' Bart reached for a chair. 'We've found Mrs Milburn. She had an accident and died some time ago.'

Bart dropped on the chair and stared at the table: a few muffins on a wire cooling tray, two wine glasses, an empty bottle that had held Chardonnay, another half-full. He shook his head as if dislodging a fly. At length he found an explanation: 'You said she wasn't in the car.' He looked up. 'You lied?'

'She wasn't in the car,' Blake confirmed, familiar with initial denial in the face of such news. 'She did go to view a house however, and a floor gave way. She fell into the cellar below.'

'*No!*' The tone verged on hysteria. 'You don't die just falling into a cellar.'

Blake was silent. 'She couldn't get out,' Ware said.

'You're telling me that no one knew she was there? Did she – was she unconscious?'

Blake prevaricated. 'We'll know more after the post-mortem.'

Bart reached for the bottle of wine, looked at it as if considering his purpose in picking it up, and put it down. Ware hefted a kettle and pushed it on the Aga's hot-plate.

'Where did this happen?' Bart asked weakly.

'In Harras,' Blake told him. 'An old town house backing on a yard. She had the keys in her pocket,' he added, regarding the top of Bart's head as, elbows on the table, he was again staring at the wooden surface. Blake had a sudden image of the splinters in June Milburn's hands. 'Did she go straight there on Monday morning?' he asked.

Bart inhaled deeply and let it go. 'I wouldn't know.' He raised his head. 'I was in the cellars' – he choked on the word – 'in *our* cellars, here, at the Hall. I didn't see her go; Hugh and me, we were levelling the floor. Haven't I told you this already? I've told someone. I didn't see her – the last time I did must have been at breakfast. I went out – no, Hugh came, I asked if he wanted a mug of tea; she was upstairs dressing, I suppose, showering – oh my God, when did I see her last? What was she doing? I can't remember.'

Ware had made tea and placed a large mug in front of him. 'You been baking,' he said, too lightly. 'Have a bun.'

'They've been coming over,' Bart said dully. 'The women. Bringing casseroles and stuff.'

Blake thought that whoever did the baking had done it here. And stayed. Stayed a while. He didn't know how long it took to make and bake the muffins but a bottle and a half of wine took a while to get through even with two people sharing.

A mobile was cheeping. The detectives were alert but made no move. Bart looked round, bewildered. Then Ware spotted a phone on the dresser and handed it to him.

'Yes?' Bart said, blinking, smoothing his forehead with his fingers. 'Speaking.' He listened for a moment then, 'I've been told,' he said listlessly. 'The police are here now but thanks –' He checked and listened again. 'What?' he whispered. 'No.' But it wasn't the fierce denial he'd voiced at the news of June's death. Ware and Blake exchanged puzzled glances. 'When?' they heard. '. . . Yes, yes, I'm sure you did . . . yes, I know . . . my God, that poor woman! Of course I will –' He clapped his hand to his mouth, turning to Blake with wide eyes. 'Yes, yes,' he repeated, laying the phone on the table. 'Larry died,' he told them.

'I'm sorry.' Blake wasn't sorry, he was frustrated. On the way here they'd discussed just this contingency and speculated on the chances of Larry's recovering enough, or for long enough, to answer some questions, notably why he had allowed June to enter a house in such a dangerous condition on her own, for it seemed obvious that Larry must have taken the keys from the office.

'I have to go and fetch his mother,' Bart was saying. 'Poor old girl, she'll be beside herself.'

'It would be wiser for her to come home in a taxi,' Blake said, thinking that the man was in no state to drive. He had to be in shock.

'I'm all right,' he protested.

Ware put in neatly, 'You're over the limit' – gesturing to the wine. 'We'll call the hospital, get them to –'

A trim woman, flustered, middle-aged but still attractive, had appeared in the doorway. 'Bart!' she exclaimed, nodding to the strangers, 'You're needed pronto. Everyone is turning out. Kim's missing.'

His face contorted. He gave a harsh bark ending in a splutter – of laughter? Disbelief? Never amusement.

'What the hell's got into you?' The woman glowered.

Blake said, 'We're police officers, ma'am. I take it you're a neighbour?'

She nodded distractedly, her eyes on Bart who had dropped his head in his hands. 'I'm Alice Potter; I live down the green a bit.'

'We came to inform Mr Milburn that his wife has met with a fatal accident. And the hospital's just rung to say Larry – Larry?'

'Payne?' Alice breathed, taking a hesitant step forward.

'He too has passed away.'

'Oh Bart!' Her hands went out but she thought better of touching him at this moment. She remembered her own words. 'Forget Kim. They'll manage. I'll stay with him,' she told Blake. 'You'll be needed for Kim. Don't let me keep you.'

She pushed the mug of tea at Bart and stared bemusedly at the muffins and the remains of the wine.

'Who is Kim?' Ware asked.

'Why, aren't you – oh, I see! Different cases – not that Kim's a case – well, she is, but not in that way.' She stifled a giggle. 'And you're CID, they'll send uniforms for Kim, that nice Sergeant Plumpton. But it's probably no more than a ploy, attention seeking: that's Kim all over. Five years old and no one's seen her since ten o'clock. Her mother's dreading the worst and her dad's drunk and spitting blood.' She stopped. Bart seemed not to be listening. The detectives waited for her to run down. She swallowed. 'I'm sorry, it's only a minor village upset, happens all the time.' She was terribly embarrassed, going off at half-cock like that, intruding on a man suddenly – and doubly – bereaved. She went to continue, glanced at him, at them, and closed her mouth like a trap. Blake knew she was dying to ask about June. He turned to Bart.

'Did your wife have a mobile phone, sir?'

'Yes.'

'We haven't found one.'

'She didn't take it with her. The battery was flat. She left it on charge.'

Chapter Eight

Alice had exaggerated when she said that everyone was searching for Kim. With her special knowledge she did know that when small children disappear it's vital to find them quickly, yet she wouldn't have been thinking along those lines had it not been for Hugh Butler. His panic was infectious. In the normal way he would have collapsed on his return from a midday session in the town's pubs, and slept off the effects. Today he had to keep going and he did so by stealing a bottle of vodka from the bar when everyone was occupied elsewhere. Now, drunk and panicking, raging at Sergeant Plumpton for turning up on his own, Hugh was swearing that if Kim hadn't been taken by Housby's dog then a paedophile had got her.

His Land Rover was outside the pub, the bottle of vodka on the floor. Every so often he would return to it and drink from a glass, also filched. 'Water!' he hurled at Plumpton. 'I'm de –' He struggled with the word and settled on 'thirsty'. Plumpton, who had glimpsed the bottle, waited for the fellow to drop, when he might be deposited in his house in Dubb's Close out of harm's way.

From the people Plumpton had talked to there were conflicting statements – information rather; 'statements' implied a more serious situation than he was ready to accept. Maureen, drained and grim in the face of her husband's condition, but more reasonable, now dismissed the question of Housby's dog; it was just rough, she said. She was more concerned with her own guilt, not watching to see that Kim had joined Jason. She reckoned the child was in the ghyll, she'd fallen and hit her head.

The ghyll had been combed. There *were* big boulders, even little crags, all choked by timber and a luxuriant ground cover, but Graham's Labrador had found nothing. Observing the bitch – young, lean and eager – the sergeant knew that, had the child been there, unconscious or hiding, she'd have been found.

Jason, following his own paths in the ghyll and else-where, visiting places known only to him and his sister, when asked, didn't think Housby's dog would kill her; he'd just knock her over like he did last night, he wouldn't savage her. All the same, Plumpton thought that Jason was running scared.

The sergeant went to find Housby and was met by the dog in the drive. He knew it was the right dog by its strange appearance – something like an otter hound – and its intimidating roar before it thrust its head through the open window, grinning and dribbling. Plumpton, a coun-tryman, had no hesitation in stepping out, sternly ordering the brute to stay down, asserting his authority. Ignoring the front of the house, as would all country folk and any policeman worth his salt, he went round the back, accom-panied by the gambolling Baz.

The rear door was closed, guarded by a small tabby cat that snarled at the dog but otherwise remained immobile, not even shifting from the step when Plumpton banged on the door. There wasn't much fear around Lonning Head, and the sergeant held that where animals were well treated so were people. (But Alice Potter could have told him of at least one murderer who had loved animals.)

A girl rode into the barnyard on a tired pony. 'No one in?' she called cheerily as she slid down and flexed her knees. She came over, the pony plodding behind her. 'My dad'll be shepherding,' she told him, glancing at a Land Rover and an old van. 'Can I help?'

He introduced himself and told her that a child was – missing. He hesitated over the word, not liking it.

'Who?' she asked quickly.

'Kim Butler.'

She gave a snort. 'And her dad sent for you! Typical.

He'll have given her a belting – no, he wouldn't belt Kim – but her mother would have laid into her for some crime. She's a wee monster. She's hiding to give everyone a fright. She'll be in someone's shed.' She became aware that he was regarding her too intently. 'You're taking this seriously?' She was amazed.

'Her dad's bothered about your dog.'

'This dog? Look at him.' Baz had collapsed in the shade beside a number of somnolent hens. 'How did he greet you?'

'He was friendly.'

'You see. You could have walked in this house and walked out with the TV. He'd have helped you carry it. Hugh will have told you about last evening. What happened was that Kim fell over. Baz might have licked her a bit juicily, that's what he does, but if she was grazed it was from the fall, and I could see no mark; the paths are deep in dust.'

'The dog's harmless,' he conceded, 'but her mother maintains the child's terrified of something.'

He accompanied her as she led the pony to an open stable. She tied the animal to a ring in the wall and reached for the girth buckles, her mind elsewhere. Plumpton was expressionless. She pulled off the saddle, set it on the half-door and eyed her mount's steaming back. 'Ask Jason what they were fighting about when I came on them in the ghyll last evening,' she said.

'Fighting?'

'Shouting at each other.' She bit her lip. 'Threatening.'

'What was the threat?'

'They're only kids.' She tried to backtrack, then thought that Jason was only ten, they couldn't *do* anything to him. Aloud she said, 'Kim threatened "to tell" – she didn't say what; he said he'd kill her if she did. It was just a kids' quarrel, that's all, I promise you.'

'Two duck, one salmon,' Joely announced, coming in the Stag's kitchen, collecting dishes of game chips and asparagus, using her shoulder expertly to sidle through the swing door, back to the dining room.

'She looks sort of dreamy,' Alice observed. She was sprawled on a chair with a mug of tea.

'Speak for yourself.' Win turned from the Aga with a tray of duck quarters. 'You should go home and have a lie-down.'

'I'll revive; it's nice and cool in here now you've got the fans. We ought to find Kim before dark – although it is high summer; she'll survive one night out if she has to.'

'Where can she be?' Win forked duck on to plates. 'The ghyll's been done, all the sheds and barns –'

'You can't do them all in a few hours,' Alice protested. 'They've eliminated the ones around the village certainly but now they're having to work outwards. Ted Brunskill's looking, and chaps from Dubb's Close and so on.'

Freda came in. 'Lemons! Do we have a lemon? Hi, Alice, take a drop of something hard in that tea, you look as if you could use it. D'you know what? There's a bottle of vodka missing.'

Win looked blank. 'I haven't used any vodka.'

'It'll be Hugh Butler.' Freda was vicious. 'I wouldn't serve him so he must have helped himself when my back was turned. I saw him drinking through the window. I thought it was water then. Water! Hugh Butler never touched it in his life.'

'The man's lost his kid.' Win was reproving.

'For pity's sake, Win! Don't put it that way.'

'Well, she's lost, that's what I meant.'

Joely came in. 'Since ten o'clock,' Alice mused. 'It seems impossible that no one saw her after ten.'

'Maybe someone did,' Win said grimly.

Joely picked up plates of duck and went back to the dining room. Freda found a lemon and returned to the bar. Alice said, 'I suppose I'd better shift myself – but it's hard knowing where to look next. We've got no method, you know. Graham accounted for the ghyll but that's the easy part, now we have to do all the isolated bothies and field houses, not to speak of holiday places – I mean, unoccupied, of course' – as Win looked up sharply – 'she could have got trapped, like cats getting themselves shut in when visitors leave.'

'Is it deliberate or accidental, d'you think?'

'You're asking me?'

'You're the expert, well informed anyway; you have to be. All you ever read is crime.'

'But we're not talking crime here!' Win was silent. Alice's expression changed from denial to helplessness. 'I don't like it,' she admitted. 'Maureen insists the kid's terrified of something, wouldn't leave her side –'

'Something or somebody?'

Alice signalled caution as the door opened and Joely crossed to the sink with used plates. They shouldn't speculate in front of her; at sixteen she was only a child herself, and if one small girl could go missing . . . Alice thought of serial killers, and as her tired brain recalled the serial *accidents* overtaking the villagers Joely said, 'Can we save some duck for Bart? He won't feel much like eating but we should make the gesture, don't you think?'

'He's got the casserole from last night,' Win reminded her.

'He's – he'll have wolfed that. Of course, if you don't want to –'

'Poor Bart,' Alice broke in, trying to ease the tension, 'if there's some duck to spare, I'll take it over. He can put it in the freezer if necessary.'

'I'll take it,' Joely said. 'You look for Kim; we ought to find her while it's still light.'

'Do you realize,' Win said, her eyes on Joely's back as she went out, 'we've got Rachel to watch out for now as well. Maud's with her but she can't stay at Todbank, she has Ted to look after.'

'I was over at Todbank,' Alice told her. 'Rachel was asleep. I told Maud I needed to look in the Paynes' garage and shed. She said Rachel was upstairs, flat out. I guess the Brunskills will handle the funeral arrangements for her. Maud's already contacted Rachel's two sisters.'

'And then there's June's daughter.'

'Carol's abroad, in Australia or somewhere, with her husband. She has to be told. I'll see if Bart's going to phone them. If not, I'll do it when I go across – oh no, Joely's going over. That child's being a bit proprietorial, isn't she?'

'It's her chance and she's taking it. She was always mad about him.'

'Puppy love.' Alice sighed heavily and stood up. 'Where shall I go? Kim hasn't gone far, little kid that age, she'd never go on the fell – surely? She might have gone down to the road but then someone would have seen her.'

'Someone might have done, and picked her up.'

'Then he – they'd bring her home.'

'Or *take* her home.'

'Win! We don't have to – Ah, Graham!'

The Labrador pushed in the back door followed by her owner. They didn't ask if he had any news. Win poured a large mug of tea and added a fair measure of whisky. He held up a protesting hand. 'It's all right,' she told him. 'You're not driving.'

'No. She can't have gone far. Jon's going through the ghyll again. The lad feels guilty: been out all day, come home to this. Swears he'll thrash young Jason within an inch of his life when he finds him. Not Jason's fault of course. My, but they're an excitable family, the Butlers.'

'Where *is* Jason?' Alice asked.

'Disapp –' He stopped. 'He's off on his own: searching. He'll know all their little hidey holes, won't he? In fact, he could be the most likely one to find her. What are the police doing?'

Win said, 'Plumpton went to Brimstock. He said they're short of cars, implying he had to go back in order to bring more men here. Sounds a bit odd.'

'He could have gone back to get access to a computer,' Alice said.

Graham goggled at her. 'What for?'

She shrugged. 'There were Hugh's accusations.'

'The dog? The fellow's drunk, and you know what he's like with Kim: his baby doll.'

'Actually I don't think Plumpton will be thinking in terms of dogs. He's more likely checking whether anyone in the locality has a record for offences regarding children.'

'Have you looked at the father?' Brimstock's chief inspector asked.

'Suspected, pulled in, never charged.' Plumpton was terse. 'Nothing involving children.'

'All the same, like spouses, isn't it? First suspect is always the nearest and dearest.'

'He's dead-drunk,' Plumpton said. 'He won't be in any state to answer questions until tomorrow.'

'I just hope she's found before tomorrow.'

Blake received a preliminary and verbal report on June Milburn later that evening; he'd asked specially for it. Her injuries were consistent with the falls: both legs broken and the right wrist; internal injuries would have to wait for the post-mortem. There was a depressed fracture to the vault of the skull: the top of the head, the pathologist translated. Could that have been the cause of death? Blake asked.

'Eventually, not immediately – but there again it depends on the internal injuries. There was considerable bleeding from the head wound so it occurred some time before she died.'

Blake was in his own living room. He replaced the phone, stood up and, regarding the carpet, visualized a gaping hole in its place, a drop of eight or nine feet below. You fell feet first, right? Or forwards, striking your face on the edge of the hole (her face wasn't lacerated) – no, the floor gave way, she'd have *dropped*. So how was it the top of her skull came to be fractured?

Chapter Nine

Blake slept badly and woke to a feeling that something was wrong: he'd missed a cue or committed an error, but before he could associate this with the nature of a head wound, the phone rang. After that June Milburn was yesterday's news and it was back to Culchet to find a missing child.

Briefed by Plumpton the detectives went straight to the Butler house, arriving as Jon was leaving. His tension was obvious but they knew him as a thief and not one with a record of violence, and certainly not a child molester. They would keep him in mind but at this moment their business was with his father.

Hugh sat at his kitchen table in a grubby singlet, barefooted, smoking, looking at *The Sun*. It was a moot point how much of the man's wretched appearance could be attributed to concern for his daughter and how much to a thumping hangover. As if he needed reminding Blake told him that Kim had wanted to go to Brimstock with him yesterday but he'd gone alone. 'What time did you leave here?' he asked casually.

Hugh passed a large hand over his face. 'I can't remember. Ask the wife.'

'Where is she?'

'Out. Looking for my little girl.' The eyes, already bleary, watered. A sob turned to a snarl. 'You come about 'er? *Plain clothes?* You'm asking where I were? I'm 'er dad! You reckon as how I done summat to my –' He was rising.

'Calm down.' Blake didn't move but his immobility was a threat in itself. 'We have to ask everyone. That is, all the

98

men. That's what you want us to do, isn't it? *All* the men.
So we start with you, for elimination purposes. You know
how it's done. Sometimes it's a member of the family.
Elimination, Hugh.'

He gave a derisive snort. 'Alibis, that's what you're after.
So,' he grated, 'I left here late on; she were with her mam
here in this same kitchen when I went. I drove straight to
town to me cousin's house and from there us went to Pack
Horse. And then to Brindled Bull – an' White Lion –' His
eyes were glazing.

'You were with your cousin all the time?'

'Him and others. Them's the places where I drink.
I know all t'regulars. An' they knows me!' Defiantly.

'Right. Give the names and particulars to this officer –
and the times, where you were, while I have a word with
your boy.'

'He's away out.'

'The young one: Jason.'

'Him too. Them's all out searching, like I'm about to –
and you should be. It's what you'm here for.'

'And that's what we're doing.'

'Then look in right place, not at 'er grieving family!' He
was enraged again. 'I'll tell thee where tha should be
looking – at yon Housby. Why'd he keep that girt savage
dog except to stop folk visiting – him living up there all
alone? Unnatural. And that Payne – a poofter – what's he
at, living with his mam? Who's he –'

'Larry Payne died yesterday,' Blake said firmly. 'Before
that he was in a coma for two days. He had nothing to do
with Kim going missing.'

'Milburn then. That Hall's full of cupboards and such,
I work there; I know. And Bart and Larry's like that.' He
pressed his palms together and grinned slyly, then remembered Kim and glowered. 'I'll come with you, show you
where to look.'

'We'll do it our way, thanks. Now you just give those
particulars to Mr Ware and I'll look for Jason.'

'You won't find him then.' Crowing now. It would seem
that obstructing the police meant more to him than locat-

ing his daughter. 'Jon took his belt to 'un.' He stopped, he hadn't meant to come out with that. Blake waited. 'For losing his little sister,' Hugh blustered. 'Supposed to look after her, wasn't he?'

'I thought she was in the pub with her mam.'

'That's right.'

'But she sneaked out the back way.'

'Maybe.' He was wary.

'How could that be Jason's fault? Kim escaped from her mam, not from him.'

'He blames himself. She were *supposed* to go out to him and she didna. He thinks it's his fault.'

'And so does Jon?'

'No! Yes – I dunno. He cheeked Jon – well, he would, wouldn't he, being blamed for summat he didna do?'

The detectives left after Ware had obtained details of times and the man's drinking companions. Out of earshot Ware said, 'Think he's in the clear?'

Blake halted with his hand on the car door. He blinked, changing mental gear. 'Oh, regarding Kim? Yes, he's clear – if all those witnesses stand up. But he's lying about Jason. Maybe it was himself who thrashed the lad, but what for? Certainly not for losing Kim, he'd have been condemning the boy from the start if he thought it was him at fault. Could Jason be in trouble for something else – involving Kim?' They regarded each other over the top of the car.

Ware said thoughtfully, 'According to Plumpton the first thing Hugh said – when he was raving drunk and after he said a dog killed her: Housby's hound Plumpton says is harmless – next thing Hugh's saying is that a paedophile's taken her.'

'No paedophiles in Culchet.'

'To our knowledge. He favoured Larry Payne. Forgot the guy had been in a coma. So Payne was gay. We didn't know that.'

'We haven't been here that long. Most of what we know comes from Plumpton. So maybe *he* didn't know. We'd soon have found out of course, someone would have told us – and there you are: Hugh did. But whichever way you look at it, it has no bearing. Larry's dead.'

'Hugh implied a relationship between him and Milburn.'

They got into the car, which was like an oven. They lowered the windows and opened the sun roof. 'Drive to the green,' Blake ordered. 'I don't like talking here in the close. Someone might know how to lip-read.'

Ware drove off, turning right and right again, squeezing between two cottages to park on the green in the shade of a horse chestnut.

'Can we have come full circle?' Blake mused. 'We've left June Milburn, transferred to something apparently unrelated, and within an hour June Milburn's name – well, her husband's – turns up again.'

'Coincidence,' Ware said. 'And Butler was throwing accusations around like confetti. It's a small village, everyone knows everyone else so people will all be connected. It's like a web.'

'We'll see Milburn, but right now let's try to find Kim's mother before Hugh unscrambles what little brain he has and gets to her first. Perhaps we'll find her more accommodating.'

Hugh had said his wife was searching for Kim but they had no idea where to start except by way of their own men. Seeing a number of stationary police vehicles on the grass Ware pulled over to them to find they were parked at the mouth of a narrow track between two cottages. Blake spread a large-scale map on the bonnet and they saw that the track would take them to a ravine: Culchet Ghyll.

'You'll be with them,' someone said abruptly.

They straightened and turned to see a heavy woman in her forties wearing tight jeans and a grubby T-shirt, her hair strained back and tied with what looked like a bootlace. 'I'm the mother,' she told them in the kind of brittle tone that masked desperation.

Blake introduced himself. 'We'll do everything in our power,' he assured her, clamping down on a grimace as a dog started to bark excitedly beyond the end of the track.

She heard it too. Hope flared in the plain face, followed by anguish. She turned and ran amazingly fast down the track.

They followed, within a few yards coming on a transverse lane that ran along the rim of a densely wooded gorge. Now they heard men calling and bodies crashing through vegetation. The dog had stopped barking.

The ghyll was fenced. Maureen gripped the top strand of barbed wire and shouted: 'Kim, Kim! Kim, baby!'

Blake tried to ease her hands from the wire. Ware was running down a path into the ghyll. 'Listen!' Blake demanded. 'Listen to what they're saying.'

She stopped shouting but he couldn't shift her hands. There were sounds of movement below but no cries. 'Now,' he said comfortably, 'my colleague is going to find out what's happening and he'll let us know. Shall we walk along a little – maybe see something . . .' He had to get her hands off that wire.

'I doubt there's anything to see.' She sounded drained but she moved away, her hands hanging limply, blood dripping off the fingers.

'We've been talking to Hugh,' he told her chattily. 'I'd like to have a word with Jason too; he might have some idea . . .'

'They were always together,' she said sadly, staring into the green canopy below the fence. Now the silence in the ghyll was full of menace. 'Except this time,' she continued. 'Jase thinks he knows where she is and he keeps looking but he don't find her. Butler's certain someone's took her.'

'Sergeant!' It was a bellow: Ware's voice.

'What?'

'Dogs found a dead sheep.'

'Right.' He turned to Maureen who was staring at her hands. 'Come along and let's get you cleaned up.' He started to steer her back to the green. 'Who does Hugh think took Kim?'

'Larry Payne.'

'He died yesterday.'

'I told him. He were so drunk he couldn't take it in. Now he'll go round accusing every chap in the village. The trouble is' – she stopped and faced him – 'if he hits on the right man by chance, him what's holding her, he could panic.'

'We've told him to leave things to us.'

'And what are you doing?'

He hesitated but there were no witnesses to any indiscretion on his part. 'What would you suggest, Mrs Butler?'

'You mean if it is a man, not that she's fell and hit her head?' He was surprised at the speed with which she'd regained control. 'Someone she knew or a stranger?' she asked of herself. 'Well, if you was looking at Culchet folk, there's Bart Milburn' – she shuddered – 'Rob Housby – but I got nothing against him. Ted Brunskill now, he hates Jason – and Jon – so that'd hold for Kim too. Mr Carrick at Stag? I dunno. Why'd he want a little girl? There's our neighbours in the close of course.'

'Bart Milburn,' Blake repeated thoughtfully. 'Your husband's been working with him.' She said nothing. 'Laying a cellar floor,' he elaborated.

She knew exactly what was in his mind but there was no reaction: no horror, no pain. On the contrary, she relaxed, looking down at the dust at her feet. 'If she's there,' she said, 'then it's over and she don't feel nothing no more. But if she is there I'll kill him.'

Jason had been looking for Bart but there was no one at the Hall even though the back door was unlocked. He was used to that and he went through the house: the bedrooms, the attics, the queer dim parlours which you couldn't call 'lounges' because that was reserved for new places like those in the close. He gave the cellars only a cursory glance, he knew she wouldn't be there. They were the first place he'd looked. He returned to the kitchen, found a congealed stew of sorts in the fridge and dismissed it. He looked no further. The Milburns never had crisps nor

103

Coke nor any kind of decent drink. He walked out of the front gate as if he owned the place, aware of the police vehicles a few yards away but secure in the knowledge that searchers (and wasn't he one?) could go anywhere, do anything without question. He went next door to Todbank.

Rachel was standing at the sink drinking water when he passed the kitchen window. Their eyes met, hers expressionless in a face so pale it looked enamelled, framed by the coal-black hair. Jason was momentarily awed until he remembered that he had the whiphand although he wasn't sure how to use it. He clenched his jaw; he'd see how it went. He kept going to the back door.

She didn't ask him what he wanted. She regarded him with those lizard eyes and waited.

'I need to look in your shed,' he told her. In his effort to sound confident it emerged rather too loudly.

'What have you done with her?' Rachel asked, without curiosity.

'Kim?' His voice rose. 'I'm looking for 'er.' Praying that she'd interpret his shock at the question as righteous indignation.

'What did she do? Threaten to tell on you?' Her lips stretched, her teeth showing in a grin like a dog's snarl. Jason took a step back.

'You got something to hide,' he snapped, but there was a crack in his voice.

'Scum,' Rachel said coldly. 'What are you going to do, eh? What *can* you do now? I've got no animals, no pets, nothing for you to hurt. Nothing.' A light leapt in her eyes. 'Ah, but I do! I have – an ambition? A wish? A dream. I have a dream.' She rolled it out slow and deep. Jason had never heard of Martin Luther King but it was a fair imitation and he was petrified. 'I dream,' Rachel intoned, 'of little children, of one little child; of putting these hands' – she showed him her palms – 'round the sweet soft throat of a little boy and gently squeezing the life out of him. And no one would ever know. Do you know what little boys look like when they're dying that way, Jason? Their tongues come out all blue and swollen like balloons and they wet themselves and –'

He was retreating, his hands on his own throat, unable to tear his eyes from hers. 'You're mad,' he whispered, tripping, turning, starting to run. At the corner of the house he stopped and glanced back. She was standing there, grinning.

'Mad!' he shrieked. 'You'm as mad as he were! Him what were killed dead!'

'There's Jase,' Maureen said. 'Why's he running? Jase, come 'ere!'

But Jason, who had been racing down the green as if heading for home, only swerved as he came level with the pub and, slowing down, jogged in the direction of the car park at the back.

'I need to speak to him,' Maureen said, taking off across the grass.

Ware came up, panting and flushed. Blake told him what he'd learned from Maureen, which didn't amount to much, only that Ted Brunskill hated the Butler children – they must follow that up – and that Maureen, like everyone else, had considered the possibilities of the Hall's cellars.

'Hugh hasn't,' Ware said. 'He's not interested. He was there, pouring concrete. He'd know. He mentioned the Hall but not the cellars. And even mentioning the Hall was only to distract us from himself. He don't suspect Bart.'

'No. He appears to favour Housby – after Housby's dog. The man's widowed.' Blake paused at that, then went on, 'We'll be seeing him but first I want a word with young Jason. Like his mam said: what's he running from? Or to?'

There was a gate at the back of the Stag's car park giving access to what they saw from the map was Back Lane, and that contoured the village. Hedges and high walls made it a secretive place. They didn't reach it because, through the open windows of the pub, they glimpsed Maureen at a sink, another big woman beside her. Thinking Jason would be with his mother they approached the back door as a third woman came along a passage from the front of the house. There was the sound of a vacuum cleaner in the depths. 'Come in,' she called impatiently. 'The bar's being cleaned but if it's only the two of you, there's tea in here.'

Content to be taken for members of the search team Blake and Ware followed her into the kitchen. Jason wasn't there and no introductions were made, apparently deemed unnecessary by the women. As for the police, the formality of announcing themselves – as detectives – could be counter-productive. They deduced that the woman with authority was the publican, Freda Carrick, and the one tending Maureen must be Win Langley, the cook. Freda had stared at Maureen's hands in horror – she'd be thinking of slashed wrists – but Win shook her head in reassurance. Freda grabbed mugs and a bottle of brandy.

'Let's have the First Aid box,' Win said calmly, and Blake saw that Freda wasn't the only authoritative woman here. 'We'll get you bandaged,' the cook went on, 'and then you can go home, have a –'

'I'm staying,' Maureen said. 'I'm not going home till she's found.'

Blake opened his mouth but Freda was quick with distraction. 'Here's Mr Plumpton. He looks exhausted, and there's all the rest of them will be coming in some time. Now what are we going to give them to eat?'

'Sandwiches,' Win said, picking up her cue. 'We're going to need stacks.'

'Maureen will help, won't you, love? Drink your tea while it's hot.'

Maureen could be of little assistance with those bandaged hands, evidently what Freda was concerned with was keeping the woman here under watchful eyes rather than roaming the countryside cutting herself to bits.

Plumpton was in the doorway. 'Room for one more, Sergeant,' Freda told him cheerily. 'The bar's not available at the moment. Tea?' Blake was startled before he realized

106

that the bar must be in use as an assembly point and café rather than a saloon.

The men and Maureen sat at the huge table, the detectives a little awkward in the circumstances (CID, but where was the crime?), Plumpton accepting their presence without comment, apparently unaware of any tension, and Maureen: if she was lost in her thoughts the nature of them was concealed; she could have been alone in her own kitchen.

A girl came in: slim and alluring in a tank top and thin cotton jeans, appalled at sight of Maureen's bandaged hands. The woman raised her eyes. 'I fell,' she said, in a tone that discouraged further fuss, then: 'You should be riding.'

The girl stared, frowning; the others were bewildered, then tense. What was this?

'Joely hasn't got a horse, Maureen,' Freda said gently.

'It's a good idea.' Plumpton nodded approval. 'Anyone who can ride would be an asset. Cover more ground.'

'Thornthwaites will let you have their pony again,' Freda urged. 'You and Jill: keep together.' She threw a startled glance at Maureen but the woman had missed the significance of girls being advised to stay together, not to stray.

'You were riding with Jill Housby yesterday?' Plumpton asked genially, and the detectives turned to him with interest.

'No,' Joely said quickly.

'But –' Freda began.

'I changed my mind,' Joely snapped.

'Then where –' Freda checked, aware of her audience.

'I was visiting friends. Look, do we have to –'

Maureen turned to Blake. 'You'd best go up to Lonning Head,' she said harshly. 'I'd come with you but I need to find Jase –'

'Thank you, Mrs Butler,' Plumpton said loudly, rising, addressing Blake. 'I'd like a word.'

They walked across the car park, Ware following. 'This Jill Housby was out yesterday,' Plumpton told them. 'I was at Lonning Head in the evening and she came in with her horse. The animal was exhausted. I reckon she had to have been out several hours. If Joely wasn't at the Housbys' place that puts Rob Housby there on his own at least for the afternoon. What Maureen's saying is that men on their own is suspect.'

'We're going to see him,' Blake said. 'What d'you make of Bart Milburn?'

'Feckless, skint, weak.'

'Gay?'

'What? Never. The opposite, I'd say. Not that he runs after women but he's got those sort of looks . . . His wife was much older of course: big heavy woman, rather plain.'

'We've seen her – her body, rather.'

'She had the money.'

'Yes. Was Larry Payne gay?'

'I didn't know him. What's this got to do with a little kid gone missing?'

Blake didn't answer immediately. Ware, too, was thoughtful. Plumpton looked from one to the other. 'It occurred to me,' Blake said at length, 'that the two – events – might be connected.'

'What?' Plumpton was astonished. 'June Milburn's accident, and Kim disappeared? How could they possibly be connected? They got nothing in common.'

Blake regarded him morosely. 'Nothing obvious,' he amended, 'but there are threads.'

Chapter Ten

Bart was not at home. There was no reply when they knocked on the back door and the Land Rover was missing from the yard. The door was unlocked. They looked at each other quizzically.

'Check it out,' Blake said. 'I'm going to take a look at the cellars. Don't look too hard; he knows we're searching, he'd never leave the place unlocked if she was here, alive or dead, even a trace of her. The dogs would smell her out.'

He descended an outer flight of steps to a door at the bottom thinking that there were too many cellars in this case – and then he remembered that there were two cases – with threads. Was this door unlocked? He looked back at the cement mixer. They'd recognized the potential significance of new concrete when it was June who was involved, and dismissed the possibility, and been right to do so. But – Kim? They must find out if she was seen after Milburn stopped work here. Too obvious? They'd said Hugh Butler would have to know, but then Milburn was missing . . . Had they been working together down here? If separate, then Butler could be back in the frame, except that he wouldn't have stayed in Culchet, he'd have done a runner . . . Why did he get so stinking drunk yesterday?

The door yielded. He stood at the head of another flight of steps, a light switch where it should be, on his right, a hand-rail against the wall on the left. All relatively civilized; lights came on when he depressed the switch and he descended, calling 'Kim' loudly because that was what he should do, but there was no response.

There were several cellars, although those furthest from the steps were more like walk-in alcoves, without doors and all cleared of clutter. Uncovered bulbs hung from the ceiling, beams and boards covered with whitewash that reflected the light. They showed him a level grey floor reaching to the steps and dry to the touch. Set in the surface were the imprints of a small shoe.

The depth and the direction of the marks indicated the movements of the wearer. She – Blake corrected that quickly in his mind – a small child had jumped off the lowest step on to the surface when it was wet, and sunk in and panicked – there were the prints of hands where she had overbalanced – had scuffled her feet free, turned, making clearer prints, and retreated up the steps. Yes, there were the grey footprints, fading as she climbed to the top.

'Nothing,' Ware said, emerging from the house to find Blake sitting on the mounting block and staring at swallows swooping through an open stable door. 'You find anything?

Blake told him. Ware was puzzled. 'What does that tell us? Apart from the fact that she was down there soon after they laid the concrete?'

'We need times. If she went missing while it was still wet, why would she come here? To hide?'

'She didn't. Didn't hide if you say she didn't cross the floor but turned round and left the cellar.'

'But she came here in the first instance. She knew the place. And even if she came at some earlier time, before she was ever missing, what's she doing here at all? And where's Milburn?'

'In town.'

'What? How d'you know that?'

'I don't. I'm guessing. Someone has to identify June's body.'

Blake sighed heavily. 'God, this heat! I'll be glad of my holiday. I'm compartmentalizing all too well: concentrating on one thing at a time, forgetting that there's a parallel – situation? I was going to say "investigation" there, as if

110

June was the victim of foul play.' His eyes followed the flight of a swallow. 'She lived here,' he mused. 'And we're at her house looking for signs of Kim.'

'That head wound's bothering you.'

Blake stirred restively. 'Go on.'

'And Kim's accustomed' – Ware's voice rose – 'accustomed to visit at this house?'

They looked at the back door. 'We'll wait for him,' Blake said.

'Do we question him about June or Kim?'

'You're jumping the gun. We proceed very cautiously. And we keep quiet where everyone else is concerned, like Plumpton. Any mention of a connection and we'll have Bell here within the hour.' Bell was the inspector at Brimstock. 'Not to mention the media.' Blake was grim. 'No way do we want a suit for defamation on our hands.'

Joely helped prepare the food and when policemen started to drift in for a break, she tipped a plateful of sandwiches into a freezer bag and slipped across the green to the Hall. No one noticed her go; the bar was full of people, reporters now as well as searchers.

The back door was closed, not locked – as usual now that June was no longer around. Joely was too elated to notice that there was no Land Rover in the yard. She burst into the kitchen, laughing, her eyes shining – and gasped. Strangers – no, those two cops – were at the open cupboards, turning at her entrance, the older one certainly interested but the younger, the one with the body and the eyes, making like a teenager. She was excited and resentful, revelling in the attention but they had no right poking around in his cupboards. She took a grip on herself and asked coldly, 'What are you doing here?'

'Waiting for Mr Milburn,' Blake told her. 'I see you're filling the gap.'

'What the hell d'you mean by that?'

'Food.' He was bland. 'He won't feel like cooking for

himself. He told us the neighbours were looking after him.'

Joely swallowed and went to the fridge. She rummaged inside, rearranging the contents fussily. She stowed the sandwiches and turned, her face softer now, child-like. 'Where is he?' she asked.

'You don't know?' Blake's innocence matched hers.

'I thought he was here.'

'I expect he went to town. As her husband he has to identify Mrs Milburn's body.'

'That was sad.' She lowered her eyelids and sidled towards the door.

'Don't go,' Ware pleaded. 'Sit a while and have a chat.'

'I don't think – Can you . . .'

'Can we what?' Ware's tone was insinuating.

She eyed him speculatively and then she beamed. 'I'm only sixteen,' she told him, wondering if she should insist on someone else being present, someone on her side.

'Really?' Ware breathed. 'Hell, I thought you were eighteen at least.'

'Flattery'll get you nowhere.' She preened herself, sitting down, supple as a cat. Her glance travelled over his shoulders, down the muscular arms. 'What d'you want Bart for?' she asked pertly.

'We thought he might be able to tell us something about Kim,' Blake put in.

She glanced at him as if he were a fly on the window pane. 'Everyone knew Kim,' she told Ware.

'And she knew everyone?' Ware was diffident, as well he might be, receiving no direction from his more experienced partner. 'She visited people?' he hazarded.

'Naturally.' Joely shrugged. 'She went into everyone's house. Some of us still leave our doors unlocked; it's an open invitation to kids, isn't it?'

'Don't they – pick up things?' Blake asked.

'Don't they just!' She stopped flirting and proceeded to instruct the old man. 'Jason,' she told him flatly, 'goes round to people in the village cadging clothes and stuff for non-existent jumble sales, takes his haul home; his mother sorts it, keeps the best, and bins what she doesn't want.'

Ware said, 'If it's public knowledge why do people tolerate it?'

'He only does it once: with newcomers and holiday people. Mind you, he gets belted for it when he's caught, but he starts up again, selling stuff to his mates, not taking it home because his dad laid into his mum as well. Of course, Hugh's a villain too but he doesn't want attention called to himself. The Butlers are a problem family.'

'All of them?' Blake asked, thinking of the elder son.

'Oh yes, Jason takes Kim with him. He looks after her, you see' – turning back to Ware – 'they're always together. Never apart – till now.'

'She was here,' Blake said.

'Yes.' She accepted it as a question but then stopped short, her eyes suddenly jumpy.

'In the house?'

'No.' She stared at him. 'I didn't see her in here.'

'In the cellars then.' She gulped at that. 'We know she was in the cellars,' Blake said gently.

She nodded and shrugged, implying it was of no importance. 'I came over to do some baking for him. I thought he must be in the stables so I went across and when I was inside, just happened to glance out of a window and saw Kim sneak up the cellar steps and run away.'

'Where was Bart?' Ware asked quickly.

She turned her dazzling smile on him. 'Out looking for June. He came in sometime afterwards.'

'What time did you see Kim?' Blake asked.

'Oh, around eleven, half past.'

Ware drew in his breath sharply. Blake said sternly, 'You saw her at eleven?' She nodded, stiffening at the change in mood. He said, 'Until now no one's come forward to say they saw her after ten.'

'So? Why's it important?'

'You know why it's important. A little girl's missing and

we're concerned for her safety. We're trying to trace her movements.'

'Well, you're doing that. Now you have to find the next person who saw her – oh!' Her hands shot to her mouth.

'Yes.' Blake nodded. 'As of now you're the last person to have seen her.' His guts contracted. Had he gone too far? But she was smiling sweetly at him, a mercurial child.

'That makes me involved? Do I come to the station with you?' Now, of course, she was addressing Ware, flirting again, nothing to hide. But Ware's eyes went to the window, alerted by the sound of an engine. A Land Rover pulled into the yard and Bart Milburn got down from behind the wheel.

Joely jumped up, seized a kettle and crossed to the sink. Bart appeared in the doorway. 'Company,' he said superfluously. 'Sorry I kept you all waiting. Tea, Joely? That'll be welcome.'

'Where d'you keep the tea?' she asked. He looked at her blankly. 'Ah, I remember!' She plunged towards a cupboard, found a packet of tea bags, hesitated, went to the correct cupboard for mugs, the by-play deceiving no one.

Blake wasn't distracted. 'Why didn't you tell us about seeing Kim before now?' he asked her, ignoring Bart who evinced only mild curiosity.

'No one asked me.'

'I don't think that's quite correct.'

She glowered and said sullenly, 'My dad says I come over here too often; he says it looks bad.'

Blake raised an eyebrow at Bart who, seeing that something was expected of him, nodded confirmation. 'Any dad would feel the same way: a man on his own, women bringing food over, including this one. Look at her: if she was my daughter I'd put a stop to it.' He was morose. 'I keep telling her, she's asking for trouble, but from her mother, not her dad. Graham's pretty casual about things.'

'We all come over.' Joely was indignant. 'You've got

114

no heart; you're cops. Alice comes, and Win; Rachel would but she's got her own problems. And Maud's got enough on her plate looking after Rachel. We look out for each other in Culchet. You wouldn't understand, you're townies.'

Blake said, lying through his teeth, 'We're not concerned with appearances and relationships, we're here to find a little kid who's been missing over twenty-four hours, and we're worried about her well-being.'

'She's not here.' Bart sounded exhausted. 'Search the place. Tear it apart.'

'She was in your cellars.'

'I *know*! You think she's under the floor?' He laughed angrily. 'Like my wife? That's what you thought, wasn't it? Missing wife, fresh concrete –'

'When did you finish pouring the concrete?' Blake broke in, checking the other in full flight. Bart paused, glaring, trying to think.

'Monday,' he said slowly. 'Hugh left me on my own. I went to town for cement, and I finished the main cellar in the afternoon. With everything that's happened I've not worked down there since.'

'And you saw Kim come up the cellar steps at eleven,' Blake said to Joely.

'On Wednesday.' She was emphatic.

'Ah yes, Wednesday. The concrete would have been dry by then so she was down there either Monday evening or Tuesday morning. It wouldn't be set Tuesday morning?'

Bart said tightly, 'I didn't go down to look. I had other things on my mind, like my wife being missing, her car found burned out, and my friend dying in hospital. It didn't occur to me to go and look to see if the concrete had dried in our cellars.' He went to a cupboard and wrenched open the door. He swore angrily.

'You need a drink,' Joely said, glaring at the police. 'Come across to the pub. You're among friends there.'

'He doesn't need her protection, nor anyone else's,' Ware

said as they emerged from the gates of the Hall. 'If he came home shortly after Joely saw Kim alive then he can't be involved with the kid's disappearance.'

'Use your head, man. We don't know when Kim went missing, nor yet what's happened to her. What was Bart doing all the rest of the day? How long did Joely stay at the Hall?'

They paused in the deep tree-shade, eyeing the increased number of vehicles on the green, Blake thinking that with luck the media people were preoccupied with the searchers. 'We should split up,' he said. 'You find this chap Brunskill and I'll see Housby. Now where do we find them?'

'Housby farms at a place called Lonning Head; Brunskill I'm not sure about – hello! That's Sowerby and Elliot; what are they doing here?'

Two men in plain clothes came towards them. 'What's going on?' Blake asked as they approached. He was full of curiosity and some resentment, thinking that they were making for the Hall.

DC Sowerby grinned. He was considered academic, a man on the fast track. 'The body in Harras,' he said, 'Buncle's Yard. That skull fracture: it's in the wrong place for a fall, isn't it? A short fall.'

Blake was enraged. '*I* said that! It's our case!' He glared at his partner as if he were responsible. 'We got the call; we had two days on it –'

'Priorities,' Sowerby reminded him. 'And you've got seniority. The woman's dead, the kid could still be alive.'

Neither Blake nor Ware liked that but the statement did underline the urgency concerning Kim. Blake said grudgingly, 'You could be right but we're not at all sure there isn't a tie-in between the two cases. We've just been talking to Milburn. The kid's been in his cellars, but he's got an alibi for the crucial time –' He stopped; they didn't know the crucial time.

'Milburn?' Sowerby was dismissive. 'We're not interested in him. It was Larry Payne she was having it away with.'

'What?' Blake snapped, overlapping Ware's 'Who was?'

Elliot, a tough fellow with a chip on his shoulder concerning seniority, was happy to be one up on the more experienced men. 'The garage cleared Payne's car of personal possessions,' he told them, 'but they left what they thought was rubbish, and so did our people. Big mistake. We found an envelope under one of the seats: screwed up and mucky where someone's big feet had trampled it. It held the keys of Buncle House: labelled and all.'

'June had the keys.' Blake was contemptuous. 'They were in her pocket.'

'I mean, it *had* held them. So Larry was in that house with June.'

Blake and Ware said nothing, their brains racing. 'So we're away to see Larry's mum,' Sowerby said. 'Find out what she has to say about the relationship between her son and the dead woman.' He smiled, knowing that Blake was considering how he might muscle in on the interview. 'We'll leave you to your own investigation,' he said indulgently. 'See you later, bring you up to speed.'

Rachel and Maud Brunskill were in the back garden at Todbank, a Spode coffee pot and cups on an iron table, an umbrella shading them from the sun. 'I feel sleepy,' Rachel murmured. 'Is it the heat or those tablets?'

'Something of both.' Maud was reassuring even as she racked her brains for something to occupy the woman; it was too soon to suggest they start to sort Larry's clothes. A figure appeared at the corner of the house, framed by yellow roses.

Maud struggled to her feet. 'This is a private garden,' she cried. 'Leave it this minute or I'll send for the police.'

Sowerby produced a thin smile, presenting his warrant card like a weapon, Elliot following suit, scowling because he was impressed by the delicate china, the manicured garden.

'What is it you want?' Maud wasn't giving them an inch.

'A word with you, Mrs Payne.'

'I am Mrs Brunskill.'

His eyes went to the woman on the chair behind her. 'Then may I –'

Rachel stood up and came forward. 'What kind of word?'

Sowerby felt at a disadvantage but he wouldn't show it, and if they weren't going to be asked to sit down, he'd conduct his business standing up. It was difficult: two old bats, both highly stressed (he rationalized), one a bereaved mother . . . 'About your son, ma'am.'

Rachel raised plucked eyebrows. He thought it was a good thing she didn't try to dye those like the remarkable hair. She smiled as if she knew what was in his mind. 'Whatever he's done,' she said, 'you'll have a hard job convicting him.'

'Rachel!' Maud murmured, shocked. 'Don't let this fellow –' She rounded on Sowerby. 'Have you no feelings?'

Rachel ignored her. 'I like talking about my son.' She was too serene. 'What is it you'd like to know?'

Maud shot her a suspicious glance. Sowerby said, 'What was his relationship with Mrs Milburn?'

'Ah.' Rachel considered. 'You think that it was more than just a matter of taking her to view a house; that it wasn't a professional meeting? You're thinking in terms of something more informal, an affair perhaps?'

'I'm asking you, ma'am.'

Rachel thought about it, watched uneasily by Maud. 'I couldn't say. She didn't come to his bedside. Is that significant?'

'She was – incapacitated.' Maud grimaced at her own choice of words.

'Was she, dear? I'm confused over sequences. I've no idea what happened to June, or when – as if I cared. How long did I have with Larry?' she asked, addressing

118

Sowerby. 'Not as long as I could have had. I lost hours. I left him.' She turned to Maud. 'I was asleep when he went; not even the fire alarm could wake me so I never heard my boy calling. There wasn't even a nurse, no one, no one there to hold him at the last –' Anguished, Maud took a step towards her but Rachel raised her bent arm in a stiff, hostile gesture. She told Sowerby harshly, 'Whatever he did or didn't do is finished, over. You can do *nothing*. You can't even hold *me* responsible, although you can try.' Her mouth stretched in a rictus. 'You think I care? It should have been me who died, not him.'

Ware drove smoothly away from the other vehicles unnoticed, circling the green as Blake was finding Lonning Head on the map but having no luck with the Brunskills' house because they didn't know its name. 'Right,' Blake announced, 'if we stop at the pub we'll have the media on our backs. We'll both go to Lonning Head and Housby can tell us how to find the Brunskills.'

'It's Housby who has the dog.'

'What dog – oh, the one Butler maintains is a killer and Plumpton says is harmless. What kind of dog is it?'

'We'll find out soon enough.'

From the top of the green and again at Back Lane neat signs directed them to a track and a substantial farmhouse. No dog came to meet them and there was no answer when they used the iron knocker on the studded front door. They walked round to the back to find the woman who must be Housby's daughter cutting nettles in a stack yard using a small scythe. There were cats and hens about but no dog.

They waited for her to notice them, not wanting to startle her; it might be a smaller version of a man-size scythe but the blade was still long and looked as lethal as a machete. At length she paused, wiped her forehead with a forearm and caught sight of them.

Her father was out searching, she told them, not with the others because he'd taken the dogs and Baz would have created mayhem among the police Shepherds. 'So Dad's on the fell,' she said. 'I'll be out on my pony later. It's too hot at the moment.'

Blake was puzzled. 'You think a small child would go on the fells?'

'Well . . .' She looked doubtful. 'Along the bottom of the scarp maybe. You can't eliminate anywhere. There are the old kilns and shake holes and all the field houses – barns to you. Isolated, you know? There's the church. I'm sure Jason and Kim would have been in the church if they ever went that far. It's not locked.'

Ware frowned, trying to visualize the map. 'I don't remember seeing a church.'

'It's between us and Long Skelton: it serves both villages. But someone will have covered it: Ted Brunskill or Carrick from the pub.'

'The child has to eat,' Blake observed.

'We've been talking about that, Dad and me.' She went to a shed with the scythe, emerged and shut the door. 'Eating wouldn't be a problem for Kim; she'd just slip into a place when no one was about and raid the fridge. Sleeping's rather more difficult; on the other hand Jason would know every window in the holiday lets that looks as if it's secure and isn't, or can be eased open with a knife or a bit of wire. And if he knows, so does Kim.'

'She's five years old!' Blake protested.

'Ye-es.' She drew it out. 'And she's missing and' – defiantly – 'I prefer to think she's scarpered of her own accord. I don't want to think about the alternative. But – on that score' – thoughtful again – 'she's terrified of something. She wouldn't leave her mother yesterday morning.'

'But she did leave her.'

'I know. Then she must have seen something – or she imagined something – or misinterpreted something she saw? Or heard? That child has the most vivid imagination, you wouldn't believe! She only has to hear Carrick's Lab in the ghyll and she says she's seen the Big Cat (you know the Big Cat myth that surfaces every summer?) – or a dragon. She's into dragons in a big way. And then there's

120

Baz: her own fantasy killer dog. The reason why she ran away is anyone's guess.'

'Except that she ran out into the open where you'd think the imaginary monsters might be rather than staying in the pub where it was safe – and with her mother.'

'Perhaps the monster was indoors.' It was said lightly but Blake took it seriously.

'Who was in the pub at the time?'

Jill laughed. 'I wasn't there. The Carricks, no doubt, Win Langley, Maureen. My' – she paused but only fractionally – 'my dad delivering the eggs.' A sudden shiver was superseded by an enchanting smile. Ware bloomed, thinking his job had few such rewards.

'Joely would like to speak to you,' Alice Potter said breathlessly, having waylaid them in Back Lane as they came down the farm track.

'Of course.' Blake was affable, concealing his gratification. 'Where can we find her?'

'Well, actually' – Alice was embarrassed – 'if you wouldn't mind hanging on here for five minutes I'll – er – set it up.' She giggled. 'It's rather – she doesn't want her parents – it's by way of being confidential, you see. You can park your car in the lane where the path goes down into the ghyll and come through our back garden. There's a laburnum inside our back wall. You can't miss it.'

'We'll do that,' Blake said benignly, as if clandestine meetings were commonplace among police.

She left, herself keeping to the back way. As she went they saw her take something out of her jeans and put it to her ear. 'Phoning,' Ware said. 'What's going on? Are we going to be ambushed?' He looked delighted at the prospect.

'Joely,' Blake murmured, ignoring the question. 'What's she up to now? She already good as told us that she and Bart are lovers.'

'She's going to give Bart an alibi for Kim. Another one with a vivid imagination. She's sixteen. Dangerous age.'

'In this village all the females seem to be at a dangerous age. If it isn't the menopause, it's teenage neurosis, or tiny children or small boys, and all at their most vulnerable.' Blake's tone changed. 'We have to speak to Plumpton about that church, make sure it's been covered, and – what did she say? Shake holes? What in hell are shake holes?'

Ware didn't reply. He was chewing a blade of grass and frowning fiercely at the bend in the lane where Alice had disappeared. 'What?' Blake asked, following his gaze. 'You seen the Big Cat?'

'I'm thinking: if this lane goes right round the village –'

'It does. We know that.'

'And it's accessible to vehicles, which it is, then it's not only people on foot who can use it without being seen, what with all these back gardens, but folk can drive it.'

'And?'

'With passengers – or cargo – like little kids.'

Blake reached for the map, folded to show the village. He found their present position. 'The lane runs down the west side of the village after that bend . . . the Paynes' place must be round the corner, and then comes the Hall: next door – close, aren't they, the Paynes and the Milburns? Then more houses, a green dotted line: that has to be the footpath through to the ghyll down on the right, so Alice's place is there. The lane continues down to the bottom of the village, curves left again, joins the road where it narrows between those two cottages. You're right, it accesses rear gardens all the way round. Interesting.'

'I bet it's seen some comings and goings at night over the years.' Ware put the car in gear. 'No street lights either.'

They crept along the lane below walls cushioned with yellow stonecrop and swathes of blue campanulas, noting that at the back of the Hall (identified by its many chimneys and cluster of outbuildings) an ungated entrance debouched on the stable yard. Ware continued and parked as directed. They walked back under a fine laburnum, turned up the side track and found the garden gate. Delphiniums in shades of blue bordered a flagged path and there was a strong scent of honeysuckle.

Alice must have heard them latch the gate. She was waiting at the back door and ushered them to a shaded room where Win was standing with Joely at the window. The whole effect was one of careful stage management. Alice disappeared but Blake acknowledged the presence of 'an appropriate adult' with a formal nod. Ware was poker-faced.

'You wanted to see me?' Blake asked Joely. 'Shall we sit down? Be more comfortable.'

They sat at a large polished table, a bowl of sweet peas on a cork mat. Evidently this was the dining room. Joely said, 'I'm not saying a word unless you promise not to tell my parents.'

Blake thought that Win suppressed a sigh and guessed that this wasn't how it was supposed to go. He said, 'If there's nothing criminal –'

'Oh, there isn't! The opposite in fact. That's why – But my dad would *kill* me.'

'Joely!' Win exclaimed.

'Well, he'd ground me for ever – and I can't, I just can't afford to be grounded at this – I'll run away sooner than be locked in my room.' She was threatening Blake as if he were her father.

'It's not criminal then,' he stated pleasantly.

'*No!*' She threw a wild glance at the open window and hissed fiercely: 'I was with Bart all day yesterday.'

'Where?'

She inhaled sharply, channelling embarrassment and fear into anger. 'In bed then! At the Hall! Satisfied?'

'What time did you leave him?' Blake asked calmly.

She shrugged, the hardest part over. 'Six-ish.' She looked at Win. 'I had to help with the dinner.'

'You came over at half six,' Win said.

'So,' Blake's tone was light, 'he could have had nothing to do with Kim's disappearance.'

'That's what I'm telling you! It's ludicrous anyway. What on earth would he want – But you suspect all the men, and there's this business of the cellar. I saw Kim myself: at eleven, and that was just before he came home!'

'Well, that seems to have cleared up things.' Blake was expansive, seeing Joely soften and relax, a happy girl again, aware that Win was regarding him shrewdly, reading his mind, both of them thinking that a youngster, head over heels in love, would die to get her lover out of a tight corner.

Chapter Eleven

By lunch-time that Thursday most people admitted, at least privately, that since Kim hadn't come home of her own volition, something or someone was preventing her. Either she had met with an accident or she had been abducted. More people joined the search, those with dogs kept separate from the police with their German Shepherds. Alice borrowed Thornthwaite's pony and, despite the heat, rode the woods and intake below the scarp with Jill Housby. They took it easily and anyway you couldn't go fast when you were looking for clues like a hair ribbon or a little shoe.

Ted Brunskill, searching on his own because he was that kind of man, came to the top of a small conical hill midway between Culchet and Long Skelton and settled on a sun-warmed slab to study the terrain. He faced south, the two villages to his left and right, the church a few hundred feet below. The sands of the Solway estuary showed pale through the haze but he ignored the grand vista and, like the falcon he resembled, concentrated on what was immediately below his eyrie.

He had brought his powerful binoculars. Through them he could see every field house, cottage and ruin that wasn't masked by trees. He saw vehicles in lanes which were usually quiet on a summer's afternoon and where they were stationary he could distinguish people moving about a barn or a house. He could discern no pattern to the search but then this situation bore no resemblance to his own methodical quests for nests or a badger sett. He knew the habitat that bird or badger favoured, he went straight to a likely site and cast about for clues which were conspicuous to his trained eye. Everything was predictable, but not here. Looking for a child with no clue as to what had happened to her, where or why, when the child might not be here at all but hundreds of miles away – if she wasn't buried – this was a hopeless task. And yet, he thought, surprised, they'd find her; usually they did. Ted's lateral thinking was geared to Nature: to fauna and flora and rocks; people were a closed book to him.

He dropped down the front of the pike, using his stick but still spry for a man pushing eighty; he crossed a beck by two great slabs of rock, pausing to glance at the mud but seeing tracks only of fox and mallard. He passed an alder wood, glimpsing riders on the slope above, one on a piebald, the other on a chestnut – Alice and Jill – and he came to the old drove road. This ran along the foot of the scarp, at one time serving farms built on a line of springs; now these were ruins or, if in good order, were locked and shuttered against vandals. He looked in the byres and stables, thinking that if she were here she had to be incapable of movement, had fallen through a ceiling perhaps – now what did that put him in mind of?

He climbed a stile and crossed a meadow where sleek red bullocks dozed in a grove of sycamores. Beyond was the back gate to the churchyard – and Plumpton, standing there watching his approach. 'Saw you on the pike,' the sergeant told him. 'You got good glasses there.' Admiring the Swarovskis.

'For all the use they were. What's the police thinking, Dave?'

'About the kid?'

'Who else?'

'June Milburn. The thinking there is she didn't fall, she was pushed.'

Ted was confused. 'But' – he gestured to the church – 'aren't you searching for Kim?'

'Oh yes, that hasn't changed.' He waved his mobile. 'It's

that I just heard the post-mortem results on June Milburn. It's come as a surprise.'

Ted sat down on a slab-tomb. 'It's a shock,' he agreed. 'How did they arrive at foul play? How can they tell?'

'The skull was fractured.' Plumpton fingered the top of his cap. 'Wrong place to be injured in a short fall. And there's rust in the wound. No sign of rusty objects where she was found. She was hit with something and it's missing.'

'She must have walked in on a tramp – or a drug addict?'

'She'd gone there with Larry Payne,' Plumpton said meaningly.

'Ah.' Ted blinked. 'He'd taken her to view the place – now where did I hear that?'

'Wherever, you're right. The house is on Wharton's books and Larry worked for Wharton, and he crashed in a spot that indicated he was coming away from there – but this is the clincher: they found the envelope that had held the keys to that house in Larry's car.'

'How d'you know all this?'

'Blake and Ware came in the pub for a bite – the chaps who were on the case till the kid went missing – and they're not in the best of tempers because the DI – Vince Bell – he'll be taking over the Milburn case. Blake had his own suspicions about that head wound but the powers that be didn't see it that way, and thought the missing child was more urgent anyway. They did put a couple of junior chaps on June's case but for my money they'd have preferred it to be an accident. Got enough on their plate here.' He looked towards the church where light showed behind clear window panes.

Ted was following his own tack. 'Why on earth would Larry kill June?' He was mystified.

Plumpton shrugged. 'You knew them. I didn't. The first suspect's usually the husband but apparently he was in his own cellars at the time, or in Brimstock. He's in the clear.'

'It's my wife who knew the Milburns, and the Paynes.

127

Oh, I knew them but she's into all the gossip. Doesn't interest me, gossip.'

Vince Bell, the DI, was a large man nearing retirement and deeply thankful that, if the Milburn case were a murder inquiry as the pathologist's findings implied, winding it up was no more than a formality. Circumstantial evidence pointed to the estate agent, Payne; all Bell had to do was to find something a little harder and the investigation, as such, would be over by the weekend. 'Just as long as we don't get switched to the other one,' his driver warned, weaving the police car expertly through lanes on the way to Culchet. DS Helen Dodd was lithe, sharp and ambitious. Each deplored the other's lifestyle; she looked on Bell as a slob, he rated her a workaholic. For all that, they were mutually respectful of each other's abilities on the job.

'The kid?' he asked. 'No, that's Blake's pigeon.'

'If they don't find her – or find her dead –'

'Don't borrow trouble. What we have to do now is discover the relationship between Larry Payne and June Milburn. Now she lived at Culchet Hall and he was next door – as if that isn't significant.'

'We were friendly,' Rachel said. 'Naturally, we were next-door neighbours.'

Maud was dispensing coffee and shortbread. This was a formal visit so they were in Todbank's sitting room. Helen was the first policewoman to come to the village on this occasion and, with Bell sunk in a shadowed armchair leaving the floor to her, the atmosphere was relaxed so far. The detectives had been briefed by Sowerby on Rachel's precarious balance.

'We often had them over for a meal,' she was saying. 'In fact they were here last weekend.' A spasm contorted her face.

'More coffee, Mr Bell?' Maud asked quickly.

'He was a brilliant cook,' Rachel mused.

128

'Unusual in a man.' Helen was indeed surprised: this was the rural North, macho to its heels. 'How many men in this village do the cooking?'

Rachel shrugged. 'He was an unusual boy. How many sons prefer to live with their old mothers? Not that he was tied to me, mind; he was the head of this household. I relied on him for everything.'

Helen was looking at photographs on a sideboard. 'You'd have missed him when he married,' she said.

'He wouldn't – have left. This was his home.'

'Really? So when he did marry you'd all have lived together.' Rachel stared at her. Pleasantly, sympathetically, Helen tried again: 'Did he bring his girlfriends home?'

Bell's eyes only appeared to be sleepy, he didn't miss Maud's start at the question.

'He didn't have any girlfriends,' Rachel said.

Helen's eyebrows shot up. 'He didn't like women? But what about . . .' Her eyes wandered as if she were at a loss. 'You said the Milburns came over. He must have –'

'Oh, he liked June – well, he tolerated her.'

'Only tolerated?'

'It was Bart who was his friend. June was much older.'

Maud said brightly, 'Different generations, you see. A boy in his twenties would look on June as his mother's generation. In any event men do things together, don't they? Ladies have their own interests.'

Helen stood up and approached the sideboard where the photographs in silver frames stood among bowls of roses and white lilac. The pictures were a sequence from infant to young man. 'He was very handsome,' she said approvingly, although 'pretty' was the term that came to mind.

'Those are old,' Rachel said. 'Where did I put my bag, Maud?'

The handbag was found and she produced a bulky Kodak folder. 'These are the most recent ones,' she said. 'I can't look at them again but I like to keep them close. They're part of him, like his clothes. Bart says he'll sort them for me and I let him start but then I changed my mind. It's too soon, I told him.'

Helen was shuffling through the photographs. There were some of gardens but mostly they were of Larry in a black vest with spiky yellow hair and an ear-ring, posing to show off an intricate arabesque tattooed on one arm. He looked rather soft. Rachel was watching her closely, forgetting the fat man in the corner. 'What do you think?' she asked sharply.

Helen looked up, got a nod from Bell. 'Was he gay?' she asked on a casual note.

'Gay, dear?'

'Homosexual.'

'You youngsters nowadays: you think any boy who lives with his mother, takes trouble with his appearance and – oh yes, who cooks – can't be normal. Straight – is that the term? Of course Larry was straight. Ask Bart Milburn, he should know. They were best friends.'

The police dogs and their handlers emerged from the church and the rest of the search team moved in, which seemed to Ted a superfluous action when the dogs had found nothing. Hastily the animals were pushed into their vans as Graham Carrick approached with his Labrador. 'Rob's doing the drove road with Baz,' he said, meeting Ted at the front entrance to the graveyard. 'You been inside?' Nodding to the church.

'The police team's in there. The dogs found nothing.'

'They wouldn't. They're exhausted. You can't work dogs for hours at a time and expect them to stay keen. Sable's tired too' – the bitch had dropped in the shade – 'I'll take her home, let her rest. This is a bad business, Ted.'

Ted, who truly wasn't a man for gossip, forbore to tell him that the business was considerably worse than he knew, if June Milburn had indeed been murdered.

'You're very quiet,' Graham said.

'The heat's getting to me,' Ted lied. 'I was on the fell and

I've been looking around some of the places on the drove road. Rob's duplicating my work.'

'No, he's got the dogs. Baz has a good nose, not as good as Sable's, mind.'

The bitch sat up at the sound of her name. 'I'll try her in the church,' Graham said as the police appeared and moved down to the gate.

'Dogs have been inside,' Plumpton told him.

Graham nodded but kept going towards the porch. Ted followed, as much for something to do as anything. Despite the nature of the search men, like the dogs, had lost their edge, and with every hour the feeling was growing that they were looking in the wrong places. Increasingly, and particularly here among the graves, they wondered if the child had been buried.

The church was small: an oblong without aisles or a tower, only a modest bellcote. Very plain, only its walls dated from medieval times, most of the rest was mid-nineteenth century. Unlike many churches nowadays it was kept unlocked, at least in the summer, but everything of value had been removed, that is, everything that could be carried by thieves. A rough piscina remained, almost certainly pre-Reformation since such stone bowls were used to wash the holy vessels after a Mass. The only other feature worthy of notice was a small dark coffer, less than five feet long, with a roughly carved front and an iron lockplate. Graham lifted the heavy lid and Sable leapt inside, sniffing excitedly at a stack of old hymn books. 'Mice,' he said dismissively as she jumped out and dashed between the pews. 'Smelling the other dogs,' he observed. 'There's nothing here.'

'What's this?' Ted murmured, stooping over the chest, probing delicately at a rough plank. It was dark here on the shaded side of the nave, the bulbs giving little light. He straightened and went to a plain window, full of sky. Between long fingers he held a wisp of fine flaxen hair.

Jason crept through his empty kitchen to the front room.

The television was switched off and in the light from carelessly drawn curtains he saw Maureen on the sofa, her head in her hands. He moved to her knees and at his touch she jerked into life with a gasp, saw it was him, not her lost baby, moaned on a high note and pulled him to her.

They didn't speak. Maureen held him as if she would crush him, making small whimpering noises. Jason shivered spasmodically. After long minutes he squirmed away. She stared at him. 'We'll find her,' she said heavily.

'I'm scared,' he whispered, and he looked it, no colour in his face.

'We all are – we're worried, but the p'lice is here –'

'I'm scared what Dad's gonna do.'

Maureen wasn't. Why should Jase be bothered? He watched her eyes. 'What he'd do to me,' he elaborated. 'I didn't tell un what happened.'

She gaped, then seized his wrist. 'You know what happened!' she hissed. 'You tell me or I'll throttle you.'

'No, no! I mean once – it happened just the once, not *now*, not this week. I mean when them – he tried to get us to go indoors, upstairs – Kim, not me. *You* know: like I were only asking for old clothes but he said Kim were to go upstairs and play with him.'

Maureen was taut as strained wire. 'Who?' she breathed.

'That Bart Milburn,' he told her.

The church had been sealed off and fresh dogs sent for. The searchers were called in, those who could be raised on their mobiles, preparatory to working outwards from the church, but having to wait to let the dogs go in first. They looked for Maureen to show her the hair but she was nowhere to be found. Hugh, not drunk but not sober either, said yes, that was Kim's hair, and had to be restrained although there was nothing he could do. He had no more idea than the police how to proceed from the church and he wasn't allowed there. Kim's hair brush was taken away for comparison.

At four o'clock fresh dogs arrived, were given one of

Kim's shoes for scent and started to track away from the church, followed by men now grim but eager, revitalized and so focused that it was a while before anyone noticed smoke, too black for a garden bonfire or heather, rising above Culchet's horse chestnuts. Shortly afterwards they heard the sirens. The Hall was on fire.

By the time Bart arrived the Hall was blazing. The fire chief was greatly relieved when he identified himself although the firemen didn't need assurance that there was no one else in the building. People had already told them that Bart lived alone – now – and that there were no pets. So they concentrated on trying to save the Hall but with all its panelling – and petrol, the chief told Bart, there was a strong smell – they stood no chance.

Bart was sitting in the passenger seat of the Land Rover watching the flames when the windscreen shattered. He had no sooner got out and glimpsed the half-brick on the bonnet when a great weight landed on his back and there were claws at his throat.

Shouts erupted from the people who had been watching the fire, there was a concerted rush, more cries, someone screaming foully, and the weight was pulled off him. He held his painful throat and turned to see Maureen Butler struggling on the ground, held by several men and Win Langley. 'Why?' he croaked. 'What have I –' His head turned slowly to the fire. '*You* did that?'

Maureen stopped struggling. Win's hands loosened. The others stood up but they stayed close.

'You took my baby!' Maureen hissed.

Faces turned to Bart in consternation. He cried, incredulous: 'You torched my house!'

'You're mad!' Win said, and wondered which of them she meant, or could it be both?

'The chief says it was set with petrol,' he told her. He turned back to Maureen? 'Why?'

'You took –'

'Oh, for God's sake! This is my home you've destroyed.

133

If I had Kim would you set the place on fire, with her inside? Come off it.'

'It were Hugh set the fire,' Maureen cried. 'You got her somewhere else.'

Win said quietly, 'Who put this idea in your head, Maureen? That Bart took Kim?'

'Jason.'

Bart nodded. 'It would be Jason, wouldn't it?' He addressed Win. 'Perhaps some of the ladies would take her home?'

'Not before I –' Maureen started to get up.

A woman was shouting. Freda was running up the green from the pub. 'Kim, Kim! They've found Kim. She's alive! She's fine –'

Maureen fainted heavily.

The fresh dogs had been good. They took their handlers to new patio doors on an old house called Ravenstone, a place bought for the owners' retirement and lovingly restored. How the doors came to be unlocked was anyone's guess but grandchildren had been the last to use the place . . . No one was apportioning blame however because, when the doors were opened and they went upstairs, the dogs went straight to a wardrobe. It was Plumpton who looked, dreading what he might see, but she was there, standing up, swathed in hanging clothes, her face and T-shirt smeared with food, mostly chocolate, her hair in a mess, clutching a doll with flaxen hair. She glared at them, frightened and defiant, but once she realized that the dogs were held securely and she was high in Plumpton's arms, she became furiously angry. A man put her in the cupboard, she said, her dad would kill him.

'A man,' Plumpton repeated comfortably, holding her tight. 'Now who would that be?'

'He'll come and get me,' she said. 'No way am I going home.'

Bart wasn't off the hook, but that held for all the men in

the village, visitors too for that matter. Kim remained adamant that she wouldn't go home, a resolve which fitted well with the programme that must now be put into operation: the medical examination and questioning. As for the latter, Kim couldn't talk enough about her abductor but there were contradictory features. Not the least of these was the rage and even terror the child manifested when she was told her mother was coming to take her home. By this time Kim was in hospital, Helen Dodd in attendance, but at this stage mainly to listen, not to question. It was a nurse who told the child that Maureen was on the way. Seeing the reaction that this produced Helen was appalled: was it one of *those* ghastly cases, with not one but both parents involved? Did Kim –careful question – not want to see her mam? 'Yes,' she shouted, 'I want my mam!'

Maureen came, closely followed by Hugh, and the eagerness with which Kim flung herself at her mother was matched only by the obvious delight with which she clung to Hugh. Helen, ostensibly a benign observer, was covertly alert for any sign of tension or self-consciousness on the part of child or parent but the excess of emotion shown by the adults must surely be attributed to relief. It was the word 'home' from Hugh that produced more drama. Kim pulled away, glowered at him, and announced that she wasn't going: 'No way,' she shouted. 'Never! I'm staying here.'

Shocked, Maureen looked to Helen for guidance. The sergeant shook her head, trying to signal caution, and Maureen interpreted it correctly. 'Come here, love,' she coaxed. 'Tell Mam what's wrong.'

'He's there.' Kim was suddenly piteous. 'He's going to get me. He knows where I live.'

'Who?'

'Him what took me.'

Hugh started to shout. Helen said, 'Mr Butler, we'll never find out if you can't – if you're so noisy.' Meaning to imply he was only terrifying the child.

Hugh didn't lower his voice. 'If you think I'm going to

stand here and my baby says as how some – some *monster* took her, you got another think coming –'

A doctor appeared: white, elderly. Helen thanked her stars; an ethnic medic at this moment might have inflamed Hugh to the point of hysteria. The doctor took in the basic situation at a glance.

'Mr – er, the little girl has had a traumatic experience; shouting isn't helping her. We'll leave her with her mother for a while, shall we?' It was an order, not a suggestion.

Hugh, the bully, turned to him for support, allowing himself to be eased out of the room but muttering urgently. '. . . no knowing what . . . She's . . . and her's petrified . . . back there in village . . . have to find out before . . .'

Helen and Maureen exchanged glances, Maureen's guarded. She turned to Kim. 'You don't have to go home, love.' She looked at Helen who nodded agreement.

Kim asked suspiciously, 'So we can stay here?'

Maureen blinked, nonplussed. Helen said gently, 'Where would you like to go?'

Kim turned to her. 'We'll go to Aunty Bet. Me and Mam and my dad – we'll all go there.' She paused. 'Where us'll be safe.'

'His cousin,' Maureen explained, jerking her head at the door. 'Bet lives here in town.' Her tone changed, became playful: 'And who's going to look after Jon and Jase?'

'No!' Kim shrank back from her mother, retreating until she was against the wall.

Maureen moaned, tried to turn it into a cough. 'What the – what did Jon do?' Helen had the same thought.

'Nothing,' Kim said, seeming surprised.

'What did Jason do?' Helen asked.

Kim turned on her, the little face shocking in its hostility: 'I hate you! Fucking old slag! Go away, get out of here! A man took me!' And shouting between sobs she flung herself at Maureen who gripped her in powerful arms and stared at Helen in utter bewilderment.

'What did you make of it?' Bell asked. 'Is she terrified of

136

her brother? For pity's sake, he's only a child himself! Or is she sticking to this story of some man taking her?'

'Or both,' Helen murmured, voicing a private thought.

They were in the hospital's cafeteria waiting for the result of the medical examination. The church and the house where Kim had been found were being gone over for traces, the owners contacted, the grandchildren questioned. On the face of it none of them was implicated; over the period of Kim's absence all of them could prove their presence elsewhere.

'When you say "both", you mean a man *and* Jason?' Bell was appalled.

'Not in collusion but – at different stages? Like she was frightened by one and, running, ran into the other one.'

'You insist she's not afraid of her parents or her big brother, but she won't go home and she threw a tantrum when you asked her what Jason had done. I'll hang on here for those results, you go back to Culchet and find that boy.'

'Do I bring him in? We have Maureen here. Leave Hugh with Kim, question Jason in Maureen's presence?'

'We'll cross that bridge when we reach it. Find the young bugger, tell him Kim's safe and well –' He stopped, ruminating.

'And talking?' she suggested.

'That could keep him away. Play it off the cuff until we have him in the station.'

'I'd like to hear the medical results as soon as you do. It could make a huge difference: negative or positive.'

'Odd,' he mused. 'Plumpton said she didn't act like she was scared of strange men. And she don't seem to have been hurt.'

'As in rape, you mean? If she was, it was unusual to let her live afterwards.' Helen became thoughtful. 'We know Jason lied when he said Bart Milburn had Kim in the Hall, but was he lying when he said Milburn once tried to lure her upstairs? If the medical results are negative, if Kim is building a fantasy about a man having abducted her, then

137

Bart and anyone else, any *man* is in the clear. There never was an abduction. She's running from Jason.'

'Was. Was running. We've caught her. You reckon she's terrified of her brother. You find him and let's get to the bottom of this business. And then we can get us back to June Milburn, where we should be, and wind that one up before the weekend.' As the senior woman available Helen had been the immediate choice to handle Kim, not to mention her mother.

There was no one at the Butlers' house. The back door was unlocked, the television dark and silent. Helen went upstairs and glanced in the bedrooms. Two were in a state of chaos: the parents', the boys' – the latter identified by the heavy rock posters and the clothes. The third room, little more than a box-room, was painfully neat: the smooth duvet, stuffed toys and dolls on the painted chest-of-drawers: all carefully arranged by Maureen against the return of her youngest. Helen opened wardrobes, looked into alcoves behind curtains, glanced in cupboards. Finally she drove to the Stag.

Smoke still rose from the ruined Hall and the air smelled sour but the village was celebrating – and why not? What was one building destroyed (no doubt insured) beside the recovery of a child feared dead, and worse. Helen parked on the grass and sat for a moment thinking how she should approach Jason, who could be with his brother, thinking of connections, associations. Jason telling his mother that Kim was in Bart's house, the Hall catching fire – but Kim hadn't been there. Apparently Maureen had thrown a brick through Bart's windscreen and he had accused her of setting the fire, which was ridiculous if she was thinking that Kim was inside. Indeed, Maureen had accused Hugh – which was equally ridiculous and for the same reason – but the fire appeared to have been arson, Bell had it from the fire chief that there was a stink of petrol.

Connections, connections. The Hall was owned by June

Milburn, *had* been owned by her, now, presumably, inherited by Bart. June was (possibly) murdered by Larry Payne, the next-door neighbour: everything, every bloody strand was connected. One big tangle. June's death, her home – torched? If Kim hadn't been abducted, where did she fit into this – apart from being connected with everyone concerned, at one or two removes? I need a drink, Helen thought: malt preferably, a double, and she opened the car door.

Jon was in the Stag. The happy recipient of as much free drink as he could hold, he was no longer in full command of his senses. Jason, he told Helen, was safe. Asked if the boy had been in danger, the elder brother told her never, they were always together, it was Jason's *job* to look after his kid sister. Helen sighed and looked about at the company. Someone said sharply, 'Who's Jason?' Press, she thought, and moved to the bar, asking a woman with an expensive haircut and a Prada top for Glenlivet, and had she seen Jason Butler? 'No,' Freda said. 'Who's asking?' Helen palmed her warrant card.

'Now what's he done?' Freda asked, resigned.

'Nothing.' Helen was cool, relishing the first taste of the good malt. 'It's just that he might be able to help us with Kim.'

People were listening. A stranger asked, 'Who're you with, love?'

She held his eye: overweight, over-confident, sweaty. She considered whether to put him down, knew that any reporter of his age would bounce up again, took one last leisurely taste of whisky, showed her card, and started to trawl the bar, abandoning subterfuge, trying to trace Jason.

Jon disappeared but some of those who were more inebriated were eager to talk. No one had seen the boy recently. He had come home because he had been in the house and spoken to his mam, that was common knowledge, and there was some tale about Bart, nothing in it of course; Kim was half a mile away in Ravenstone. Speculation ran through the bar. Someone said it would be a while

139

before Jason showed, scared at what would happen after he'd tried to finger Bart, but he'd be sneaking home by way of Back Lane soon as he got hungry. Certainly he wouldn't show his face in the village proper after the fire and all. Maybe he set the fire. Hugh would have it in for the kid when he did show. If Jason had any sense he'd go missing now; it would be a way of getting folk's sympathy.

Helen's mobile was chirping. She went out to the privacy of her car. It was Bell; preliminary results were negative: no bruising, no trace of semen, no traces at all. Kim's clothes had gone to the lab but it looked as if they were clean, although filthy in the conventional sense, but so far there wasn't a speck of evidence to show that the child had been molested in any way.

'So she's fantasizing,' Helen said.

'It looks like it. You find Jason?'

She told him. 'Keep looking,' he said.

Chapter Twelve

On Friday morning Culchet's village hall was comman-
deered as an incident room. Bell was in charge at the start
but well aware that he would shortly be superseded
because several crimes were involved here, including vio-
lent death. For the moment he held the threads, super-
vising teams. Blake and Ware were back to probing the
relationship between June Milburn and Larry Payne while
Helen was at the hospital waiting to question Kim. Meanwhile uniforms were to search for Jason, working outwards from house-to-house inquiries, and then there was
the fire. Investigators from the Fire Service and insurers
were due this morning. DCs Sowerby and Elliot would be
in attendance.

Blake and Ware were leaving the village hall considering
how they should question Maud Brunskill with regard to
June when a sleek silver Jaguar emerged from the gap they
called the Narrows and prowled up the green to stop
outside the gates of what had been the Hall. The car was
the new S-type and the detectives lusted after it, envious
and surprised that arson investigators could run to such an
elegant machine.

A woman climbed out: large, powerful, wearing a cream
trouser suit that even at a distance spoke of money. It
didn't suggest a person who was going to rake through
ashes and soot.

She stood in the gateway flanked by Sowerby and Elliot.
'BBC?' Ware hazarded. Blake didn't answer. The trio
turned and all looked down the green, Sowerby gesturing.
The woman got back in the Jaguar, swept round, careless

of bumps in the grass, and came back. She stopped level with them and Blake, enlightenment dawning, stepped to the driver's window.

'I'm Carol Hammond,' she told him. 'And you're Detective Sergeant Blake.' She looked past him. 'And DC Ware.'

Ware was gaping. Blake said smoothly, 'I'm sorry about the loss of your mother, ma'am. And now' – he looked up the green – 'another shock on top of that.'

'The house doesn't matter; I never liked it.' She opened the door, emerging neatly for all her weight, her movements suggesting muscle rather than fat. She reached back for a large straw handbag. 'Perhaps you'd take me to Inspector Bell,' she said.

Bell's eyes narrowed at sight of her, widened at Blake's introduction. 'Please accept my sympathy, ma'am,' he announced stiffly, adding belatedly, 'for the death of your mother.' He was embarrassed; in police minds the fire had superseded the death of the Hall's owner.

'Thank you.' Carol was cool. 'I've had some time to absorb it although I find it difficult to accept. It seems utterly bizarre. What was she doing in that house? Maud Brunskill said it had been empty for ages.' She spoke with an old-fashioned public school accent, none of your mid-Atlantic or fake Strine for this lady. Bell put her age around thirty: lovely skin, unobtrusive make-up, an air of authority. 'Please sit down, Mrs Hammond,' he said, and to Ware: 'Go and ask the Stag if they can produce a pot of tea.'

Blake brought a chair, everyone punctilious and alert, aware that she might hold clues to the mystery of her mother's death.

Bell was circumspect. 'Your husband is with you?' he asked politely.

'No, I left him in Australia; he had business in Sydney. I can cope with the funeral on my own. And my mother's solicitor is competent, I can call on him if necessary.'

'The inquest is on Monday,' Bell told her. 'It will be adjourned.'

'Adjourned?' She was puzzled.

He realized that she might know nothing of the suspicious circumstances. 'You've been travelling.' He was gentle. 'It appears that your mother didn't die by accident.'

'The cellar floor gave way, so Maud – Mrs Brunskill said.'

Not Bart, Blake noted; wasn't he in touch with his stepdaughter? 'The kitchen floor gave way,' he corrected. 'She fell into the cellar. But there's a wound on the top of the head that isn't consistent with the fall.'

'I don't understand. She was with Larry Payne, wasn't she? He was showing her over the house.'

'There are a number of questions that we'd like to have answers to. Larry *had* been with her but it seems he'd left the house – left her in the house; he'd driven away and crashed his car. He died without regaining consciousness. We can only deduce what happened from the evidence. There were no witnesses.'

'How do you know he'd been with her?' She was confused and angry.

'The keys to the house were on her person, and the envelope that had contained them was in his car.'

'Are you saying he – that there was something – You said it wasn't an accident?' Without giving him a chance to respond she rushed on, 'A blow to the head? Larry *hit* her?'

'He might not have intended to kill her.' Bell watched her eyes. 'It could be manslaughter.'

'Why on earth should Larry Payne hit my mother?'

'A sexual entanglement?'

She gasped in derision. 'Larry! The boy's gay! Mum couldn't stand him and probably he felt the same way about her. Some kind of entanglement, sure, but not sex – not between June and him.'

'Between who then?'

Carol's eyes shifted to Ware, stepping gingerly over the door sill with a tray. She said coldly, 'It should be easy enough to find out.'

'Mrs Payne tells me Larry and your stepfather were the

best of friends.' Bell was casual, standing and making room on a table for the tray.

'Are you trying to tell me that Bart is gay?' Carol asked tensely.

'I wasn't. What's your opinion?'

'The agenda behind this squalid subject, or rather your harping on the subject, is that you're thinking in terms of an affair between Bart and Larry, right?'

'We consider all possibilities.'

She accepted tea from Ware, so lost in thought that she didn't thank him. 'Of course you've tackled Bart.'

'Not yet.' He was bland.

'He married my mother for her money,' she said distantly. 'She'd be a rich woman in his book. She had some money but a lot is tied up in the Hall – or was. Bart would never have risked a liaison with the boy next door. He had expectations.' The tone was ironic.

'Such as?'

'Why, the cash: a nice little nest egg, and the Hall of course. And now the insurance.'

'Do you know what it was insured for?'

'Not really. There's some land, and the outbuildings, I'm told those are still in good condition. The insurance on the Hall itself – I don't know, I haven't spoken to the investigators. Two, three hundred K?'

'A quarter of a million's a respectable sum.'

She shrugged. 'Well, it's early days. Obviously I can't collect from the insurers *and* make a packet from a builder for the site.'

'Ma'am?' It was a bark.

She raised delicate eyebrows. 'I'm certainly not going to rebuild that place myself, far too much –'

'Are you telling me you inherit?'

'Naturally. I'm an only child.'

'But – the husband – Are you sure of this?'

'Of course. Mum and I were close and we kept in touch.'

'Does your stepfather know?'

She gave a sly smile. 'I doubt it. He wouldn't have

stayed. But my mother knew the marriage wasn't going to last, you know. She'd come to accept that he married her for what he could get out of it and when she bought the Hall and he had to do all the work because she said there was no money left, things got pretty rocky. He was much younger than my mother and he was greedy. She knew he'd be away as soon as another lady with a bit of money came along which is how I know Bart wasn't having it off with Larry Payne. He wouldn't be interested. Bart's not gay.'

Carol needed accommodation. Finding the Stag fully booked she turned to the Brunskills and Maud installed her in their guest room. That settled, she returned to the ruins of the Hall and spoke to the insurers' representative, thus learning of the likelihood that the fire had been set, something Bell hadn't seen fit to tell her. The information occasioned her some amusement. The owner being sometimes the first suspect in a case of arson it was a relief for this one that she was thirty thousand feet in the air when the match was struck.

Maud told her that Bart had found temporary quarters in a holiday cottage across the green from the ruins. Carol glanced at it as she came away from her meeting with the fire investigators but there was no sign of her stepfather. A pretty girl in a cropped tank top and very short shorts was unlatching the cottage gate. She was carrying a large bowl and a plastic carrier containing something heavy. Carol's eyebrows rose fractionally before she slid into her car and left for Brimstock to view her mother's body.

Joely stowed the salad and cold roast chicken in the fridge and went upstairs to the master bedroom where Bart's discarded clothes struck an alien note. He was awake but bleary-eyed. She sat on the side of the bed and stroked the hair back from his forehead. He smiled sleepily. 'You'll have to get up,' she told him. 'People are arriving over at the Hall. And Carol's landed – just like the eagle.'

'Shit!' He pushed her away and flung himself out of the bed.

'It's not that urgent,' she protested, pouting at his naked back, cursing herself for her carelessness, anguished that they weren't going to make love at this moment with all the bustle about to start, and him the centre of it. 'She's left now,' she assured him. 'Off to Brimstock I expect. She's got a car to die for: a silver Jag. Dad says it must have set her back close on thirty thou. She was after one of our rooms but we're fully booked.'

'What's she want to stay here for?' He was towelling his face in the bathroom. 'There's nothing for her in Culchet, and she always loathed the place, said it was the sticks.'

'So what? It's your home, not hers.' She followed him back to the bedroom. He snatched up his jeans. 'Bart! Those stink of smoke!'

'I've got nothing else till I go to town. I lost everything, remember?'

'I'm sorry, it's just –' Just that she didn't want him meeting people in dirty clothes. She was proud of him.

He pulled back the curtain and looked across the green. She put her arms round him, under his shirt. 'Better not be seen,' he said easily, moving to the side. 'Graham would climb the wall.'

'I'm sixteen. You know what he can do.'

'Now look' – he turned and held her at arm's length – 'I have to go to the Hall now, and I'm going to be busy all day. How about you coming here this evening, bringing me something to eat?'

She was about to say she'd done that, it was downstairs in the fridge, but then he might tell her not to come, it would attract attention, twice in one day. 'If I can work it with Mum,' she said.

'If you can't, then come after you've washed up, when they're busy in the bar. I'll be waiting.' He kissed her lightly but she clung to him. 'I'll always be waiting,' he assured her, holding her face, kissing her eyes. 'You know that, don't you? Now let me go; the sooner I can wind

146

things up across there, the better. What?' Seeing the question in her eyes.

'Well, before, I saw us living in the Hall together. What do we do now?'

He hesitated and her face started to crumple. He said thoughtfully, 'I'm not straight in my head yet. We're not going to rebuild the place, that's for sure.' He grinned. 'Do we take the money and run? Go abroad? Canada? New Zealand?'

She was beaming. 'When? How soon?'

'Ah, that depends on the insurance pay-out. And that's what I have to go and discuss right now.' He turned to the stairs.

'You haven't had any breakfast!'

'I'll be back shortly.'

Although the panelling in the Hall and the furniture had burned and the roof had collapsed, walls were left standing and men moved with circumspection among the remains, watched from the gateway by two observers who turned at Bart's approach. 'Don't go any further.' The sharpness of Elliot's tone was occasioned by the state of Bart's clothes.

'I don't need to,' he retorted. 'And you are?'

Sowerby's stare was as stony as his partner's. 'Police,' he said, with the air of one accustomed to use the word as a weapon.

A man in a hard hat came over from the ruins. 'Two seats to the fire at least,' he told them, evidently mistaking Bart for one of a team. 'A room on the left, another on the right.' He gestured. 'Probably a lot of old panelling, wooden furniture, flammable upholstery. He knew what he was doing.'

'He did,' Bart said grimly. 'He'd been working here.' He had all their attention. He shrugged. 'It was his wife who named him: Hugh Butler. Didn't you hear about it?'

'Who *are* you?' Elliot blustered.

147

Bart smiled wryly at the wreckage of his home. 'I'm Milburn. I'm the owner.'

'But –' Elliot began.

'Go' – it was almost a shout from Sowerby and Elliot stopped short – 'and report to DI Bell,' Sowerby finished, holding his partner's startled gaze. The fire investigator turned and walked back to his colleagues.

Sowerby, alone with Bart, asked, 'What was that about Hugh Butler?'

Bart said, 'I came home to find the place blazing and while I was watching, Maureen Butler heaved a brick through my windscreen *and* accused me of abducting her child, and God knows what else. So I retaliated, said she'd torched my house. You have to understand, everyone was shocked and hysterical at this point: her over the kid, me seeing my house go up in flames. And that was when she said it had to be Hugh who set the fire.'

'So who did start it?'

'Hugh's the most likely bet. He's an alcoholic and if he thought I'd taken Kim, he wouldn't stop to think the child could be in the house when he torched it.'

'Fortunately for everyone Kim was found.' Sowerby smiled thinly. 'All the same, you'd best come down to the hall and make a statement.'

'The Hall?'

'Village hall, sir.' That 'sir' wasn't respect but prudence; Sowerby didn't know what he was dealing with here. 'We've set up a temporary incident room. There's the problem of young Jason now; he didn't come in with the rest of the searchers. The inspector's down in the hall. He'd like a word with you.'

'Of course.' They started to stroll down the green. Bart was embarrassed. 'I've got no other clothes; I lost everything in the fire.'

Sowerby's eyes were on the geese as they threaded their way through cars parked untidily outside the Stag. 'Insured, I hope,' he murmured.

'So do I.' The words were heartfelt but the tone was

casual. 'My wife – late wife – looked after the business side. I'm hopeless with money.'

The village hall appeared abandoned but the door was open. Inside, Bell and Blake sat at tables, ostensibly engaged on paperwork. Elliot and Ware were nowhere to be seen. At Bart's entrance the police stood and Blake performed the introductions. Bell regarded the newcomer benignly. 'A shock for you, sir: your home on fire.'

'Torched,' Bart stated. 'They say petrol was used.'

'It's insured.'

'No doubt.' But it hadn't been a question.

'Oh, it is. Mrs Hammond thinks the sum will be upwards of two hundred and fifty thousand.'

Bart made a subdued sound, his expression implying that the sum was immaterial. 'I lost my home and all my possessions,' he pointed out.

'Sit down, Mr Milburn.' Bell shifted papers. 'I'm sure Mrs Hammond will be compensating you for your loss.'

Blake, watching like a cat at a mousehole, caught a movement, a tensing of the jaw muscles. Bart seemed to stop breathing for a moment. 'That was only clothes and books and a house. I also lost my wife.'

'Indeed. Nothing can compensate for that. Although young Joely might make a good substitute.'

Bart's eyes were shocked, then venomous. 'I loved my wife,' he grated. 'But she didn't care for – a close relationship. We lived our own lives. Had to, in the circumstances.'

'You being considerably younger.'

'She had a number of interests outside the home.'

'So it wasn't the worst kind of blow when she died.'

'Of course it was! She was my wife! It was a hell of a shock.' Bart's tone flattened. 'I find your attitude offensive.'

'What was she doing there in Buncle House?'

'You tell me. I'm as much in the dark as anyone –'

'As Larry Payne?'

Bart was silenced. After a while he shook his head as if denying a thought. 'I don't understand. Larry knew what he was doing there but I don't.'

149

'You didn't know that your wife was going to view a house?'

'No – yes. *A* house, but not that particular one. If I'd known would I have been searching everywhere for her?'

'Sitting by your friend's bedside,' Bell mused. 'And no idea that he was involved.'

Bart said firmly, 'You've no proof of any involvement. The floor collapsed certainly, but Larry wasn't there, couldn't have been there or he'd have gone for help. He was in a hurry to get to another job so he left her at Buncle's. If he hadn't crashed his car he'd have raised the alarm immediately he heard she hadn't come home.'

His speculations could be wrong but he was right when he implied that they couldn't prove foul play, not on Larry's part, not on the site of a head wound alone, and the suspect dead. 'And what would his motive be anyway?' Bell asked, as if in agreement.

'None. He had no motive.'

'No. It would be ridiculous to suggest that, with your wife dead, you stood to inherit a fortune.'

Bart smiled and shook his head. 'What fortune?'

'And that she was killed because you and Larry were lovers.'

'First I'm having an affair with little Joely, now Larry.' He was still smiling. 'I'm not gay.'

'A quarter of a million's a lot of money.'

'Not much these days. It'll enable me to start over.'

'Except that you don't inherit.' The silence lengthened. 'Your wife left everything to her daughter,' Bell said.

He didn't slump, rather he seemed to harden like a stone man. Otherwise he made no sign until he blinked and said calmly, 'It makes sense; they were close, her and Carol, and she'd never told me she was going to leave the place to me.' He sighed heavily and fingered his shirt. 'This is all I've got left: the clothes I stand up in – oh, and a Land Rover. I forgot, it's registered in June's name.'

'You're lucky that Kim was found,' Bell told him.

'What? Why lucky? I've had some *luck*?'

150

'Her footprints were in your cellars. And she's adamant that a man abducted her. And Jason named you.'

'Fingered me, you mean. The Butlers are a problem family; they've got it in for everybody.'

He was allowed to go. They knew where they could find him – and he had no passport, Bell said.

'Only if it was burned along with everything else,' Blake pointed out. 'He wriggled away from every awkward question you put to him, and if he did set that fire he'd have removed his passport first.' Bell regarded him morosely. 'Insurance scam,' Blake said smugly.

'He doesn't own the Hall.'

'He thought he did.'

They were quiet for a while. Bell spoke first. 'Suppose he had known that Carol would inherit, what other motive could he have had for torching the place?'

'To hide evidence that Kim had been there?'

'The kid was found safe –'

'– but she could have been in the Hall at one time.'

'She was: in the cellars.' A pause as they considered this. 'He's having it off with Joely Carrick,' Bell said. 'The fellow likes them young.'

'Young, but not virtual babies. And those footprints in wet cement need mean nothing more than she was in the cellar, and only once.'

Ware came in, closely followed by Elliot. Ware said, 'DS Dodd wants to speak to you, sir. Kim's talking.'

Elliot said, 'The search team's arrived. Where do they start?'

'Hold them while I speak to the sergeant.'

From the hospital Helen gave him a rundown on the curious story Kim was telling, curious because although it went further than Jason's tale to his mother, it stopped short of an ultimate revelation. The child was now saying that men, not 'a man', had taken her 'upstairs', given her sweeties and played with her. She named the men: Larry, Bart, Mr Brunskill, Housby, Mr Carrick. She had named Sergeant Plumpton and retracted as quickly. She had named several of the neighbours in Dubb's Close. 'In other

151

words,' Helen said, 'all the men she knew by name. Her mother would believe her if it was only one or two but naming everyone she could think of was a dead giveaway. Oh yes, and when I asked her how she got past Housby's dog she said they visited him when the dog wasn't there. She's saying Jason was with her.'

'You're trying to tell me something.'

'It's a theory but it won't gel. It goes like this: Jason was running a scam, using Kim to distract men while he pocketed small items or cash downstairs. But no responsible man is going to take Kim into another room, let alone upstairs. As for paedophiles: firstly she hasn't been abused.'

'Wouldn't show necessarily; doesn't have to be penetration. And secondly?'

'No amount of persuasion can get her to explain the term "play" except one thing. They went upstairs to "play stations". The child has a vivid imagination but it doesn't stretch to any form of sex play. In the experts' opinion here she's not only innocent – in this respect – but totally ignorant.' Helen snorted derisively. 'Not innocent in other respects. All the time they were searching for her she was dodging from one unoccupied cottage to the next, raiding larders and fridges. She boasts that she can use a can opener. She said that people left their windows unlatched and we know that the patio doors were unlocked at the place where she was found, but for my money those kids know every insecure house in Culchet. I wouldn't be surprised if Kim can use a knife on the latched windows.'

'Jason could have been using her in some way,' Bell said flatly. 'Is she still frightened of him?'

'She's not terrified but then they're not coming home, her and her mum. They're staying in town with Hugh's cousin. What's the news on Jason?'

'None. We're starting the search now. We have a few questions for the men in the village. Something was going on here. No smoke without fire.' He stopped short on that, thinking of fire. Helen had talked about threads . . .

'Question the women too,' came her voice. 'They see

152

more,' she added, reminding him that she didn't know about Carol's arrival on the scene and the revelation that she inherited the Hall, and therefore the insurance, not Bart. She thought that amusing. 'There's your motive for the fire,' she said, 'if he thought he was going to inherit.'

'That's what Blake said.' But Bell was thinking of other motives for arson besides an insurance scam.

Chapter Thirteen

Helen was drinking coffee in the garden at Thrushgill, gossiping with Alice Potter and Win Langley. Bell had summoned her back from Brimstock because in his opinion she was the most perceptive member of his team. Another officer stayed with Kim and Maureen: an expert on hand to pick up anything, fact or fiction or nuance, that could be relayed to Culchet immediately in the hope that it might be of assistance in finding Jason and, equally important, what he was about.

'He's the priority now,' Helen told them, turning serious: 'not the fire, or June's death, but Jason.'

'So this isn't a social visit.' Win was resentful. Helen had spent some time admiring the garden, apparently relaxing in the sunshine after a gruelling time with Kim.

'She's on the job,' Alice pointed out and, to the visitor: 'Do you suspect foul play?'

Helen thought about it, and about discretion, but a small boy's safety could be at stake and she'd had no guidance from Bell . . . 'Two things,' she said. 'Jason wasn't your local cub scout by any means – and Kim's frightened of him.'

'From what we gathered she was terrified,' Win growled. 'And Jason was delinquent, not that he could help it coming from that family.'

'Even Kim?' Helen murmured.

'Jail bait.'

'Oh, come on, Win!' Alice wasn't amused.

'You implied it yourself: only that time when she was in the ghyll with Larry. Jason was –'

154

'She wasn't "with him". He followed her out of the ghyll –'

'So they were down there together. Immaterial in this case of course.' Win addressed Helen: 'Larry wasn't interested in little girls.'

'Little boys?' Helen came back, sharp as a nail.

'We-ll' – Win turned to Alice – 'it sort of crossed our minds.' She sat up quickly and her chair creaked alarmingly. 'That can't have any relevance now, with Larry being dead.'

Alice said, unaware of any offence: 'You've left our guest way behind. What she says is right, Helen; if Larry had been a paedophile which he wasn't –'

'You don't know that,' Win countered.

Alice glanced at her doubtfully. 'Anyway Jason's been around for days since Larry died so if there has been foul play . . .' She trailed off as her own words struck home to her.

Win shrugged. 'Maybe Jason was selling himself to –'

'Win!'

'Sorry.' She bit her lip. 'But there are children that age in the Third World . . . All right, all right, I'll be serious; no more gallows humour.' But they were uncomfortably aware that she hadn't been joking.

Helen said, 'Tell me about Jason and Larry – and Kim in the ghyll.' She looked down the garden to the trees on the rim of the ravine.

Alice obliged, telling how one afternoon Kim had come up out of the ghyll talking to her doll, maintaining she hated 'him' by which they realized now she had meant Jason. She'd been with him but he sent her packing when they met Larry. Alice had learned this from the man himself who, without any initial embarrassment but puzzled, told how Jason's conversation was innocuous until it appeared to take on a sexual slant, as if he'd seen or heard something at home that he needed explained.

Win broke in at this point. 'She thought there was something going on but she couldn't put her finger on it.'

'It was the two of them together,' Alice explained: 'a

155

volatile combination. Of course Larry's gay – you know that' – she didn't pause for confirmation but rattled on – 'but he's naive, knows nothing of the darker side of life.' Helen's eyebrows climbed. 'You know what I'm on about.' Alice was impatient. 'Larry is – was – innocent but perceptive, rather like Ted Brunskill – on different levels, you know: innocence and perceptiveness. And Larry said that although Jason was knowledgeable he didn't have the experience to apply that knowledge. He said that if Jason was ever to try blackmail he – Larry – would put his money on the blackmail*ee*.' Alice stopped and eyed Helen expectantly.

'Why were you talking blackmail?'

'Because I'd told him to watch his back at the times when he was alone with Jason.'

'But Kim wasn't involved.'

'Not that time. No. She'd run away, or been told to by Jason. Which was why she was so resentful. What you should do,' she went on earnestly, 'is talk to Jill Housby. She came on them quarrelling in the ghyll, threatening each other; one of them – I think it was Kim, yes – saying she'd tell on Jason, and him saying he'd kill her if she did.'

'She knows about that,' Win said, watching Helen's face.

Helen nodded. 'Jill told Plumpton, the uniformed chap. When we were searching for Kim and Jason was absent at the same time I mentioned those threats to my boss, but he was focused on an adult perp. Men are more likely, you see.'

'Perp?' Win repeated.

'Perpetrator.' Alice was dismissive, concentrating on Helen: 'You mean you thought Jason was after Kim, not searching for brotherly reasons but just the reverse. He wanted to reach her first.'

'Alice! Your mind!'

'It had occurred to me,' Helen agreed.

'So Jason had done something bad, and Kim knew . . .

156

and could tell! She said so. Jill heard her. You reckon Jason –' Alice checked, her eyes glazed.

'– could have run away,' Helen supplied smoothly, but what she was thinking, remembering Kim's talk of playing with men, was that Jason (knowledgeable but lacking experience) had come up against someone proficient in both.

She left Thrushgill by the back way. Although some members of the Press were trailing the search teams, others – circumspect rather than indolent – remained on the green, sitting in their vehicles, doors wide, or outside the Stag, their attention on comings and goings at the village hall. There were few of those; Bell remained there like a spider, his web spun along telephone lines. Blake and Sowerby with their partners were going door-to-door, ostensibly seeking any information that would help to locate Jason but covertly interested in all males between sixteen and sixty. Women were left to Helen. She followed a sketch map of the village drawn up by Plumpton, walking up Back Lane, past walled gardens, the ghyll on her left, and coming to outbuildings and a wide entrance through which she could see the grotesque ruins of the Hall. Plastic tape was strung across the gap.

She walked on, past the end of the buildings, and came to a small gate in a hedge of flowering hawthorn. A lawn showed beyond – in need of mowing – and a rockery with cushions of alpines in pastel shades and a sprinkling of Gold Dust. An arbour was draped with wisteria, mauve and white. Helen was oddly touched to think that the gardener would never see it again.

'Larry did the mowing,' Rachel said, apologizing for the long grass. She had received her visitor like an old friend. 'I'm no good with machinery,' she confessed. She took Helen round the garden, identifying the plants they had bought to celebrate each other's birthdays, Mother's Day, the Christmas gift bulbs Larry said should be given their chance to make it in the wild. 'Tender-hearted even towards plants,' his mother said. 'He talked to them, you know.'

'Some men prefer plants to people.'

'Present company excepted.' It was quick but then Rachel fell silent. 'No, not Larry,' she went on after the pause. 'He had his friends.'

'Ah yes.' Helen's eyes strayed to a row of lilacs, charred rafters rising incongruous above blooms and butterflies. 'He's moved to a cottage across the green,' she murmured.

'I have the room' – Rachel had heard an implied criticism – 'but it's too soon to have another man about the house, too poignant. I couldn't bear it.'

'Of course.' They strolled on and stopped at the rockery. 'Carol went to Maud Brunskill,' Helen said, as if making conversation.

Rachel inhaled sharply. When she made no comment Helen continued chattily, 'Did you know that she inherits everything?'

'From June?' Rachel stared, then smiled. 'I don't think June had much to leave; she'd sunk everything in the Hall. They couldn't even afford a firm to do the renovating; why, Butler told anyone who'd listen that Bart couldn't even pay him!'

'There's the Hall.'

'Was,' Rachel corrected. 'Now it's a matter of insurance.'

'But Carol collects that because June left the Hall to her.'

'Not so.' Rachel was firm. 'Bart –' She stopped. Helen thought that if she were a mite more perceptive she would hear the sound of gears meshing. Rachel went on slowly, 'Bart loved that house. Maybe I got the wrong impression, confusing references to his house with his home. I'm sure he thought – but then how would I know? Except that Larry always assumed that Bart was joint owner.'

'Who could have hated him enough to set it on fire?'

'That's something you must ask him, my dear.' Showing no surprise at mention of arson.

'I wonder about Jason.'

'What about him?'

'He made trouble.'

A light leapt in Rachel's eyes. 'Let's hope it's rebounded at last. Not before time.'

'You were a victim.' It was a statement, not a question, and Helen gave her no time to consider. 'How many others were there?'

'We don't talk about it.' Rachel was stiff and angry. 'Monster! A person's old so in their minds they think you're vulnerable. Oh yes, he tried it on. I threatened him and he turned tail.' She grinned wildly. 'You know something? Ted Brunskill says no way will he join in the search; whatever's happened, that boy had it coming. Poetic justice, Ted says.'

'You can't call it poetic in this case.'

'Retaliation! Jason would victimize people who he had a grudge against; it would be poetic if someone turned on their tormentor and put an end to it – and him.'

'And Larry was so vulnerable.'

'But gone, my dear. You can't blame Jason's fate on Larry.'

'Bart then, on Larry's behalf.' Their eyes held. 'Such close friends,' Helen said.

'Ah –' It was half gasp, half sigh. 'Maud asked how a child could be so vicious, but children are the worst, think of child killers. Jason didn't care if Bart was inside when he set fire to the Hall – he'd have preferred it, *enjoyed* it. Ha! This time Jason miscalculated.'

'Jason was blackmailing Bart.' It wasn't a question, it was the wildest shot in the not-quite-dark but it kept the innuendoes going. Helen didn't stop to analyse them, time enough for that later.

'He had no success with me,' Rachel said, seemingly at a tangent. 'And as for Larry, he couldn't fathom what the little bastard was about.'

'But Larry wasn't involved in a crime.'

'Jason could make it look bad, which is what he said, can you believe that? Almost as if he'd been instructed. He was right too; in today's climate a court would believe him. He only has to make the accusation . . . Mud sticks.'

Helen thought of the photos of Larry; he'd have made a

159

poor showing in the dock: the yellow hair and black vest, the tattoo, the ear-ring, but then he'd dress conventionally for a court appearance. 'It would be his word against a little boy who might be clever but –'

Rachel wasn't listening. 'Kim was the focal point. Jason was the entrepreneur.' She laughed harshly. 'You can't believe it, can you?' – seeing Helen's expression. 'You thought this was the simple Cumbrian village: all lilac and roses and good neighbours, geese on the green, children growing up in a caring environment, and here's a boy of ten who's a blackmailer, and pimping for his little sister.'

'A bit of an exaggeration,' Helen told Bell. 'He was only *playing* the pimp: a child's version of the badger game. He didn't have to ensure that Kim was left alone with a man; all he thought he had to do was *accuse* a man of actions when alone with her and then demand money for his silence.'

'He tried that with Larry?'

'No. With Larry Jason used himself as bait. Rachel's story is that he tried to blackmail Larry on the grounds that he'd made overtures to the boy. She says Larry laughed at the kid, I think there was more to it than that; Rachel's holding back. What I think happened was that Jason heard talk at home about Larry and was warned to keep clear of him, which would have had the opposite effect. So Jason got Larry on his own and that was all he needed. Subsequently he would have come back with the demand for money.'

'More likely he'd tried that already, judging from what you say about Rachel's hostility. So where does Kim fit in, and Jason being a pimp?'

'*Playing* the pimp,' she persisted. 'He tried that ploy with Ted Brunskill, who loathes all the Butlers; he blames Jon for the destruction of birds' nests evidently. Brunskill told Jason to go to hell and take his sister with him. Ted told Maud. Maud told Rachel.'

'Why did no one tell the Butler parents?'

160

'Difficult in a small village. In public Maureen and Hugh would side with their kids, even if Hugh thrashed 'em in private – for getting caught: thrash Jason, not Kim. But a fraught situation would escalate, and then there's retaliation. Better to hope a warning to the children would be enough.'

'D'you think any other men are involved?'

'We can eliminate Housby because both kids are scared of his dog. There's Graham Carrick; someone should talk to him but he'll be out looking for Jason. There's Bart Milburn of course, if Jason tried extortion there and Bart resisted, Jason could have set the fire. Rachel thinks so. There are the men in Dubb's Close but I doubt that very much, they'd go straight to Hugh.'

Bell glowered at her across the table. She wasn't intimidated although his first words were critical. 'The trouble with you is that you're hung up on the sex angle. It's understandable but from what you've said so far, if it was true, that Jason was trying a version of the badger game, it didn't work. Now suppose –'

A telephone was playing a silly tune: his. He answered, listened, took a long slow breath, staring grimly at Helen. 'I'm on my way,' he snapped, and to her: 'They've found him.' Her belly contracted at the tone. 'In a chest,' he said. 'In that church we searched for Kim.'

'And?'

'He's been strangled.'

They went out to her car. 'What were you about to say?' she asked, easing off the grass. 'Fasten your seat belt, please. You said, "Now suppose –"'

He struggled to find the attachment. 'Very relevant,' he wheezed. 'I was going to say suppose, in playing his nasty little game involving Kim, or on his own, Jason had uncovered something else, something that one of his victims couldn't laugh at and send him packing, some secret that was worth killing for?'

Chapter Fourteen

The chest was small but so was Jason. He fitted, and fitted perfectly, having stiffened in position. Rigor mortis fully established, said the doctor, so he had been dead at least ten hours. Since Jason had been with Maureen between four and five yesterday afternoon, time of death was between then and around one this morning. So where were the men of Culchet during that time? Bell asked facetiously.

'And women,' Helen pointed out. 'Some of the locals are pretty powerful.'

He blinked at her. They were sitting on a tombstone in the churchyard, waiting for the arrival of SOCO. He said, 'They would need an alibi for the trip too. They didn't carry the body across the fields. A vehicle was used.'

'"They"?'

'He or she, it serves for both. Jason could have discovered a woman's secret certainly, or a woman could be protecting a partner. Male or female partner.'

Helen's thoughts flew to Alice and Win. 'No,' she said. 'Women don't kill to conceal a lesbian relationship. I doubt if they are anyway, and if they were, who cares?'

'Quite. What about gay men?'

'Larry and Bart? Bart's having it off with the girl from the pub.' He said nothing. After a moment she said, 'You've met him. How does he come across?'

'Clever, scared, on the make.'

'If he's on the make, what does he expect to get out of a liaison with a sixteen-year-old? I'd have thought that would be asking for trouble. Incidentally, since we know

162

about it, and Win and Alice do, how come Joely's mum and dad don't? Or do they?'

A man with a camera emerged from the porch and made for the parking space outside the gate. Bell stood up. 'Come and look for tracks. Your eyes are as keen as anybody's.'

'The ground's bone-dry.'

'Yes, but remember: something's always taken away –'

'– and something's left behind. But if it's a smear of rubber or a drop of sump oil we still need a match. Do the Carricks know?' she persisted, holding the gate for him.

'They will soon enough. And when the media gets a hold of it, there'll be complications.'

'Jason will occupy them for a while yet.'

After the body was removed dogs were brought in but without much hope, the killer almost certainly having used transport. In fact tracks were plentiful in the dust: of boots and trainers, tyres and sheep. Blake was left in charge of a team combing the churchyard and the meadow outside its walls. Bell and Helen returned to Culchet and the cottage where Bart had spent the night. They found it unlocked and unoccupied, the keys, labelled, on the kitchen table. There was nothing of Bart's in evidence but then he had nothing after the fire.

'He could have gone to town to buy some clothes and food,' Helen said doubtfully. The fridge was empty, the door open.

'And left the keys there? Who owns this place?'

They went to the pub which was relatively deserted, the Press having decamped en masse to Brimstock following the body. They would have a brief respite from media hassle before it was discovered that the man in charge was still in Culchet. The owner of the cottage lived in Harrogate, Freda told them; she kept the keys and looked after the place and no, she didn't know where Bart was. Joely might know; she'd taken some food over at breakfast time.

163

Helen found Joely in the kitchen, introduced herself and asked if she knew where Bart had gone. Joely snatched deep breaths. Win shot her a glance while carefully peeling zest from a lemon. 'Isn't he at the Hall with the insurance people?' Joely asked in a little girl's voice.

'No, he's been talking to us since then. He's had a bit of a shock.'

'We all have! It's gross. Jason was a little devil –'

'Whatever he was,' Win broke in loudly, 'he didn't deserve what happened to him.'

Joely was watching Helen like a rabbit cornered by a stoat. 'Bart won't know about Jason yet,' she breathed. 'So what was the shock you meant?'

'Oh, something to do with the Hall.' Helen was vague, as if it was grown-up stuff.

'Right, that *is* a shock: seeing your house and everything go up in flames.' Relief flooded her face belying the words. 'And Maureen Butler heaving a rock through his windscreen. If he'd been in the driver's seat she could have brained him!' This was one very impulsive girl: switching from fearful concern to relief to furious indignation as image succeeded image in her consciousness.

'Where did he say he was going?' Helen asked, as if for the first time.

'How should I know? I took some stuff up there to put in the fridge and that's it.' Joely looked past Helen.

Freda said from the passage, 'He'll be needing clothes; he'll have gone to Brimstock shopping.'

'A bit more than that,' Bell said cheerfully, crowding Freda into the kitchen. 'He's done a runner.'

'He hasn't!' Joely cried. 'Why on earth should he?'

'Because he's scared of becoming involved?'

The girl gaped, shaking her head weakly. Freda glanced from her to Bell and back. 'Involved with whom?' she asked, suspicion dawning.

'You're his alibi, right?' Bell addressed Joely, as if he didn't know already.

She blinked, trying to orientate herself. 'I was.' She wanted to ask on what occasion but daren't.

'When Kim was missing.'

'Oh, *then*!' A gasp was followed by tension as she saw his interest and realized she'd made a mistake.

He gave her no chance to identify it. 'There were other times?'

Freda said, 'What *is* this? How did you alibi Bart? He had nothing to do with Kim being missing.'

Joely had had time to think but not long enough. 'You see, when Kim disappeared, all the blokes in the village were suspected, right? I guess' – smiling shakily – 'they even suspected Dad. It looked bad. I knew Bart was in the clear because he – I was with him when she went missing, and I said so. I told that nice sergeant, the man.' She ended on a high note.

Freda swallowed and glanced at Bell but said nothing. Joely was going to have some explaining to do in private.

Bell turned to Freda and smiled. 'Nothing to get excited about.' He moved closer and murmured, the others straining to hear. Freda exclaimed, 'No, that was Larry! Why, Bart was a married man –'

'The information came from June. By way of Carol.'

'I don't believe it!' Freda swung round on her daughter. 'You knew Bart was gay all along?'

Joely licked her lips and studied their faces – Bell's, her mother's – trying to gauge potential reactions. She said carefully, 'He was always very kind,' as if she were protecting his memory.

Bell didn't seem interested. He said, with an air of finality, 'So you stand by your alibi.'

She shrugged. 'If that's what it is.'

'If you don't mind giving the times to the sergeant here . . .' He left. Helen followed orders, wondering, noting the times the girl was with Milburn on the day that Kim went missing. She caught up with Bell in the hall. 'What the hell was that about?' she demanded. 'It had nothing to do with Jason. We *know* what happened to Kim.'

'But what she was doing that day could have something to do with the motive for killing Jason. Why was Kim hiding from Jason? Discover that and we may have our murderer. What I need to know now is whether Bart and Larry were lovers.'

'But we agreed –'

'No, *you* kept harping on about the affair with Joely – and there's Freda pointing out that he was married, but the fellow could be bisexual. He's an opportunist, and one who marries a woman for her money is going to have ulterior motives coming out of his ears. He could have been conducting affairs with Joely *and* Larry. It happens. What I want to know is which affair was genuine and which had ulterior motives. Oh yes, and what part did Jason play?' He grinned at her across the table that had become his desk. 'Carol's back from Brimstock. Bart *has* left, although doing a runner was my interpretation of it: to see what kind of reception it got from young Joely. He's gone but he left a note for Carol with the Brunskills.' He handed her a sheet of paper. 'Now Carol's saying he's gay,' he said mildly. 'She said he wasn't before. It put her mother in a bad light – humiliating; but now that Milburn's scarpered there's nothing she won't accuse him of, even murder if I didn't insist he had an alibi.'

'For Jason?'

'For June.'

She gasped, holding the note but not looking at it. At length she asked weakly, 'Can she back up her charge that he's gay?'

'June had her suspicions. Apparently she wasn't bothered. June doesn't seem to have been interested in sex. Of course she was getting on.'

Helen's shoulders slumped, then she sighed and gave her attention to the note:

Dear Carol, ,

I wanted to see you but I really cant hang around its too devastating. June always gave me to understand that she would leave the Hall to me and the news that I lost my house as well as my home after the misry of her death and the fire have shattered me completely. I have gone

166

away for a week or two get my breath back. Ive borrowed the Landrover, hope you dont mind. Its in Junes
name but all the papers are burned like everthing else.
We talk when I come back in around a fortnight.

Yours Bart

'He left school early,' Helen commented.

Bell ignored that. 'Joely didn't know he was leaving,' he
said thoughtfully.

'Not necessarily. She denied he'd done a runner but he
could have told her he was going away for a week or two.'
She put the note on the table. 'He emptied the fridge,' she
went on, and frowned. 'It couldn't have held much. What's
he going to do for food? For petrol? He's supposed to have
lost everything.'

He shook his head. 'Not if he set the fire himself: for the
insurance. He'll have removed valuables, like credit cards,
first.'

'Of course,' she breathed. 'He *has* done a runner. Where
was he between five and one?'

'That's what I – Five and one? I see, you're thinking of
Jason, and taking his body to the church.'

'The fire needn't have been set as an insurance scam. He
could have started it to destroy evidence that the boy was
killed in the Hall.' Helen's eyes were like saucers: 'Jason
had stumbled on Bart's secret!'

'Which was?'

'That he was gay! An affair with Larry,' she elaborated,
but was as quickly deflated. 'No. Who'd care about that?
June was dead. He thought he was going to inherit the
Hall; he couldn't be cut out of her will *now*. He had nothing
to fear if the whole world knew he and Larry were
lovers.'

'And yet,' he reminded her, 'the boy was strangled. We'd
assumed it was because he'd discovered something and
could use blackmail. Is that too specific? There have to be
other motives for killing small boys.'

'The one that springs to mind is to conceal the identity

of a rapist. But that doesn't hold nowadays. His DNA can identify him.'

'If we have a match. We'll know more after the PM. And then there was the scam where Kim was used.' Bell was talking to himself now. 'We mustn't allow ourselves to be side-tracked by sex; it doesn't have to be sex at all. What else is there?' And with that question he came back to her. Helen blinked guiltily; she wasn't paying attention; it seemed airless in the hall even with the door and windows wide open. She felt lethargic.

'Someone killed him,' she said inanely.

'You get back to Kim. If she knows that she don't have to be scared of Jason any longer maybe she'll feel like talking.'

'I'm not sure I can tell her he's dead, given her age; I certainly can't tell her how he died –' She stopped short, then said tightly, 'If he was killed because of what he knew, she could be at risk too. Don't we need to put her in a safe house?'

'You're getting carried away again. Kim will be fine as long as she stays with her mother. You get off to town now; if she does know something, the sooner she talks the safer she'll be. I want another word with young Joely.'

Helen thought he'd get nowhere with the girl, it wasn't as if he could charm her into giving him more information on Bart; she should be the one interviewing Joely, but evidently he thought a woman would be better with Kim. Certainly he'd be hopeless with a five-year-old. Driving between banks of cranesbill and meadowsweet she grimaced at the thought of little girls and old men. She reached for the radio switch; maybe he was right when he said she was obsessed by sex, at least where this case (cases?) was concerned.

Kim had been told about Jason, Aunty Bet informed Helen, closing the front door behind them, preceding her visitor to the kitchen: a woman built like a Hereford cow with the same bright curls the colour of raw beef. Maureen was in bed, she said, sedated, and she'd taken it on herself to tell Kim that Jase had gone away, meaning to imply that it was temporary, a holiday like; there'd be time enough later to suggest he wasn't coming back. Kim however had asked anxiously if he'd gone for good and when her aunt hesitated, asked if he'd been murdered.

'Look at her!' Bet hissed, gesturing to the window. In a stark patch of garden Kim was playing in a sand-pit with a plastic spade and buckets of water. 'Happy as a pig in muck – now,' Bet observed. 'Murdered indeed! Where did she ever hear the word?'

'Television?' Helen walked outside and across the brown grass to ask Kim what she was doing. Building a castle, she was told, but it was dead boring and had Helen come to take her home because Mam had taken a tablet and she could follow on when she woke up.

Helen said, 'Didn't Mam ever say you shouldn't go in cars with strangers?'

Kim started to slap at wet sand with her spade.

'I suppose there's no harm done if it's a lady,' Helen mused. The slapping lessened enough for Kim to catch this but there was no response. 'Ladies are boring anyway,' Helen ventured, adding – but unhappy about it: 'Not like men.'

'Them's no good neither,' Kim said with an emphatic slap.

'They don't want to play?' Thank God there were no witnesses to this conversation.

'Shit, no!'

'Why not?'

'Them's old. He told us to go to hell.'

'Who?'

'That Brunskill.'

'He wouldn't play after all.'

'Jase said he would if I asked nicely. I thought he'd hit us. Jase tells lies.' Kim poured water on dry sand and started to prod and turn the result.

'You're mixing cement,' Helen said idly.

'That's daft. You need a proper big mixer, like my dad's.'

'Was he cross when he saw your foot-marks in the cellar?'

'He never said nothing.'

'Bart would have been mad.' Kim was silent. Helen thought the child might not have seen Bart since the police dogs found her at Ravenstone. 'Do you go – with Jason to the Hall?' she asked.

'Only when them's away. I wouldn't never, ever go inside when he's there. He's got a dungeon where he ties littluns and thrashes 'em with a bike chain.'

'Oh, how ghastly!' A pause. 'Mr Carrick would never do that.'

'No.' There was no emotion – and no surprise. Helen pushed it. 'Did you ask him to play: Mr Carrick?'

Now the child was surprised. 'Us never tried. Mam works at t'pub. And Jase said us had to be careful there. It were our secret.'

'You're telling me.'

'I can now. Jase can't hurt me. He's dead. He won't come back no more.'

'That's what you were quarrelling about in the ghyll. You threatened to tell on Jason.' Kim nodded, glowering. Helen went on, 'You were having fun. You'd have spoiled it for yourself if you'd told –'

'He wouldn't let me stay, said I'd to go home. He didn't want me.'

'So – he – could manage without your help; he said a little kid would be in the way.'

'You reckon. We was a team. He said so.'

'But not that time.' The child nodded, sulking, recalling the slight. 'Like the other time down in the ghyll,' Helen said. 'The time he met Larry and sent you away. You hated him that time too.'

'He said I were too little. It wasn't fair. We was a team.'

Helen sat down on the edge of the sand-pit. 'You know what I think? Jason had another game he was playing, a different one. There was the game you played together: leaving Jason downstairs, you going upstairs –' She couldn't go on with that. She shouldn't. She resumed smoothly, 'But now he was into a grown-up game; he'd have let you into it when you were a little older. Or you might even have found out yourself: spying on him.'

That didn't work. Kim shook her head. 'I were too feared of him. I scarpered.'

'I think he was feared of you,' Helen said.

So it looked as if Jason had indeed started another scam. Having failed at his nasty little badger game, too young to realize it would have alerted even a paedophile who would suspect he was being set up, the boy had found something else. Something that must exclude Kim because she might talk – and be believed. With the original scam Jason might deny everything, maintain his little sister told porkies. Helen returned to Culchet wondering what Jason had on Larry Payne.

'Not that he was gay,' Bell growled when she found him, hot and disgruntled, at a table outside the pub. 'Everyone knew.'

'His mother –'

'She knew. She was just trying to keep it from us. She's that generation: keep it quiet, none of our business. She's come clean – in a defensive manner: it didn't do anyone any harm, she maintains.'

'What does she have to say about Bart?'

'Now that did shock her. She gave me a lecture on the subject: just because you are friends with a person doesn't make the other chap – Bart – "of the same persuasion" – her words.'

'She's saying Bart's straight?'

'That's the implication.'

Helen studied his face, considering the words. She said, 'When Jason talked to Larry in the ghyll, perhaps he wasn't concerned with the man himself but was pumping him with a view to finding out about Bart. But surely Jason wasn't old enough to understand that if June knew Bart was gay she'd disinherit him.'

'The boy wouldn't think that far. Larry told Alice Potter he couldn't fathom what the boy was on about. To do with sex, he thought, and then he got cagey – Larry did – as if it suddenly dawned on him what the kid was after. Jason was probably fishing, looking for something that could come in useful: dangling a hook.'

'And a big shark came along and took the bait and pulled him in the water.' Helen's eyes sparkled, then she sobered. 'Funny about Joely though. Did you get any further with her?'

'She's not here. She's gone walkabout.'

'A pity. I'd like to tackle her when she comes back.'

'Her mother gets first call. She's climbing the wall; the girl's supposed to be here for the lunches. The only consolation for Freda is, Joely's not with Bart.'

They were all tired. Just as things were hotting up, probably *because* they were hotting up with the murder of Jason, the last spurt of adrenalin had dried, the next not kicked in. They sat outside the Stag and relaxed, ostensibly reporting to Bell and comparing notes while they feasted on Win's ciabatta with fresh butter and ham, big fat olives on the side. It could have been Italy. Helen was drinking Chianti, the others were on real beer. Helen had had a twinge of guilt, which passed with the wine. She saw that the men were somnolent, even Bell, that despite everything, they would love to stay here throughout a long and lazy afternoon, getting pleasantly drunk. She wondered what might happen to disturb them.

They didn't have long to wait. The first interruption came from Bell's phone. The autopsy report on Jason showed no signs of sexual abuse, neither recent nor at any time. His last food (crisps) was still in the stomach but that was little help since there was no knowing when he'd eaten. Maureen had left him in the house around 4.30 p.m. If he ate then, he was killed long before dark. 'Daylight,' Bell observed. 'Someone must have seen where he went.'

'He could have gone anywhere by way of Back Lane,' Helen pointed out. 'He was small enough that he wouldn't show above the walls.'

Bell pulled the crumpled sketch map from his pocket. 'He's still got a long way to go from the close to the Hall,' he muttered. 'Someone *must* have seen him.'

'It was tea-time,' Helen said: 'high tea. People would be preparing food, eating, watching telly –'

'Walking dogs?'

'Not in Culchet. You just turn them out in the back garden. I don't see Culchet people walking Back Lane for fun.'

'Something wrong, ma'am?' Bell was alert, focused elsewhere.

They looked up, interest kindled, lethargy forgotten. Freda stood in the shadowed doorway, white-faced, clutching a piece of paper, Win beside her, a meaty arm round her shoulders.

Freda held the paper out like an offering. 'At least she told me!' She laughed wildly and choked as she fought for breath. Win held her tightly. 'Read it!' the chef ordered, as if the police were at fault.

Helen jumped up and brought the paper to Bell. He read it in silence, the focus of all their eyes, colour returning to Freda's face as she built up towards rage. Bell passed the paper to Helen, Blake and Ware crowding round. It read:

Mum and Dad – I have gone to join Bart and we will make a new life together in London. We love each other very much so you need not worry. We will keep in touch promise.

Love Joely.

Chapter Fifteen

Joely had taken her mobile, a soft suitcase, and several hundred pounds from the tills. Probably she had been wearing navy shorts, a pink T-shirt and fuchsia thongs decorated with sequin butterflies. 'Thongs?' Bell queried. 'Flip-flops,' Helen interpreted. 'In that outfit she's not going to get far without someone seeing her. Either she called a taxi or she's hitching.'

'Or he was waiting for her.'

No one liked that. The police were fully alert now and, much worried by Joely's risky behaviour, tacitly acknowledging that Bart was a suspect for Jason's murder.

'Someone,' Bell grated, 'saw that man between five o'clock yesterday and when he turned up at the fire. He came from somewhere. Where? Who saw him arrive?'

'Maureen?' Helen suggested. 'If Jason spilled the beans to his mother at tea-time, she'd surely have gone looking for Bart immediately.'

'Ask her.'

'She's sedated.'

'Ask Hugh. She could have told him.'

Hugh wasn't at his house in the close. Jon was, sullen and defiant, and seemingly untouched by the death of his brother, not, at any rate, grieving, but young villains learned how to hide their feelings. He reckoned that his father was in town 'seeing to the funeral and that'; Bell forbore to point out that it would be a while before the body was released. He was considering how to ask a question that wouldn't be a leading one. What he needed to know was Bart's whereabouts during that crucial period last evening. He tried to play it foxy but his age was telling as the after-effects of the lunch-time beer kicked in. 'Think about last evening,' he said heavily. 'We're looking at people's movements.' Jon stared at him, waiting. Bell tried again. 'Your mother went looking for Milburn?'

Jon considered this. 'I weren't here.'

Well, it was a start, sort of. 'Where were you?'

'How can I remember . . .' He trailed off as he realized that last evening wasn't that far back. 'I were in t'pub,' he muttered. 'I been looking for Jase, hadn't I?'

'What time did you go to the pub?' Helen asked, startling him. Women weren't meant to interrupt when it was business.

'How in hell would I know?'

Bell sighed. Helen said quickly, 'Was Milburn there?'

Jon blinked, obviously trying to work out what lay behind the question. 'He'd be at the Hall,' he said carefully.

'Why would you think that?'

'Because Carrick saw Jason go by.'

Bell said incredulously, 'Graham Carrick saw Jason pass the Stag?'

'By Back Lane.' Jon nodded emphatically. 'Me dad told us.'

'Told you *what*?' Bell was losing it.

'That Jase went up Back Lane. Carrick saw un from t'car park, going to t'Hall.' Jon's eyes were wide. He could be deeply in earnest or scared stiff.

'How did Carrick know that?'

Jon swallowed and shrugged theatrically. 'He coulda been going to one of them holiday places but why would any of them want to harm Jase? He weren't going to Housby's, not with yon girt hound loose; and why should un go to Todbank? He were on t'way to t'Hall, them had summat going.'

Bell's face reddened. Helen rushed in, but quietly: 'We know about Jason's scam.'

175

'Well then.' Jon sat back in his chair with an air of finality.

'They were into something together?' she asked gently, praying that Bell would keep quiet.

'Don't know what it were. He didn't tell me everything.'

'What did he tell you?'

'Nothing. No details. He said as how he expected to come into some cash.'

'He was ten!' Bell exploded. 'You're an adult, his brother! Couldn't you make him tell you? You had to know it wasn't – that it was dangerous: a little kid and a grown man!'

Jon's face muscles stiffened. Helen dropped her eyes. Stupid old git, he'd ruined it. How did he ever come to make DI? If this was what she had to contend with on her climb to the top the future looked rosy. But now – now it was back to salvaging what she could out of this abortion and try to bring home the murder to Bart.

'He's lying,' Bell said as they came away.

'He's got more to tell us – with careful handling.' If he caught the rebuke, he disregarded it.

'It'll only be more lies. Let's find Carrick.'

'*What!*' Carrick was indignant. 'I never saw Jason. How could I? At that time I was serving in here.' They were in the bar at the Stag. 'If Hugh said I saw the boy, that's Hugh projecting, or whatever you call it, for his own ends. Or Jon got it wrong. It would be Hugh saw the boy, or is saying he did and Jon twisted it for some reason. I tell you: I didn't see Jason!'

'You see?' Bell said to Helen, out of earshot. 'Jon's lying in his teeth. Arrest him.'

'On what charge?'

'Obstructing the police. OK, we'll have him in to help us with our inquiries. I want to question that lad in the proper surroundings, off his home turf. He's played into our hands.'

'He's scared.'

'What's he scared of then?'

'Small-time thieves always are but right now it's probably the same thing that terrified Jason.'

She prevailed on Bell to let her conduct the interview, assuming that Jon had a poor opinion of women officers. She asked if Ware might partner her and Bell, too tired to protest or argue, agreed.

Seeing she was to be his opponent Jon started out cocky in the interview room, confident he could run rings round the filth. Helen recognized the attitude as plated armour and was alert for cracks. She began by conforming to his image of women in authority, asking him how he looked on Jason's use of their little sister as sex bait. Not that she called it that but employed euphemisms: 'persuading men to forget themselves' was how she put it.

Jon registered bewilderment. 'How: forget themselves?'

She was pleased. He was going to talk, to play games. '*You* know' – she was suggestive – 'enticing them, luring . . . Of course it was only a distraction . . . You fenced the stuff.' There was no change in tone.

'That were –' He stopped, puzzled, suspicious; he'd be going over her words. She was opening a file on the table in front of her. He tried to read a page upside-down and failed. 'He'd stopped thieving,' he said. 'That were history.'

'Naturally.' She was smooth as silk. 'The money the men parted with was a small fortune to Jase compared with what he made through thieving. And Bart wasn't the only one by a long chalk.'

'Bart was cool.' It meant nothing. He watched her too fixedly, never glancing at Ware, thinking he was giving nothing away but body language betrayed him. He was keeping tight control on himself.

'There were better targets,' Helen said.

'Always are.' He was merely agreeing with her.

'But he went and died. You made a mistake there.'

'*I* did?' Innocence and shock were demonstrated but not convincingly. 'It weren't nothing to do with me. It were all Jase's idea.' He hadn't asked who died.

It was her turn to simulate shock. 'You're telling me Jason discovered how to blackmail blokes sexually at ten years old?'

'It weren't like that.' He sounded – surprisingly – sincere. 'It just come about – natural, like I said. It started with them going into houses, holiday folk, visitors, and Kim all over the place, into everything – bedrooms like, anywhere, and folk'd do anything to get rid of her, give Jase summat to take her away. Some give cash and o' course Jase, he started asking for it, and then finding men – men on their own – they'd give even more. It grew, see!'

A neat little protection racket and big brother was fostering it. Aloud she said, 'You didn't think it might be dangerous where Kim was concerned?'

'Nah. Not in middle of t'village. And she didn't know what she were doing.'

'Jason did –'

'Not really –'

'– and you didn't see any danger in it for him? Even when he started operating on his own.'

'I didna know about that.'

'It was innocent up to that point: a kids' game, the two of them working as a team to shake down people with plenty of cash: more money than sense.'

'That's how they saw it.'

'And you.'

'Yeah, well, it didn't do no harm. Kids making a nuisance of theirselves – pay 'em to go away. Kids do it everywhere.'

'But Jason ran into difficulty with the new scam.'

'I wouldn't know nothing –'

'You do know. He was murdered.'

'I mean I didn't know what he were into.'

'It was to do with Bart Milburn, you said.'

'I didna.' He couldn't resist a glance at the tape recorder. He could deny everything he'd said before coming here; now there was a record.

Helen leaned back in her chair. Ware, the silent observer, glanced at her and then kept his eyes on Jon. Helen said,

'Jason was using his little sister to lure men into compromising situations so he could blackmail them. She's five, he was ten. You were the one behind it, they acted on your instructions. Kim has a vivid imagination and no one will believe her if she talks, but Jason decided to shake you down, and people would believe *him*. He was a plausible little rogue. So you had to silence him.'

'I what?'

His surprise appeared genuine this time. Unbelievable: he hadn't seen what she was leading up to? He was that thick? 'You didn't mean to kill him. You lost your rag but then you had to cover up, so you fingered Milburn.'

'You're daft.' A long pause. 'Prove it.'

She looked at the machine. 'We've got all we need.' Like hell they had. She went on coolly, 'You've confessed to the scam, scams rather, admitted you knew about them, condoned them, encouraged, suggested improvements?'

Jon grinned savagely, his face alight. He'd thought of something. 'You go to that old witch at Todbank. Her threatened to strangle our Jase. Spooked 'im, her did. He come home and told us. 'Cos of Larry, see. Jase tried it on with him thinking as a poof would go for little girls like. I told him that were daft, try it t'other –' He stopped, gaping.

'Try it t'other way.' She knew a glow of triumph. 'So he offered himself to Larry instead of Kim.'

'He laughed at un! That Larry did. So he weren't no good for a shakedown but after he died Jase went to see his mother – like saying Larry had interfered with Kim, see, but the old witch, her sent him packing. An' said as how she'd enjoy squeezing life out of un, what he'd look like, swelled tongue an' all. Jase run for his life.'

Rachel sipped her sherry, relaxed at least superficially, even seeming pleased to see them. 'I take it that, because this time Mr Bell is with you and you both decline a drink, that your business is more formal.'

Helen thought, she's recovering fast and she's a very

179

different proposition from Jon – and did she feel she had nothing to lose? But she was a small woman with small hands; had she the power to strangle a boy of ten?

Bell was looking at her hands too. He said, 'Jason talked to his brother before he died.'

Rachel nodded. 'I did wonder. Jon was the instigator?'

Bell looked round the room as if pricing the contents. He smiled. 'You live a blameless life, ma'am.' A pause. 'What did Jason have on you?'

She sketched a shrug. 'Nothing.' Her face changed, contorted. 'I did have a hostage to fortune.' It sounded proud but then she added, 'Not any longer,' and Helen knew that recovery was no more than skin-deep.

'He was getting at you through your son,' Bell said. 'But Larry couldn't be hurt any longer. What enraged you so much *then* that you wanted to kill a small boy?'

'That was it, Inspector: rage – and grief. His appearance was a kind of relief, a release rather. He had threatened my son; I put the fear of death into Larry's tormentor.' She saw their attention was on her hands. 'I would have been happy to strangle him,' she said, and her lips stretched like a wolf's. 'I wouldn't have gone to the trouble of putting him in the church chest however.'

Bell was silent for so long that Helen wondered if he were dropping off again; he'd confessed that he'd taken a nap while she was in Brimstock. For herself she craved a drink and her eyes wandered to bottles on the sideboard. Someone sighed. Rachel said firmly, 'You could both do with a pick-me-up.'

She served them with a marvellous malt, something Helen indulged in only at Christmas and on holiday. She felt herself blooming, knew that had been the intention and wondered how Bell was dealing with it.

'About June Milburn's will,' he said conversationally, turning to his partner. 'Mrs Payne told you that Larry understood that Bart was to inherit everything.'

'That's right.' Helen glanced at their host who looked politely interested. 'That is, to inherit the Hall. Mrs Payne

180

thought there wasn't much more –' She stopped. Why didn't he address Rachel directly?

He said easily, 'No doubt at one time this was what June intended, but she changed her will?'

'Either that,' Rachel said, 'or there was only ever one will and Bart didn't know its contents. June didn't impress me as being particularly frank.'

'So she allowed her husband to think that the Hall would be his eventually.'

Helen stifled a gasp. Would Rachel get the inference? But Bart had alibis for the time of June's death.

'She distrusted him,' Rachel said coldly. 'And he's much younger – and very handsome. It would be a way of holding him: letting him think he'd inherit if anything should happen –' She stopped. The inference had reached her.

'Bart was in Brimstock when June died.' Bell spoke with finality. 'The question I need answered is where was every-one when Jason died?'

Helen blinked and then wondered if he were being deliberately confusing in reverting to Jason.

'Jason assumed Bart was gay because of his friendship with your son.' Bell was informing Rachel as if she didn't know.

She licked her lips, seemed to collect herself and said coldly, 'The car crash was a catalyst. Bart didn't care any longer. I'd always known of course, but I'd been discreet, had to be because of June – thinking she'd cut Bart out of her will if she found out. Larry wasn't bothered about money but he couldn't bear to see Bart hurt. He set so much store by his home. Larry and I didn't talk about – the relationship. But after the crash, sitting there beside him, unconscious, nothing else mattered to us, only willing him to live. Bart knew that I knew and we acknowledged each other's – devotion. And then,' she said sadly, tears trailing her cheeks, 'neither of us was there at the end. Even the nurses left. There was no one.'

'But he was in intensive care!' Helen was amazed. 'Where did the nurses go?'

181

'To the fire of course: the alarms were ringing. You forgot. I told you.'

Helen shook her head. 'The fire was here, Rachel: miles from the hospital.'

Bell overlapped her: 'No one told me. Where was this fire?'

Rachel scrubbed at her face. 'I need a drink. The fire in the hospital,' she snapped savagely, stumbling to the sideboard, splashing whisky into her sherry. 'The bloody fire that meant not even a nurse was there – a young girl, anyone – just someone to hold him, to say goodbye when he left us.'

At the hospital end of the phone there were protests, procrastination, smoke screens. Bell cut through it all like a laser and reached someone in authority. Not a fire as such, he was told: a cigarette end in a bin bag, nothing. It had been put out immediately, it hadn't even made the local news. No, people didn't stay at their posts when there was a fire alarm, that is, they dropped what they were doing – naturally – shut doors . . . No, they didn't have sprinklers, how could you have sprinklers in a *hospital*, shorting out electrical equipment, soaking patients in their – 'Stay there!' Bell ordered. 'I'm coming in.'

'A fire alarm,' he declared as they drove north. 'Rachel's left the bedside to snatch a few hours' sleep, nurses rush away at sound of the alarm, panic . . . Larry's on his own.'

Helen's eyes were fixed on the road. The man was mad. He grinned at her stiff profile. 'Bart had an alibi for June's murder but Larry was actually *with* her – although but for the car crash he would have had some alibi prepared too. There was a fire. A hoax fire? Put-up job anyway. Fire alarm sounded: enough to cause panic. Larry's left alone. Is that when he died: during the flap over the fire? Tubes disconnected?'

'Nothing was said about it. He died naturally. He was dying anyway.'

'But it was important he should die before he said anything incriminating.'

'Bart killed Larry? They were lovers.'

'You never heard of lovers killing each other? For whatever reason?'

The hospital spokesman was called Palmer. He was defiant, on the edge of panic, sweating profusely, but then it was a warm day. In the time it took the police to drive there he had looked for help and found none. He knew he had to stall but, faced with a fat, sleepy inspector and a girl, aware of the authority vested in him and the obfuscation that might be employed in respect of cardiac monitors and the running of an ICU, with luck he could win out. After all the man had been dying . . .

He was quite open about the fire. He had to be, three fire appliances had attended although by the time they got there the staff had extinguished the fire. No, there was no damping down, as such, he said, the fire was *out*. Naturally the firemen were around for a while, turning out the cleaning cupboard, making sure – yes, it was in a cleaners' cupboard; the fire had been in a refuse sack, almost certainly started by a cigarette butt or a match. People smoking? Of course. Staff do smoke.

'In a cleaners' cupboard?' Bell was incredulous. 'Where was this cupboard?'

'On B Wing.'

'What is that used for? Or whom?'

'The ICU – intensive care.'

Bell frowned. 'It must be a shock for very ill patients: a fire alarm going off in the corridor. Presumably not actually on the wards.' He grinned. It was a joke.

'Most of them are sedated.'

'What's the drill when the fire alarm goes?'

This wasn't the same man Bell had spoken to on the phone but he showed no surprise at the question nor at its repetition. He had been informed of the content of that call. 'All the doors that aren't automatic are shut immediately the alarm goes,' he told them. 'And a nurse is sent to a designated meeting point – usually near the switchboard – to find out the location of the fire. Patients are then moved to a safe area if necessary.' He spoke as if reading from a card.

'That will be difficult with all those tubes and masks and such. You must have two nurses for each patient. One for the bed – can one nurse move a bed?'

'It works.' The man was tense. 'But it doesn't – didn't apply in this instance. There was no evacuation. Almost as fast as the fire – so-called – was discovered, it was extinguished.'

'But three fire engines arrived.'

'That's routine when there's an alarm in a hospital. There's a direct link to the station; the Fire Service has to come.'

'No one went round reassuring patients? A fire alarm is a terrifying noise for anyone, let alone someone who's immobile.'

'The possibilities of a conflagration outweigh all other considerations. After all –' He stopped in mid-flight.

'After all,' Helen supplied, 'the potential death toll in a conflagration' – she rolled it out, annoying him – 'could be horrendous compared with one or two fatalities from shock on hearing a fire alarm.'

Palmer swallowed. 'I said: they're sedated, heavily drugged . . .' A pause. 'Dying, some of them.'

Bell appeared lost. 'Would it be possible for us to be shown this intensive care wing? See how it works.'

'I'm afraid not.' He'd been ready for that. His tone lightened. 'I can explain – What exactly is it you don't understand?'

'How the system works.' Bell was playing a typical puzzled pensioner. 'All the tubes and machines, the mask on the face: it's a total mystery to the layman.'

'Not a mask, air would leak round the edges of a mask.' Palmer went into lecture mode: 'The tubes come from a ventilator – the "life support machine",' he added for their benefit. 'One tube is inspiratory – it pumps air into the patient – the other is expiratory. These join at the connector and from that the endotracheal tube goes via the trachea to

184

the lungs. Then there is a cuff which can be inflated ensuring the ET tube fits snugly inside the trachea to avoid leakage. You with me so far?'

Both wore expressions of people trying desperately to follow. 'Can any of these tubes or cuffs be disconnected?' Bell asked.

'Or switched off?' Helen suggested.

Palmer frowned but didn't seem unduly worried, as if other hospitals might have accidents but not this one. He resumed instruction: 'If the ET tube were disconnected the ventilator's alarm would sound.'

'But no one was there to hear it in Larry Payne's case?' Helen sounded dubious and at this point Palmer might have been patronizing but she was intrigued to see he was watching her closely and responding with care:

'It would have been sounding when people returned.'

'Wasn't the patient dead by that time?'

'Yes, he died in the interval –'

'And no alarm was sounding.'

'Oh yes.' Palmer's eyes were fixed on hers. 'The alarm on the cardiac monitor was going. He'd had a cardiac arrest.'

They stared blankly, their minds busy. He stared back like a man without hope. Bell said easily, 'What went wrong, Mr Palmer?'

He shook his head weakly, he was only the spokesman, for God's sake. Bell stated the obvious: 'It would save a great deal of trouble for the hospital if you were to tell us now. More people are in the know than just yourself: doctors, managers, nurses. We shall interview them all. It could be that the hospital isn't to blame. The fire seems to have been set deliberately; if not, it's an amazing coincidence that Payne should have died when there was no one at his bedside. Was he smothered?'

'No!' It was a cry of indignation. 'I told you: it was cardiac arrest –'

'Everyone dies of that.' Bell overrode him. 'What caused it?'

'I can't tell you.'

185

'Can't or won't?'

'I would like to consult with my superiors.'

'Mr Palmer, I am investigating a suspicious death; you will now –'

'There is nothing – the worst it could have been was carelessness' – a shifty look – 'on the part of a care assistant, a language problem most likely, lack of communication, confusion . . . The system is intricate, involving –'

'Something was disconnected.'

'No, no –'

'Switched off,' Helen snapped.

The man's jaw dropped. 'What was switched off?' Bell pressed. 'No' – as Palmer shook his head – 'not "carelessness" again. Which tube was switched off, Palmer?'

His face sagged. 'The O_2.' They waited, no longer tense and staring, just waiting. 'It's another tube, it supplies additional oxygen,' he muttered. 'The ventilator keeps going but the blood-O_2 levels drop and the cardiac monitor shows cardiac arrest but it's not immediately apparent what caused it. Eventually it was discovered that the O_2 tube was switched off but then it could have been switched off some time after death when they were dismantling the equipment.' He was watching to see if they'd buy that.

'But you don't think so,' Bell said.

'It could have happened.'

Bell said, 'All those hours that his mother and friend spent at the bedside, the nurses would have been observing the monitors?' Palmer nodded. 'Would they have explained their function to the relatives?'

'I'm sure, if they were asked.' Palmer was morose. 'I understand what you're saying, but they weren't there. That is, Mrs Payne was sedated and Larry's friend didn't visit that morning.'

'How do you know that?'

'Well, I can't say, but I do know that no one was with him when he died.'

'During the panic that follows a fire alarm in a hospital who's going to challenge a man in a white coat?' Bell asked.

Chapter Sixteen

Bell called for a watch to be put on ports and airports. 'Too late,' he asserted. 'They'll be away by now: Newcastle to Schipol and lose themselves in Europe. He may not be using his credit cards but Joely had a few hundred.'

'That's barely enough to get them to Amsterdam,' Helen protested. 'Even if they leave the Land Rover and steal a vehicle on the Continent, her cash is going to run out pretty quickly.'

Stricken with thirst they had stopped at a motorway services café on the way back to Brimstock. They sat at a window smeared with bird droppings, watching the traffic and considering what they had learned from Palmer.

'There's no proof,' Helen said, her eyes following two eighteen-wheelers nose-to-tail. 'Everything is guesswork: the fire, Bart knowing which switch to throw, the doctor's white coat – and all the time that's supposed to be happening, he's in bed with Joely – well, bedding her – in Culchet.'

'No, he wasn't. He was out, supposedly searching for his wife. He got back to the Hall at – what time?'

'I'll check. He must have made a statement because of Kim. He was questioned when she was missing and that was how Joely's involvement came to light. She saw him coming out of Bart's cellars just before he reached home so we do have a time there.'

'And you may be sure that will alibi him for Larry's death.'

They regarded each other speculatively. Bell said grimly, 'I bet he doesn't have an alibi for Jason's death.'

'What's the motivation?'

'For Jason? We've been over that. He discovered Bart's secret – like . . .' His face lit up. 'Like Jason could break one of his alibis.'

'The word of a vindictive small boy against an adult's?' He looked surprised. 'Devil's advocate,' Helen said. 'What would be the motive for Larry's murder? You said on the way here there was a reason. So what is it?'

He looked uncomfortable about that. 'Larry knew Bart had killed June.'

'Oh, come on! Bart had an alibi for June's death, he was in Brimstock buying cement. It's Larry who's in the frame for June's murder.'

'Look at it this way. It was a conspiracy, and it went wrong because Larry crashed his car. If he was conscious he was reliable. Bart was afraid that when – if he came out of the coma he'd talk, maybe talk deliriously, not fully with it but enough to expose Bart.'

'But if Larry killed June how could –'

'I *said*: it was a conspiracy.'

She was sceptical. 'It seems so unnecessary for them to conspire. And, you know, I don't think Bart was the type – do you? He strikes me as a loner. Loners don't trust anyone.'

'He's always with someone – June, Larry, Joely – and on intimate terms with them. That's no loner.'

'Being on intimate terms with people doesn't mean you trust them, and psychopaths are good actors.'

'Bart's no psychopath.'

'I hope not, for Joely's sake.'

'That's one youngster who can look after herself.' But he was whistling in the dark and Helen knew it.

Attention was now focused on the missing pair by the police, the media and even the public. Bart was wanted 'to help with inquiries' and it was known that Joely was with him. The tabloids went as far as they dared in implying to their readers that a suspected murderer was on the loose accompanied by a teenage girl. They were in a Land Rover and the registration was circulated.

The police didn't wait for information to come in; they scoured the county and the roads linking Culchet with the M6 and routes to Newcastle, Stranraer, Glasgow and Edinburgh. They called at petrol stations, cafés, and farms where people might have been working in fields overlooking minor roads. They turned up nothing. Land Rovers were ten a penny and who looked at registration plates? Although it did seem odd that a strange Land Rover with a pretty girl as passenger hadn't been noticed at some country garage.

Helen wasn't scouring the countryside. Bell, concentrating on Larry's death, had the bit between his teeth. For all the good it did them, she thought, detailed to chase up Bart's alibi, which had been sworn to by Joely, and there they were back to square one. In lieu of the girl herself Helen went to find Blake who was the man, along with Ware, who had talked most with Joely, although at the time focus had been on the missing Kim.

She found Blake at home, frustrated and weary after the abortive hunt for one Land Rover in a county of Land Rovers. With his wife and children at a party, he was relaxing over beer in his living room, the patio doors open to a shaved lawn and herbaceous borders in tasteful shades: the work of the wife, he admitted.

The first time they talked to Joely had been by chance, he told her; they'd gone to the Hall as part of the house-to-house operation when Kim was missing. They had found Bart absent, and Joely had walked in on them.

'You broke in?' Helen asked casually, not wanting to sound judgemental.

'I'd seen the kid's footprints in the cellar, in the cement. Actually,' he confessed, 'Ware was already in the house, the back door was unlocked.' She raised an eyebrow. 'The sequence doesn't matter,' he protested. 'And Joely came in with some food for him. She knew what we were about immediately, and said she'd seen Kim come out of the cellars before Bart came home. That had happened the previous day of course.'

'It's times we're interested in.'

189

'First she said she saw Kim around eleven or half past and that Bart came home sometime afterwards. I think those were her words then: "sometime afterwards".'

'And later that was whittled down. It's in her statement.'

'She said eleven the second time, and that was just before Bart came home – she said. This was when she asked to speak to us again, and we met her in Langley's and Potter's place because she wanted to keep it from her parents.'

'In the interval Bart had got at her: he refined the alibi.'

'Expanded it. We'd left them together at the Hall. At the second interview Joely said she stayed at the Hall all day – the previous day – and left him at six. Win Langley said six thirty. Joely didn't deny that, it was the morning that mattered. She said she'd been in bed all that time. With Bart.'

'She actually said that: "in bed"? Emphasizing it?'

'That was because at the time Kim was still missing and it was thought that she'd been murdered, so Joely was concerned to alibi Bart, meaning he could have killed the child after Joely saw her at eleven, but impossible if he was in bed with Joely.'

'But the man didn't need an alibi. He had nothing to do with Kim. Joely was giving him an alibi for *Larry's* death, although she wouldn't have known that. Bart hadn't been searching for June at all; he'd been to the hospital.'

'Times. You need more times. Joely saw Kim at eleven and Bart arrived back shortly after. What time did Larry die?'

They'd learned that at the hospital. 'Two minutes to eleven,' Helen said with a sigh. 'Or rather that's when it was discovered he was dead.' She had told him generally of Bell's suspicions, now she explained in detail about the fire alarm and the possible – probable?– interruption to the enriched oxygen supply. 'It takes over half an hour to get from the hospital to Culchet,' she ended unhappily.

'Joely could be lying.'

'Of course she could!' She brightened. 'The child's besotted. Bart's using her. And that's not the only way she's being used.' She was silent, cogitating. 'Rachel too,' she muttered. 'You couldn't use sex with Rachel . . .'

'What the hell are you on about?'

'How did he know Rachel wouldn't be with Larry? OK, he planned to start a fire, cause a panic among the staff, so he knew the nurses would almost certainly leave, at least for a few minutes – long enough for him to flick a switch, but Rachel would never have left Larry when the fire alarm sounded. She'd have died sooner.'

'So why wasn't she there?'

'She'd been persuaded to lie down. They'd given her a pill. Together – her and Bart – they'd been at the bedside since the beginning.' She glanced at her watch. 'It's late; I'll see Rachel tomorrow.' She looked at Blake in some trepidation. 'How's she going to react when she sees where the questions are leading?'

'Maybe she knows by now. Everyone knows he's a wanted man.'

'But for Jason's death. Rachel thinks Larry died as a result of the car crash –'

'You've no proof that he didn't.'

'I mean to find it.'

The weather broke that night in a sudden fierce thunderstorm succeeded by long hours of rain fining to a thin drizzle. There was a lot of surface water the following morning but, despite the battering the gardens had taken, the country looked fresh and green, all sparkling in the sun.

At Todbank Ted Brunskill came down the stairs carrying two bulging bin bags. Helen was at the open front door smiling politely, trying to remember who he was. She introduced herself and showed her card.

'I know who you are.' He didn't return the smile. 'I'm Brunskill from across the way. We're helping with his clothes.' He indicated the bags. 'Rachel!' he called. 'The police are here – but it's the woman.'

'I'll be down,' came the answer. 'Take her in the drawing room, Ted.'

He motioned her to one of the front rooms, dropped the bags in the porch and followed her. Making sure I don't pocket anything, Helen thought cynically.

He told her to sit down. 'I hope you're not going to harass her. She's had enough trouble.'

About to protest, Helen hesitated. 'Not harass, but there is one question . . .'

'What's that?'

'It's to do with her time at the hospital.'

'You can't revert to that. She's getting over it, managed to bring herself to get rid of his clothes, to consider what she's going to do with his room. You can't make her recall such a painful time.'

'What's painful?' Maud asked from the doorway, bristling like a terrier. 'Ah, Sergeant Dodd.' It wasn't a welcome.

Helen said, 'Perhaps you and Mr Brunskill would like to stay while I talk to Mrs Payne.'

'Certainly we shall stay. Ted, move those bags out of sight.'

'For heaven's sake, Maud!' Rachel entered the room. 'I've been sorting his clothes; they can stay there a few more minutes surely. You wanted to see me, Helen? You don't mind if I call you Helen.' It wasn't a question. 'Shall we have coffee?'

Everyone declined. They wanted to get it over, whatever 'it' turned out to be.

'She's got a question for you,' Ted growled.

'More than one on past experience.' Rachel was tart.

Helen smiled wryly. 'In our job questions follow on from answers, I'm afraid.'

Ted glowered. 'Well, let's have it.' Evidently the Brunskills had appointed themselves Rachel's guardians.

I must get it over, Helen thought, like news of a death. 'Did Bart Milburn call the hospital around ten o'clock Wednesday morning?' she asked.

'No.' Rachel's face was blank – schooled. Helen blinked.

'He called at nine,' Rachel said. 'I was asleep. He left a message for me that he wasn't coming in until the afternoon because he felt he had to look for June.' After a moment she added, in a high thin voice, 'God knows why June was suddenly important.'

'She was his wife,' Maud reminded her gently.

'She was alive,' Ted put in, then, seeing his wife's surprise and Helen's interest: 'Meaning he might be able to help June.' What he meant was that Bart had balanced the chances of finding his wife alive against the hopelessness of doing anything for the dying man.

'He didn't care much for her when she was alive,' Rachel said stubbornly.

'My dear, he didn't know that June was dead!' Maud was bewildered by her friend's attitude. She glanced at her husband for support, ignoring Helen.

'I think,' he began judiciously, 'that her being missing came as a blow, brought him to his senses – I mean, he appreciated – I'm sure he was very fond . . .' He was floundering and made a wild grab for firm ground: 'He was away straight after breakfast and he'd have been out all day searching –'

'All morning,' Maud corrected. 'He was back by lunchtime.'

'What time would that be?' Helen's tone was too casual. That she should ask the question at all alerted Rachel.

'Why is it important?'

Helen knew that she had come so far that there was no retreat. She hesitated too long. Rachel turned to Ted. 'What time did you see him leave?'

'Who?' She'd taken him by surprise. Helen saw that he wasn't very good with people, probably better with animals.

'Bart,' Rachel said.

'Oh, him. After breakfast.'

'He means *our* breakfast,' Maud explained to Helen. 'We finish around nine. Of course we get up at a reasonable hour. We just breakfast late. After nine, dear?'

'I'd just gone out to me slug traps.'

193

'After nine,' Maud said firmly.

Helen calculated quickly. Larry died just before eleven. Bart could have reached the hospital in forty, forty-five minutes but he wouldn't have gone there direct. Ostensibly he was looking for June and – or – her car. Probably he progressed in a zigzag fashion, even stopping to check barns and hamlets, but getting ever closer to the hospital. A record in its car park? No, it was Pay and Display and there were CCTV cameras; he would have parked in a back street.

Rachel broke in on her calculations: 'You were asking what time he came back.'

'Lunch-time,' Maud said promptly, but as if it were a side issue to her own train of thought. 'What does any of this have to do with Jason?'

'They need to question Bart about Jason,' Ted told her impatiently. 'It was on the TV. Joely's with him,' he added with seeming inconsequence.

Helen gritted her teeth. 'What time do you have lunch, Mrs Brunskill?'

'Oh, we have plenty of time yet, dear. We lunch at midday and there's nothing much to prepare. We don't –'

'You lunched at midday on Wednesday?'

'Always – well, usually. If we have to go to Brimstock we –'

'She wants to know what time you saw Bart come home,' Rachel cut in loudly.

Maud gaped at the tone. 'I said –'

'*Exactly* what time.' Rachel had caught on.

Maud stared back, puzzled but not intimidated. 'I was in the garden,' she said slowly. 'Chives: I'd gone out to pick chives for the scrambled eggs, so I wasn't actually scrambling the eggs or I wouldn't have left the stove. It would be a little while before midday then: a quarter of an hour? Ten minutes?'

'Not more?' Helen asked.

'No. You pick herbs when you need them, don't you? You don't want them lying about, waiting.'

'And you saw Bart.'

'That's what I'm telling you: he came – that is, his Land Rover, him driving, came through the Narrows and turned left up Back Lane. At around a quarter to twelve!' she ended triumphantly, saw Rachel's expression and sobered. 'What's it mean?' she asked weakly.

Rachel turned to Helen. 'What *does* it mean?'

Afterwards Helen wondered how long she would have remained at a loss had Rachel not answered her own question: 'You think Bart was at the hospital. While I slept. During the fire? Bart started the fire?' Helen swallowed. 'He came for Larry,' Rachel said. There was no emotion, it was a statement of fact.

'Rachel, you don't know what – I'm sure the police don't –' Maud turned wildly to her husband.

'Yes,' Helen said, too loudly. 'That's the thinking.'

'So it does have to do with Jason. Is that why the boy had to be killed?'

'*Rachel!*'

Helen said vaguely, 'Jason could have seen something.'

'Curiously,' Rachel said, 'it doesn't matter. Larry's gone. At least he went without pain – or fear. Isn't it strange: I don't feel anything towards Bart. You're saying he murdered my son and I feel nothing. I should. I should be worried because Joely's with him.'

Chapter Seventeen

Evidence was accumulating but there was still no proof. They might discover that someone at the hospital had encountered a doctor whom they didn't recognize, or a householder might come forward to say a Land Rover had been parked outside his house near the hospital on Wednesday morning but it was all circumstantial, even nebulous. Bart's fingerprints on the switch or the inside of the cleaning cupboard would have been conclusive, but best of all would have been an admission from Joely that he had come home closer to noon than eleven on the crucial day. However at this late date incriminating finger-prints were long obscured by others, and if Bart put Jason in the church chest he'd worn gloves. And Joely, like the Hall's Land Rover, like Bart himself, had vanished.

The ports – sea and air – continued to be watched and all police officers throughout the Borders had the registra-tion number of the 'Rover, but the roads were no longer patrolled and the church was open to visitors again. The inquests were held on June and Larry, and adjourned, causing speculation on the part of the media which, so far, had associated Bart only with Jason's death.

Carol Hammond attended the inquest on her mother, then went to London to await developments, the most likely being Bart's arrest.

As for the Carricks, they could only wait for Joely to get in touch.

'Freda's putting the best face on it,' Win told Alice. 'Which is all she can do in the circumstances.'

'She could be viewing it like a Bonnie and Clyde affair,'

Alice said. 'Joely's thrown in her lot with a villain but at least they're in love. Freda will rationalize it as a romance.'

Win was inclined to argue and Alice retracted, agreeing that even a desperate mother couldn't pin hope on such a wisp. 'You see things in fictional terms,' Win said sternly. 'It's you who compares them with Bonnie and Clyde.'

'They weren't fiction –'

'No, they were real people, and look what happened to them.'

Alice flinched. They'd both seen the movie and the lovely Faye Dunaway jerking in the storm of bullets.

With no action, no new developments, and any peripheral detection confined to the detectives, police activity returned to normal so far as uniforms were concerned. But the total disappearance of two people and a Land Rover nagged at Dave Plumpton. He studied maps – large- and small-scale – and tried to fathom the mind of a murderer on the run. Joely's mind he couldn't cope with so he didn't consider her at all except to assume that Bart had hung around, waiting for her to join him – and then where would he go? Plumpton favoured Newcastle because a Land Rover would have been the least noticeable vehicle on Pennine roads. Moreover, it could have been stolen if left in a Newcastle back street, which was the most likely explanation for its disappearance. It would exist but not with its original registration.

On his day off Plumpton, starting from Culchet, drove to Newcastle, or rather that was his intention but, stopping on top of the first great sweep of moorland, cars passing him at frequent intervals, he had doubts. It was needle in haystack stuff, he had to admit; every main road had been traversed, more or less, the number plate broadcast with descriptions of the fugitives. There had been sightings – that was predictable – but none that had proved valid. Days of searching, and here he was driving to Newcastle looking for a Land Rover. Two had passed him already where he sat in a lay-by in his old Peugeot. He decided that after all he'd drive leisurely to Hadrian's Wall and pay his respects to Housesteads. He was fascinated by Roman remains. And he would get away from the traffic, go by way of the minor roads.

It was a glorious morning. He drove with the sun-roof open, the windows rolled down. Larks carolled, lapwings tumbled, a heron flapped towards the road and veered away before a couple of men at work on a wall. The road dipped to a bridge over a beck and swung right to climb out of a hairpin bend. Beyond the bridge was a lay-by. A thought struck him and he pulled in at the last moment, not looking in the mirror first, cursing his absent-mindedness. He was lucky, there was nothing behind him.

He went back to the men, evidently father and son, the likeness obvious. He had to identify himself because of the questions he needed to ask but he pointed out that it was his day off, suggesting that there was nothing official in his stopping and walking back. Had they been working on the wall last Friday? They had, but not at weekend, they'd started again on the Monday: 'Dyke were bellying and her rushed last Thursday night.' They'd had to clear the road and pull down a lot more stones and start from scratch. Father and son stood back and regarded their work morosely. Plumpton remarked how awkward it must be, working on a bank, dangerous if a chap slipped, cars passing and all.

'Not so many,' the father said. 'Mostly they take main road t'other side.' He nodded across the dale.

'I'm looking for a Land Rover,' Plumpton said, knowing how daft it sounded. 'A chap driving, pretty girl passenger.'

'We heard,' the lad said. 'It were on telly.'

'Friday?' the father repeated, eyes glazed. Plumpton felt a twinge of excitement.

'Us didna see them,' his boy told him, reminded him it seemed. Father and son looked down the road at Plumpton's Peugeot. 'They was hikers,' the boy added with an air of omniscience.

'Campers. 'Rover were still there Sat'day morning.'

'There?' Plumpton pointed. 'Did you get the registration?'

'It were local,' the lad said. 'Cumbria. Something-AO. There were curry on seat.'

'What!' The father stared at him.

'I went down to look. You remember: them come while us was home for our tea. There weren't much in t'back: tools, a rucksack, box of food – looked like.'

'You saw them both?' Plumpton asked, incredulous.

The lad shook his head. 'Us never saw hide nor hair of 'em. Just the truck there.'

'What d'you mean: there was curry on the seat?' his father asked. 'You mean like a takeaway?'

'Nah, it were in a proper box, sort what you put in t'freezer. Got a fork in it an' all. Someone were hungry.'

'How long did they – did the 'Rover stay there?' Plumpton asked.

They looked puzzled. 'We weren't here over weekend,' the father repeated. 'So them musta stayed up there Friday night because he were still there Sat'day morning –'

'Not Sat'day night,' the son put in. 'Us come home in t'evening and there weren't no motor in lay-by then.'

'You said "up there",' Plumpton said. 'Up where?'

'Why, there's a path leaves road on t'other side o' beck. You can see t'sign from where you're parked.' The father pointed. 'They'd have been camping up there. What you smirking at?' To his son.

'Camping?'

'They stayed the night, didn't they?'

'Maybe them's still up there.'

'Don't be daft. 'Rover's gone, in't it?'

'Actually,' the lad started in an artificial tone immediately suspect, 'it were unlocked. I tried it, just out of interest like, thinking it were abandoned. But if I tried door' – turning to his father – 'you reckon Ikey wouldn't?'

199

The man looked away, then stooped deliberately to pick up a stone and resume work.

'So you never saw either of the occupants,' Plumpton pressed, to receive a vehement shake of the head from the lad. 'Where can I find this Ikey?'

The farm was in a wooded hollow below the road, concealed until the last moment – which was just as well because it turned out to be a rural slum. Surrounded by a graveyard of old cars and rusted machinery and a jungle of nettles, the house was an eyesore of flaking whitewash and sagging slates. A chained lurcher watched Plumpton warily as he climbed out of his car. The place was very quiet. There was a feeling of eyes in the shadows. The dog didn't bark.

A Land Rover stood on the weedy cobbles. Plumpton noted that its registration was Northumbrian, not Cumbrian. He looked inside. There was a bale of hay in the back, straws and dried mud in the well. Behind him someone coughed.

Ikey Swailes was short, round and solid. He was heavily bearded and not at all clean. He wore a watch cap, bib-and-brace overalls, gumboots, and he smelled. He didn't think he'd seen a Land Rover parked at Haggworm Bridge on Friday, nor Saturday. He said he hadn't seen the Lewthwaite men working on the wall either, he hadn't passed that way Friday.

'But you did pass on Saturday,' Plumpton stated. Ikey agreed that he might have done at that. 'But you didn't see a Land Rover.' Plumpton's gaze wandered idly to the vehicle a yard away. He walked round it while Ikey stood back, his eyes intent. 'Show me your other vehicle,' Plumpton ordered.

'I don't have no more, only me tractor.'

'These ones.' Plumpton sauntered out of the yard, making for the decrepit shells beside the approach track. No one could call it a drive. There was a Land Rover jacked up, one wheel removed, the tilt in ribbons. 'Where are its number plates?' he asked.

'I dunno. I threw them.'

'Where?'

A dramatic shrug. 'In the rubbish. They'll be on council tip.'

'Let's have the bonnet up then.'

'What?'

'You heard.'

Plumpton might be a simple countryman but he had the animal perceptiveness for other animals' emotions. Ikey wasn't exactly exuding fear but there was an air of defeat about him. He lifted the bonnet. Although Plumpton wasn't in uniform he'd had the wit to bring his notebook. Now he produced it and made a note.

He walked back to the other 'Rover, trailed by his victim. He gestured to the bonnet. Ikey lifted it and moved away, distancing himself. Plumpton recorded more figures implying he'd found the engine number. He turned. 'This is a murder investigation,' he said gravely. He didn't feel fear then, he saw it in the other's shocked eyes.

'You're having me on!'

'You knew we were looking for this vehicle.'

'It's mine! It's me own . . .' He dried up, pointing mutely to the registration.

'Oh yes, your number plates, but they come off the car on your tip. What d'you do with the plates from this one, eh?'

'It were – abandoned.'

'Where's the rucksack?'

'What rucksack?'

Plumpton turned back to the vehicle to hide his own bewilderment. Why was it abandoned at Haggworm Bridge and not in a city back street?

'How did you know?' Bell demanded when all the fuss was over and they were waiting for the recovery truck to take the 'Rover away. In the time it had taken for reinforce-

201

ments to arrive Ikey had capitulated and handed over the rucksack and tools. There had been nothing else, he maintained: no suitcase, no kind of bag. He'd eaten the food: chicken, bread and stuff. There was some queer smelly stew he'd given to the dog but it wouldn't touch it. He even produced the registration plates; he hadn't decided how to dispose of them and they were in a cupboard in his kitchen. He'd been taken into custody but he'd be released on bail so no arrangements had to be made about his animals, something that always caused headaches for police in country areas.

'So what made you think something was dodgy?' Bell pressed.

'It was the age of the two vehicles,' Plumpton told him. 'Here's this one: not that old, in good nick – and look at this place. Chap's not got two pennies to rub together – he'll need to borrow to find his bail. Any vehicle of Ikey's would be ancient and as battered as the one on his tip. As soon as I started to get suspicious I could feel him giving in, wilting like. Of course I was lucky, seeing the chaps repairing the wall, stopping and asking had they seen a strange Land Rover.'

'Why there?' Helen asked. 'What made him abandon it there? And leave his rucksack in it.' The pack had contained personal things like shaving gear, although not Bart's wallet. Bell and Helen knew where the 'Rover had been parked because when they'd been summoned by Plumpton, he'd identified his location in relation to the men working on the wall at Haggworm Bridge. They'd had a good look at the lay-by as they passed.

'I've been thinking,' Plumpton said grimly. 'I'm wondering if he could have taken Joely up that path that starts right there and come back without her.'

'No!' Helen was amazed. 'Then he'd have driven away.'

'But he never did drive away,' Plumpton protested. 'He left the 'Rover there. Why?'

'He hitched from there,' Bell said, adding in a murmur: 'Without his rucksack.'

'The man was *wanted*!' Helen exclaimed. 'He was on the

run, dodging us, the media, everyone. He was far less likely to attract attention in a car than hitching.'

'He stole – he hijacked another car.'

'Where's the driver of that one?'

'Over the wall,' Plumpton said. They stared at him. 'At Haggworm,' he went on. 'On the opposite side of the road from the lay-by. I looked. You can't see nought, it's all overgrown but there has to be a fair drop to the beck and there are trees and undergrowth. He could have tipped a body over –'

'Joely!' Helen cried.

'No,' Bell said firmly. 'Then he'd have taken the Land Rover. More likely it's a stranger, a tourist who no one's reported missing. We'll go and look soon as Recovery gets here.'

The drop to the beck was neither dangerous nor steep, just steep enough to facilitate the passage of a body which would have slid into the beck had it not been stopped by an old holly tree near the bottom. There in a bizarre loop they found it, draped round the trunk. It was Bart Milburn.

Then where was Joely?

Chapter Eighteen

Bart had been dead for some days. He was wearing only a shirt and jeans and those had been soaked and then dried; rigor had come and gone and there was no mark on him to account for his death, no obvious bruise on the head, nothing to say why a healthy man should have slipped and died, looped round a holly tree. The police awaited the post-mortem report with interest but the nearest guess was that death was due to an overdose even though there had never been any suggestion that Bart was on drugs. They did wonder about suicide. He might, after all, have been fond of Larry yet forced to kill him to save his own skin. But if he valued that, then he wouldn't kill himself, said Bell, who clung to the conspiracy theory, that Bart had persuaded Larry to kill June. Helen maintained that no man would commit murder at the behest of his lover; a contract killing yes, but not murder for love. Bell told her to read the Bywaters case, the only difference being that there the sexes were reversed: a man murdered his lover's husband at her instigation.

Helen read, dutifully, and came into the station next morning. 'Not quite reversed sexes,' she told him. 'And it wasn't a gay case.'

'You reckon gays can't love as fiercely?'

He was right, fierce could be an appropriate term. Bart did have enormous appeal: charisma, charm, whatever you liked to call it. Look at Joely – although no one would convince Helen that the girl thought her alibi was covering Bart for Larry's death. Joely thought it was for Kim. That would be what Bart had told her, and since she was certain that he had nothing to do with Kim's disappearance she was more than happy to give him a false alibi. 'Until she found out it was for Larry,' Helen suggested.

'I'm wondering when she started to have doubts,' Bell mused. 'She thought she knew where she was in the relationship until Friday, and then I told her Bart had done a runner. It was obvious from her reaction that he hadn't told her he was about to leave. From that moment she must have been confused, fighting to stay on an even keel: protecting him, being careful of what she said because she knew something was very wrong and she loved him and he could be in danger. But she was shaken, even more so when she learned he was gay – although did she believe that? Did she think it was a trap of some kind to lure her away from him? I suspect a girl of sixteen would maintain that a man who took her to bed couldn't be gay, right?'

'Yes.' Helen was firm on that point. She remembered what it was to be sixteen and head over heels in love but – 'Oh, my God!'

'What?'

'She'd confront him with it, wouldn't she? They had mobiles, that's how she got in touch with him, met up with him, joined him. That note about leaving to start a new life with him: it was just fantasy. Maybe she was thinking, hoping, kidding herself that him being gay was malicious gossip, no more; Bart and Larry were good friends. As soon as she joined him she'd be telling him that you – and Carol and June – were saying he was gay. She'd be devastated –' Helen stopped short. 'Well, she would be if he admitted it . . . but he wouldn't . . .' She shook her head violently. 'I'm reading too much into his mind,' she confessed. 'I've no idea how they would act after they met again.'

'He couldn't let her go,' Bell said heavily. 'The point is that when she heard the broadcasts, knew he was wanted for questioning about Jason's murder, he ran the risk of her recalling Larry's death – and the alibi that she'd given him that wasn't necessary for Kim because nothing had happened to Kim. She'd alibied him for Larry's murder. So far as Bart was concerned Joely was a ticking bomb.'

There was a pause, both thinking that it was Bart who'd died, not Joely. 'Is it possible' – Helen was diffident – 'that she could have tipped him over that wall? No, she couldn't have, she wasn't big enough. And she wasn't with him at the bridge. If she had been, she'd have taken the 'Rover.'

'Can she drive?'

'I don't know, but it's immaterial; she didn't take it, so she'd have had to hitch if she *was* there, and no one's come forward to say they've picked her up. Her suitcase is missing,' she added on a low note.

Bell was grim. 'You take Plumpton, work out Bart's likely route from Culchet to Haggworm Bridge and – well, follow your nose. Look at barns close to lay-bys, that kind of thing. I'll stay on here for the PM report. I'll give you a bell if it comes through.'

It came through at six o'clock that evening. They were driving down the east scarp of the Pennines, all the glory of the Eden Valley below and the Lakeland fells a hazy frieze in the west. Plumpton was at the wheel, smooth and staid, when her mobile went off. She answered and listened. 'Oh wow!' she gasped, listened some more and replaced the phone. 'He could have been poisoned,' she said.

'What? Who?' As if he didn't know, but he was taken by surprise.

'Bart. The stomach's inflamed. No idea what it is – yet. The stomach contents have been sent off for analysis.' A pause. 'Curry!' she shouted.

'The dog wouldn't eat it.'

'Joely?'

The shining panorama of valley and fell was half their world, the other half a sky like pale gentians. They saw none of it. 'Poor sod,' Helen breathed.

'He killed two people,' Plumpton said. 'Three if Larry killed June for him.'

She gave a snort of amusement. 'But Joely got away? So where is she now?'

'We were supposed to be looking for her body,' he reminded her. They were filthy and they stank of musty hay and dung.

She ignored him. 'What did she do?' she asked herself. 'Gave him the curry and walked away? Turn round.'

'Why?'

'We need to go to Ikey Swailes' place and find what's left of what the dog didn't eat. It's in that yard somewhere. And don't tell me Ikey would have washed out the container. If he did he didn't do it properly. There'll be some left for analysis.'

There was. Ikey never threw anything away and they found the box where it had been kicked into the nettles. It contained something covered with a grey mould which was sent away for testing.

The hunt for Joely intensified, based on the possibility that she had eaten some of the curry herself, been taken ill . . . but at that point speculation faltered. Had Bart left her to die or hastened the process? What was wrong with the curry? Who had provided it? Since June died a number of women had taken cooked meals to Bart. Joely, of course, Alice and Win, Maud; all denied knowledge of any curry. Rachel was away. Having buried Larry she had gone to Edinburgh to spend a few days with a cousin. Contacted by phone she said she hadn't taken any food to Bart. So it was assumed that Joely had made the curry. Win remembered that the kitchen at the pub had smelled strongly of Indian spices at one time but she'd thought little of it; Joely was always experimenting. In advance of the analysis report Helen Dodd considered the traditional ingredients: onions, meat of some kind, innumerable spices, chillies. A lot of room for a mistake there, she thought, as she went about the more mundane investigating of urban break-ins and a spate of arson attacks in Brimstock's schools.

The reports on the curry and Bart's organs came through. The curry teemed with bacteria associated with putrefaction, with a range of organic material, with some amorphous substance that could be cream, and aconitine. As for the contents of the stomach: these were meat, bread, the various constituents of the curry, such as could be identified, and aconitine.

In his office Bell passed the reports to Helen and waited for her reaction, which was predictable: 'What's aconitine?'

From his bookshelf she took down Glaister and Rentoul's *Medical Jurisprudence and Toxicology*: 'Aconitine is obtained from the root of a plant called – I can't pronounce this, it's Latin – ah, monkshood. What's monkshood?' Bell shook his head blankly. '"Has caused poisoning",' she resumed, '"eaten in error for horseradish." And what's horseradish?'

'Horseradish sauce. Don't you have it with meat?'

'Of course: beef and horseradish sauce.' She returned to the report. 'Plenty of meat in his stomach, and that "amorphous substance that could be cream". I wonder if you make horseradish sauce with cream.'

'Win Langley would know. Perhaps she made it and gave it to him with the beef.'

'Having put aconitine – no, monkshood root – in by accident? Sounds more like some old witch who keeps bunches of poisonous plants in her larder against future contingencies.'

'Plenty of old women in Culchet who know all about plants: Maud – both the Brunskills actually – Win, Alice – well, she's not so old – Rachel . . . Freda? Someone who had it in for Bart.'

'None of them,' she countered. 'They all looked after him when June died.'

'They took him food,' he corrected. 'Poisoners do that.'

'Did you ever take him food?' Alice asked as they started down the old sledge road from the moors.

'Of course not!' Jill hooted with derision. 'I've got no time for men who can't look after themselves. Let him do his own cooking. Did you take him stuff?'

'I was sorry for him.' Alice grimaced as Jill's mount

208

pushed ahead at a marshy bit and Thornthwaite's pony threw up its head. 'Excuse us,' Jill called. The way widened again to a turfy track and Alice ranged alongside.

'D'you reckon it was accident or design?' Jill asked.

'How should I know?' Alice was snappy; her legs were sore and she longed for level ground.

'You're not usually short on opinions when it comes to crime.'

Baz came galloping down the scarp, skirted the riders by way of the bank, dropped back to the path and raced ahead. 'Win can't conceive of anyone mistaking monkshood for horseradish,' Alice said. 'They're entirely different. Roots are similar, but the foliage is a world apart.'

'So someone pulled up some monkshood by design.'

Alice didn't respond. She stared at her pony's ears, thinking about the conversation with Win, recalling the women who had taken food to Bart, which one could have hated him to that extent, the aconitine being intended for his death.

'Joely?' Jill said, as if telepathic.

Win had suggested Joely too. 'The timing's wrong,' Alice pointed out. 'She had to dig the stuff up, grate it, make the sauce. And when she left the pub to meet up with him she still adored him. She thought she was going away with him. Why should she take along a deadly poison?'

'And presumably it wasn't Win or yourself.'

'Where's the motive?' Alice wasn't in the least affronted.

'OK. Maud then.'

'The same applies.'

'Rachel?'

'Ah! But first, he'd left the village by the time she understood that he killed Larry and, secondly, she never took him food.'

'You're sure of that.'

'She was grieving for Larry; how would she find the time or the energy to cook, even for Larry's lover?'

'So who does that leave?'

'No one else who took him food, and there's no other way he could have got – Hello! What's he picked up?'

Baz had returned, dropped a small object on the track and was waiting for approval, grinning.

'A butterfly,' Jill said. 'He's always chasing them. Never catches 'em.'

He had this time and he wouldn't shift. They stopped, the ponies annoyed because they were on the home stretch. 'Christ!' Jill gasped, and slid down. She picked up the object and turned to Alice. On her palm lay a broken butterfly, scarlet sequins glinting in the sunshine. 'Didn't she –?'

'Yes.' Alice felt the tears gather. 'On her thongs: sequin butterflies.'

The ponies nudged the riders and stamped their feet. Baz bounded away, Jill mounted and, heedless of the angle, they slithered straight down the incline to the old lime kilns.

They stopped below the tall brick arches and looked for the hound, expecting to find him in the crumbling chambers, sniffing at the 'eyes' in the back where once the quicklime had been drawn out. He wasn't there and now they heard him on top, snorting loudly at something they didn't want to see.

Jill dismounted reluctantly, in slow motion; she handed her reins to Alice and clawed her way up the steep grass. Above a kiln Baz glanced at her, then down to resume his gross snuffling at a jumble of stones. The huge bowl that had once contained burning limestone had been plugged with rocks when the workings were abandoned. The rocks had been moved recently; there were raw scratches on the stones. They were heavy.

'Come and give me a hand,' Jill called.

'I can't. The ponies will run.'

'Let them. Take the bridles off.'

Alice did as she was told. The freed ponies moved away and started to trot along the drove road, making for home.

With two people working it didn't need much effort. The person who removed and replaced the stones wouldn't have had much time to spare and there was only one layer.

A brown shoulder appeared first, still unblemished except for a little dirt from the rocks: a thin young shoulder. Then there was the hair, covering her face. They were glad of that. Something was under the head, like a pillow: her soft suitcase. They stood up and looked away, towards the village.

'We have to walk home,' Alice said inanely. Someone had to say something.

'Look,' Jill said. She had stooped, lifted the long hair, not to reveal the face but the throat and a tight dark groove.

'You can't tell,' Alice said savagely, refusing to identify the mark. 'What's it matter anyway? You think she killed herself and pulled the rocks in after her?'

'Why?' Jill asked. 'She'd have died for him. Why did he have to do this? You go down. I'll hang on here.'

'You can't.'

'Someone has to because of the crows. Baz will stay with me, I'll have company.' Her eyes strayed to the small body and she shivered.

Chapter Nineteen

The inquests on both Joely and Bart were adjourned. The unofficial view was that Joely had been murdered by Bart and that the eventual verdict on him would be mis-adventure. He had eaten curry containing, or in conjunction with, a sauce prepared by Joely who had mistaken monkshood for horseradish.

Bell refused to comment on this consensus nor would he discuss it with Helen. It nagged at her: both the theory of Joely as inadvertent poisoner and Bell's lack of reaction. Delegated (in her own mind) to petty urban crime, but trading on a brief acquaintance with Win and Alice, in her free time she returned to Culchet. At Thrushgill she found the two women only too ready to talk, to have gaps filled in their own speculations: a welcome antidote to the taci-turn Bell.

They sat in the garden drinking wine. It was early evening and the swifts were out, hawking above the ghyll with high thin screams. Win was present because the Carricks were away and had installed a temporary man-ager whose wife cooked. Win was taking time out, playing around in Thrushgill's kitchen, she told Helen. Since the purpose behind this visit was to try to unravel the mystery concerning the aconitine Helen welcomed any reference to kitchens, needing to discover if either the curry or the sauce, or both, were prepared in the Stag. But any mention of Joely incensed Win for whom Bart was a monster of depravity: 'He killed Jason and then stayed in the locality and *lured* that child to join him and strangled her. That's obscene.'

'He couldn't leave her behind,' Alice said in the harsh tone that told Helen she was clamping down on pity. 'She would have talked once she realized how she'd been used: the false alibi and all that. If you ask me the motive behind sleeping with her was to bind her to him. It worked. She was obsessed with him.'

'And the relationship advertised the fact that he was straight,' Helen contributed. Noting their confusion she went on: 'He could be gay, straight, bisexual: whatever fitted the situation. Larry was used the same way as Joely, but after June's death he had to distance himself from Larry because evidence of an affair with him provided another motive for June's murder.'

'Another motive?' Win queried. 'What was the first one?'

'The Hall!' Helen was amazed. 'Didn't you realize that? Bart thought he'd inherited it. Torching it was an insurance scam.'

'We did think of it – naturally.' Alice was bewildered. 'But it's too obvious.'

'Not when you remember that all the Butler family were after Bart, thinking he was a paedophile and had taken Kim. Jason may not have known where Kim was but he hated Bart – and arson is a boy's weapon. I'm chasing young arsonists in town at this moment. But there was a bonus to Bart's torching the Hall; it meant any sign of Jason, of his being killed there, his body kept there – any trace was destroyed.'

'We did work out that Jason tried to blackmail Bart,' Alice said, 'but not what he had on him. Did you and Mr Bell come to a conclusion about that, specifically?'

'He does talk about that.' Helen rushed on before either woman could ask what he didn't talk about: 'When Kim went missing –'

'Hang on!' Alice exclaimed. 'Kim was terrified of Jason, which is why she did a runner. What was it that scared her so much? She came back happily enough when she knew he was dead.'

'You never suspected? Didn't Ted tell Maud?' Helen was

surprised; this was one piece of scandal that hadn't gone round the village like wildfire, maybe it was too nasty. 'Kim's told us. That is, she chatted. It didn't come out in one interview, and even then we let her talk. She didn't need any prompting – as if we would,' she added quickly. 'What happened was Jason had evolved this scheme to extort money from men using Kim as principal: "My little sister says you did this – or that . . ." Of course Kim didn't understand what was going on – and Jason didn't see the danger – but she knew something really naughty was being tried this time, far worse than conning clothes out of the visitors, and she threatened to tell their dad. Jason started to panic and she must have known she had the whiphand. They quarrelled violently, he cracked, threatened to kill her, and then *her* nerve broke. When she ran away Jason listened to his father raving about paedophiles and, whether or not he'd tried to extort cash from Bart before, and I doubt it, now he did go to the Hall or –' She stopped, her eyes on some mental image.

'He could have phoned Bart.' Alice was on the ball.

'Couldn't disguise his voice,' Win put in. 'Bart would know who it was immediately.'

Helen said firmly, 'Bart had to have a very good reason to kill Jason. It could have been that the boy wasn't direct, he used innuendo like: "I know what you did . . ." And Bart thought he was referring to June or Larry simply because his mind was preoccupied with them and with covering his tracks in respect of their deaths. So when Jason implied he knew something bad . . .' She trailed off.

'Maybe,' Alice said quietly, 'he came along just as Bart was dousing the Hall with petrol.'

'That child was too sharp,' Win muttered. 'He cut his own throat.'

They were silent. Bees thrummed in the lilacs, a fly-catcher jumped out from a stake and back as if on elastic. Win got up and staggered. 'Sitting too long,' she gasped, going indoors.

'It's only a scenario,' Helen said. 'We've no proof that that's what happened.'

'It makes sense: the blackmail, never mind the specifics. What would have become of the affair?'

'Which one?'

'Why,' – Alice blinked – 'Bart and Larry. I mean, with June dead, if Larry hadn't crashed his car, what then? If Bart did persuade Larry to kill June – that's what he did, wasn't it? – did they plan to set up home together? In the Hall?'

'I'd never considered it.' Helen was stumped. 'One doesn't, does one? "What might have been if . . ." No,' she went on slowly. 'With June dead, Bart thinking he owned the Hall, torching it and collecting the insurance . . . He would have left, wouldn't he? Larry's pulled his chestnuts out of the fire, he's served his purpose, Bart would take off. And he wouldn't have taken Joely, she'd have been abandoned too. But you know Bart didn't *persuade* Larry; did you never read the Bywaters case?'

'Thompson and Bywaters? It strikes a chord.'

'What's this?' Win returned with the Talisker and glasses. 'Who are they?'

'Edith Thompson,' Helen stated. 'She was in love with a steward on a liner and wrote him steamy letters in which she fantasized about getting rid of her husband. The lover, Bywaters, stabbed Mr Thompson and Edith was convicted of incitement to murder. They were both hanged.'

'My God,' Alice breathed. 'Bart incited Larry to murder June, right?'

'It's in character. If any suspicion was voiced Bart could deny everything; he would have maintained he did nothing to encourage Larry. The poor guy would have been thrown to the wolves. The car crash knocked things out of gear. Larry could come out of his coma and expose their true relationship, as he saw it, and there's the motive: a sex triangle in addition to the basic one of gain from the insurance scam.'

Win's eyes shifted. 'Why, Rachel! Hello!' she shouted on a false note. 'You're back!'

Alice leapt up. 'Come in, come in! We didn't expect you, you should have phoned, we'd have gone across and aired the house.'

Rachel, cool in blue linen, her hair shortened and tapered, dark brown with lights, opened the gate and stepped inside the garden, smiling politely. 'I saw your car,' she told Helen (she'd recognized it? Sharp eyes). She glanced at the whisky. 'A party, I see; I became quite part of the social whirl in Edinburgh myself.' The tone was brittle.

Alice rushed indoors, emerging quickly with a glass, determined not to miss anything.

'You're here on business?' Rachel asked Helen.

'An informal visit.'

There was silence, fraught except on Rachel's part. 'You don't have to give me the news,' she said calmly. 'I saw notice of the inquests being adjourned in *The Scotsman*.'

'Well, *The Scotsman*,' Alice said meaningfully, implying the baldest of reports.

'I saw the tabloids too.' She turned to Win. 'You're not at the Stag.'

Win told her about the new arrangement at the pub. 'I'm resting,' she said wryly. 'Beef olives tonight; you'll have supper with us.'

'Not to watch you. I don't eat beef.'

'A pity,' Alice said.

'I could do something else,' Win said desperately, trying to keep things going. 'Or is it that you object to the smell –' She stopped. Stupid conversation.

'Is my lipstick smudged?' Rachel asked.

Win and Alice gaped in unison and looked from her to Helen who said, 'Was I staring? I'm sorry, I was miles away. Did Larry eat beef?'

Rachel's composure cracked momentarily and they glimpsed pain at a lower level. 'He loved it, dear. I was roasting a joint that evening. The evening he – didn't come home.'

'What did you do with it?' Helen asked.

'What did I – Is this important?'

'I don't know. I feel I should know. Did you throw it out?'

'Oh no, I wouldn't throw away good food. I gave it to Bart, probably when he came over to make a start on his – on sorting Larry's clothes. Appropriate, wasn't it: giving my son's supper to his killer?'

Alice gasped. In the minds of the three of them were two words. Who would voice them? Who dared?

Rachel smiled. 'I gave him the horseradish sauce too.'

Alice said flatly, 'It was an accident. It had to be.' She turned on Helen. 'Forget it,' she ordered.

'What's this?' Rachel asked.

'Was the sauce home-made?' Helen asked, thinking that at least she had two witnesses even if she didn't have a tape recorder.

'Of course.' Rachel was cool. 'She knew I cooked beef for Larry and she gave me a jar when she was putting up a batch for themselves.'

'Who?' Alice asked weakly.

'June.' Rachel stared. 'We exchanged small gifts. I didn't care much for her but we kept up the conventions. You do in a small village. After all, you have to live with people.'

Bell said, 'We have to move on. There were five deaths. Bart was responsible for four of them, including his own wife even if Larry struck the actual blow. If he was poisoned by June I'm happy to leave it like that. The verdict will be misadventure.'

'I thought you'd be interested.' Helen was resentful. 'Someone mentioned poetic justice at one time; don't you think it's *neat* that Bart should have incited Larry to kill his wife and all the time the sauce she made is sitting in a jar waiting for him to eat it? Talk about revenge from the grave!'

Bell studied her across his desk. 'You're young; experience will come with more cases. You won't get them in Brimstock.' He shuffled papers. 'This was a one-off –

although the potential is everywhere: greedy husband, doting mother and gay son, a teenager with adolescent fantasies . . .'

'Rachel's strong on what lies below the surface of village life.'

'Rachel. Yes, she would be. It was Sherlock Holmes who said something about vile alleys in London taking second place to the dreadful record of sin in the smiling country-side.' He nodded at her surprise. She wouldn't have thought him a reader of Conan Doyle. 'Folk in isolated communities,' he went on, 'they're compelled to hide their true feelings. A village is like a volcanic field: a thin crust above a bed of molten lava. I tell you, dealing with prob-lem families like the Butlers is child's play compared with the rural middle classes when one of them goes over the edge.'

She was thoughtful, listening but following a trail of her own. 'D'you think June guessed that Bart wanted her out of the way? After all, Carol said the marriage was rocky; I'm wondering if making that sauce could have been a pre-emptive strike.'

'How do you make a case against June?' He was curious.

'I've been telling you!' She was exasperated. 'She had the motive, the means, opportunities – well, as to that, she'd intended the sauce for Larry –' She stopped. She hadn't seen it that way when she'd come rushing in with Rachel's revelations.

'Yes.' His expression said that she was confirming some-thing in his mind. 'In your scenario June is making a pre-emptive strike against Bart who she suspects – or knows – wants her out of the way. But she gave the sauce to Rachel because she knew Larry liked beef.'

'But it came back to Bart; he was the one who was poisoned in the end.'

'By accident. June had no way of knowing that Larry wasn't going to eat the beef and the horseradish, so-called – and that it would come back to Bart. She didn't know that Bart wouldn't sample it sooner, when help might be at hand, and a stomach pump. And where's the roast joint Rachel gave him? Did he eat it without horseradish?'

'I don't get it. What are you saying?'

'I'm saying your scenario is all accident and coincidence; it's contrived. Think of the facts, woman!'

'I am!' She scowled. 'There was horseradish – no, there was aconitine in his stomach?' He nodded. 'And there was aconitine in the curry. Those are facts, right?'

'Right.'

'And cream. And June gave Rachel a substance saying it was horseradish sauce.'

'That's not a fact. It's hearsay.'

'We're not in court. Rachel said –'

'Exactly.' He waited, watching her resentment fade. 'She's a very plausible liar,' he said.

'Rachel said she never took food to him. She was lying there?'

'Murderers do.'

'Curry. She put the sauce in the curry. She took it across on Friday before he left. But Rachel didn't know Bart was involved at that point. We didn't know ourselves until the following day. It was after she told us about the fire in the hospital that you started to put two and two together. I remember: it was when we were driving to the hospital to interview that Palmer chap. When I said they were lovers you pointed out that lovers did kill each other – on occasions. No one had put Bart in the frame until that moment.' There was silence. She interpreted it correctly. 'Did they?'

'It was Rachel who told us about the fire. She'd known about it all along. At the same time, early on, we'd concluded June died as the result of a blow, or rather the blow was a contributing factor to her death, and Larry had struck it. What would Rachel's reactions be to that, in her own mind: her son being a murderer?'

It was a serious question and she gave it due consideration, recognizing that this was an old hand instructing one who now felt like a tiro. 'At first she'd be in denial: he didn't do it, it was a mistake. Then she'd rationalize?'

219

'Go on.'

'She'd look for someone to blame. June? But how could she be blamed? She wasn't a bimbo who influenced Larry to perform some criminal act, or a femme fatale . . . Blame, influence – ah! She'd blame Bart; he was the person who had influence over her boy, the dominant partner in the relationship.' She stopped talking and considered again while Bell watched, benign and approving. 'Surely she wouldn't kill Bart because he was a bad influence on her son.'

'Oh no. But Rachel's got a mother's perceptiveness, and she knew far more than we did. She knew about the fire in the hospital that ensured no nurses were at Larry's bedside at a time of his choosing and, most crucially, she'd been told that Bart phoned and learned that she was in bed, sedated. Now if *we'd* known all that wouldn't we have been suspicious? As Rachel recovered from the shock – and grief – she put it together. You might even find that Maud mentioned seeing Bart come home at midday although Rachel needn't have known that Joely put his return nearer eleven. She didn't need to know that; she had enough already.'

'Blake said that. I was worried as to how she'd react when she realized that Bart could have murdered Larry, and Blake said she probably knew already. I put that down to a shot in the dark, a soundbite; Blake had got it muddled. But he was right, wasn't he? And I was so considerate with her: careful, compassionate, and at some point she went out in her garden and dug up a root of monkshood.' She was furious at her own gullibility. 'How do we proceed now? What's her weak point?'

He shook his head. 'I doubt she has one. And there's not a shred of proof –'

'But it has to be her –'

'Yes, it was Rachel, but you can't make a case against her; there are no facts other than there was aconitine in his stomach and the curry. It's happened before and been brought in as accident. Even his death could be argued as hypothermia. Like I said, we have to move on. You're not going to win 'em all; how many killers get away with it that we know are guilty as hell? But this one didn't. Look at it this way: Bart killed children, he incited a man who loved him too much to kill his wife, then killed that man. After that, where would he have stopped? He's like a tiger that's discovered the easiest way to solve his problem is to kill people. Nothing evil about the tiger, he's killing for food, but Bart had learned to kill anyone who posed a threat. He'd go on to kill people merely because they got in his way. I'm against capital punishment but when an execution is an accomplished fact, I'm not going to bring the executioner to book for stopping a murderer dead in his tracks. I know what you're thinking but it's a *form* of justice.'

2